The Dirty Version

a novel

Turner Gable Kahn

HARPER ⬤ PERENNIAL

NEW YORK • LONDON • TORONTO • SYDNEY • NEW DELHI • AUCKLAND

HARPER ⬤ PERENNIAL

FIRST EDITION

Designed by Jen Overstreet

Title page artwork © TWINS DESIGN STUDIO/Adobe Stock
Chapter open artwork © Dedraw Studio/Adobe Stock

Library of Congress Cataloging-in-Publication Data has been applied for.

ISBN 978-0-06-341496-9 (pbk.)

25 26 27 28 29 LBC 5 4 3 2 1

to
this
outrageous
joy

Director of *Big Gun* Franchise Acquires Indie-Darling Series in Surprising Streaming Deal

Much-hyped adaptation of bestselling instant-classic feminist novel *The Colony* to be helmed by old-school action legend Ram Braverman

U.S. ENTERTAINMENT WIRE, BREAKING NEWS

Weeks of rampant speculation about the fate of Sirensong Media's headline projects in the wake of the company's dissolution ended today, with the announcement that the twice-traded series adaptation of the polarizing, breakout literary sensation *The Colony* has been snapped up by Hollywood heavyweight Braverman Productions, in a major deal with streaming giant PrimeFlix that puts Ram Braverman himself in the director's chair.

Reps from both firms said action filmmaker Braverman, whose decades-old *Big Gun* franchise still holds summer blockbuster records, "can't wait to put his mark on *The Colony*"—a comment that threw the book's devoted online community into a tizzy, immediately raising concerns the director is "flat out the wrong man for the job."

The future-feminist dystopian novel found its way to bestseller lists on the blessing of several high-profile women's rights activists. The story, set on an island where men are banned, follows the heir to a female-warrior throne as, against her better judgment, she rescues a shipwrecked sailor who washes up on her clan's shores. She offers him forbidden refuge, igniting a torrid affair that leaves her pregnant. The sailor then betrays her, drawing the attention of a bloodthirsty sea monster and forcing the protagonist to face a harrowing decision when a baby boy is born.

Die-hard readers call the book's symbology "necessary, post-#MeToo art," and reacted to news of Braverman's taking control of the series with worries he'll ruin it, since the novel's narrative falls so far outside his wheelhouse.

Natasha Grover, the debut author of *The Colony*, could not be reached directly for comment, but unnamed sources at Braverman Productions say she remains attached to the series' script. Sources also say the relatively unknown Grover "is pleased to be working with such a famed director," and "is positive fans will love the show!"

Chapter One

The final bell of the university school year rang, and Natasha Grover needed the sunburnt freshmen lingering in her "Heroes and Villains" English seminar to immediately disperse.

Her best friend's glare hovered impatiently against a back wall. Tash knew better than to leave Biscayne Coastal College's chair of Women's Studies hanging—especially in the minutes before trying to bribe her. Janelle and her wife, Denise, were key to Tash surviving dinner tonight.

Sorry! Tash mouthed anxiously at Janelle through a cloud of students. Outside, jags of lightning split the South Florida sky.

A blue-tipped faux-hawk stepped into Tash's field of vision.

"Professor Grover?" The student clutched a hardback copy of Tash's novel, *The Colony*, to the peeling skin above her tank top. She thrust the book forward, over Tash's desk. "Will you sign this? I knew I couldn't geek out while we were still being graded, but I love your book. I'm so excited it's being made into a series."

Tash paused her frantic sweeping up of class notes and rearranged her panicked features into something she hoped appeared composed. She very intentionally kept *The Colony* out of her classroom in order to avoid a conflict of interest. Without a completed master's degree, Tash's adjunct standing within the English department was more of a tenuous sway.

However.

On the inside of this girl's wrist, next to a straggle of string-bracelet knots, the words *Mother Beast* were inked in a magenta gothic font.

Janelle arrived at Tash's side, and Tash saw her also spot *The Colony* fandom tattoo.

Janelle smiled placidly at the student. She offered the girl her pen. She murmured sideways at Tash: "Your message said 'emergency.' I just canceled a meeting. Where's the fire?"

In response, Tash handed Janelle her phone, where the proverbial fire raged in Tash's voicemail. And in her email. And in her texts. Earlier that day, it had raged directly in Tash's ear, as her agent, responsible for negotiating *The Colony*'s film rights, shouted words like "breach" and "noncompliance," followed by a litany of increasingly appalling consequences.

Tash pushed the thoughts momentarily away and returned to the student, scribbling a practiced signature on the book's title page, adding a scrawled *#sisterhood* and a clenched fist.

Still, the girl remained. "Professor Grover, to me, *The Colony* is canon. It means so much as a new model for female myth." Her eyes glistened. "When Noab throws her baby into the ocean . . ." Chipped nail polish rested against her heart.

Just like the tattoo, "new model for myth" came from the book clubs, and at any other time, Tash would have felt sincerely humbled. She would have slowed down for a chat. On the press tour, a publishing intern showed her a pie chart: The novel resonated deeply with progressive females and childless women aged fourteen to thirty-two. Each of these connections blew Tash away, as she'd dredged her own emotional narrative to flesh out the book's themes.

But tonight those themes were on the chopping block. The new director of *The Colony*'s streaming adaptation stood far outside its demographic. He had Tash backed into a legal corner, adamant about script revisions he deemed necessary and she deemed vile.

Janelle read all about it, her eyes wide on Tash's phone.

The student, however, kept on—oblivious to the backstage drama and unaware of Tash's desperation to flee. "Noab is heroic. *You're* heroic for writing her, Professor Grover." The girl said it just as her attention snagged on a bit of sun-bleached muscle lazily exiting the lecture hall. "Although I could probably never hack it on a dystopian island where the XY chromosome is banned." She sighed apologetically. "I like boys. I can't help it. It seems too hard to give them up."

Tash gently maneuvered the student toward the door and flipped the lights off. She glanced at Janelle, still knee-deep in Tash's mess of Hollywood texts. Right now, a world without men sounded pretty great.

It sounded better than the unexpected cult status of the little book she'd written. It sounded better than the evening ahead with a director who wanted to squeeze her heroine into a push-up bra. Better than the threats from her equally douchey film agent, who'd chewed Tash out for being unprofessional and evasive.

Because Tash liked boys, too—but she'd tired of the collateral damage men inflicted.

She exited into the hallway, half-hearting a jaded, parting smile in the girl's direction. "Nah. Giving men up is easier than you think."

The wing of Janelle's signature caftan fluttered sveltely as Tash rushed her, full tilt, through Biscayne Coastal's storm-rattled palms.

Janelle still had one ear pressed to Tash's voicemail. "Are you serious?" She turned on Tash with giant eyes. "You've been avoiding the movie studio for a *month*?"

In Tash's defense, since *The Colony* had published, its film option had been traded twice. Two other showrunners had come and gone, delivering the series' scripts into the paws of a director Tash would never have originally selected. She'd hoped if she waited long enough, *The Colony* would be traded again.

It had not; in fact, the Braverman Productions team moved forward quickly.

Now they wanted Tash to expand certain scenes into naked and steamy set pieces completely incongruent with the novel's spirit and Tash's vision for it on the screen. While her book had sex—and parts of it were very sexy—it was rendered through a female lens. The progressive film studio Tash initially sold her rights to had guaranteed her a cerebral, non-tawdry approach.

But Braverman Productions made no such promises, and Ram Braverman had bikini-carwash-orgy sensibilities.

Without the resources to legally refuse his cinematic pimping of her radically feminist tome, Tash had instead ducked the studio's emails. And their phone calls. And the messengered package they'd sent her overnight.

All while still consuming every bit of internet reaction to *The Colony*'s preproduction press. The book's fans cheered the series' casting almost as much as they denounced news of its new director. Quite mistakenly, they believed Tash had influence over those details.

In truth, Tash had such little clout, Braverman's "unnamed sources" commented to trade publications in her name. Janelle had warned Tash off the internet forums for exactly this reason—Tash cared too much, and her skin was too thin. She internalized the noise.

Unfortunately, South Florida's iconic Sweetwater Film Festival had brought Ram Braverman to town to celebrate the twentieth anniversary of *Big Gun*, his first big-budget feature. To Tash, the movie and its many sequels played like mash-ups of car-chase shoot-outs and chauvinist schlock. Braverman's splendid depiction of two-thrust intercourse betrayed a sexual illiteracy that had, in Tash's opinion, misinformed an entire generation of teenage masturbation.

This was an opinion her film agent aggressively reminded her not to express. Especially not this evening, at the dinner with Ram she'd been commanded to attend. Rather, Tash was expected to bridge the "confusion" about her tardiness in responding to the production team's requests. Her agent warned her to patch things up: "Smile and nod. Nod and smile. Do not do anything else, Tash. If you piss these people off again, the Braverman legal department will take your intellectual property and defile it in a way you won't enjoy."

Janelle's expression fell as they reached Biscayne Coastal's covered parking lot. She shoved the phone at Tash. "How could you not tell me this was happening?"

Tash shrugged the shoulders of her charcoal cardigan, yanking it off and tossing it into the backseat of her car. She unclipped her wavy russet hair from its low bun, shedding her teaching persona and returning to her unarmored self—a powerless debut author who hadn't told a soul about the Hollywood movie studio's plan to make her skankify the only creative triumph of her adult life. It mortified and paralyzed her; it would undermine everything the book was meant to be about.

"I was hoping it would go away somehow." Lame but true. "Can you and Denise please come with me tonight? We'll pretend Denise is my plus-one—I could really use her advice—and the three of us can get there early and have a drink together?" Tash gave her best friend pleading eyes. "I'm spinning out. It's a big ask, I know. I'll pay your babysitter extra."

Even though Denise's lawyering focused exclusively on real estate, and the finer points of intellectual property contracts lay beyond her daily realm, Tash itched for the backup.

Also, and perhaps most importantly, by the transitive property of Janelle, Denise's legal advice was free.

Because Tash might have talked a big game in her fearless female-warrior-island fiction—but in real life, the thought of facing the dinner solo made her want to hide under her bed. Her no-name, underdog, probably-fluke, one-book success story would not survive Braverman's blockbuster treatment. He barely gave his female characters clothing, let alone dialogue; they existed just to jiggle strategically and cheer on their male leads.

And Tash knew Braverman would strip her work and take her voice also. *The Colony* was next on his menu. Tash sensed him coming to the table hungry, sharpening his knife.

Chapter Two

Several swanky piano bars gilded the nightlife between West Palm and South Beach, yet everyone in town for the Sweetwater Film Festival seemed to be tippling at this one. Tash hurried through its velvet entrance, noting a disproportionate amount of paunchy entertainment executives beside slender stalks of actress-model cosmetic surgery. Beneath a brass-domed ceiling, jazz standards soft-trumpeted the room.

Tash slid through the crowd, searching for Janelle. She lifted the long hem of the high-neck, backless, deep-chocolate dress she'd chosen, wishing it were Kevlar instead of silk jersey. She'd tried to camouflage her nerves with winged eyeliner and glittering shadow, but she doubted that it worked.

At last, she located her best friend's jaw-length, jet-black corkscrew hair.

Tash searched the space beside Janelle for Denise but came up empty.

Janelle's habit of attracting bar strays, however, seemed very much in place. She giggled delightedly with someone on her right side as Tash wedged in on her left. Tash seized the opportunity to finish Janelle's cocktail, swallowing notes of oak and amber and black cherry, waiting for the burn of whiskey to calm her internal alarm.

"Janelle." A giant ice cube clanked against Tash's front teeth. "Please tell me Denise is coming. Please tell me it's the usual situation and she's just running a few minutes late."

Janelle swung a relaxed grin around, swiping for her emptied glass. The move betrayed how long she'd already been at the bar. "She's stuck at work." Perhaps noticing Tash's agitation, Janelle added: "But she's doing her best to get here. I promise." She straightened slightly. "Babe. Calm down. There's no need to freak out."

Tash channeled her yoga breathing. "I'm not freaking out."

"Right. Because it's just a dinner. The guy probably just wants to schmooze."

Tash should have guessed it—Janelle was already drunk. These days, she had her hands full with her children, with her promotion to department chair, with her ambitious law-firm wife. Janelle never got a night out. Clearly, she'd been making the most of this one.

Because "the guy" definitely did not just want to schmooze. "The guy" was not even just a guy. He was a powerful movie director, and he wanted Tash to sell out the soul of her story.

He wanted to "taste that army with our eyes, Natasha."

A matter of hours ago, Janelle had read that message, too.

"Hey." Janelle visibly attempted to sober. "Listen. You're here to focus on the big picture, not on one creep. Let's concentrate on what's productive." Impressively, she summoned her scholarly gravitas: "Just keep the book's overarching ideas at the front of your mind."

"Right." Tash took a deep breath.

Satisfied, Janelle signaled for another round. "And if some on-screen sex gets those ideas to a bigger audience"—she fell back into her booze-softened gleam—"then let's consider the merits of lubing up."

Tash grimaced at her in open disagreement. "Let's not."

Janelle waved it away. "For now, let me observe you." She made a grand show of inspecting Tash from every angle. "You've cleaned up nicely. Strong throat, boldly exposed spine." She tapped her glossy lips with a single, polished finger. "A defiant show of confidence. Sleek fit, without the salaciousness of overt breast."

Tash accepted this analysis. She bowed in her stilettos. "Thank you. It's hard to find something that says 'Fuck you, you fucking mother-fucker' on such short notice."

"And yet you nailed it." Janelle's praise happened to be gospel—as the author of a doctorate treatise on the Gender Semiotics of Female Costume and Armor, her taste in clothing was rarely ever wrong.

A husky chuckle issued from Janelle's other side—the friend she'd been making before Tash arrived seemed to have overheard Janelle's scrutiny. Tash peeked around and spied a man with hair like morning sex—rich brown, tousled, cut short above the ears—and ocean-blue eyes framed by tortoiseshell glasses. He wore a T-shirt and a tailored canvas jacket. Tattooed script peeked from his collarbone, illegible from where Tash made an inventory of all his handsome, hipster details.

And then slapped herself out of it—other people were temporarily irrelevant, unless they were Denise.

But Janelle had also darted a gaze in his direction. She looked at her watch and back to Tash, alight with an idea. "Twenty minutes before dinner. Let's distract you."

Tash caught on too late—Janelle had already swished a wrist, grabbing the stranger's attention as he closed out his bar tab.

"This is Caleb." Janelle said it too loudly. "He's in town for the film festival. He works in translation." She stepped back to better triangulate an introduction. "This is Tash." She swished the other wrist. "She loves subtitles. She has extremely highbrow taste."

Caleb laughed, sliding the paid billfold to the waitress ogling him from behind the bar. "Really?"

Tash shot Janelle daggers, unsettled and now annoyed, in no mood to be dazzled by grinning mischief. "No." She shifted to stare at the bar's entrance, at the burgundy curtain over the door. She willed Denise to spring forth.

Undaunted, absorbing Tash's irritation blithely, Janelle tried for another pass: "And, Caleb, which Sweetwater Film Festival highlights will you be taking in while you're in the fine bake of our beaches?"

In her periphery, Tash saw the athletic angles of his body lean in and engage.

"Well, since you ask . . ." He settled in to play along, the calligraphy on his collarbone disappearing behind his jacket collar. "I'm pretty focused on *Vaudeville Striptease*. Have you heard of it? It's a documentary about burlesque."

Tash couldn't help herself. She all but snorted. She kept her face turned toward the door.

"Janelle? Did your friend just snort at me?"

Tash sensed his gestures.

Janelle sighed into her drink. "No. She would never do that. She's unfailingly polite."

Janelle was overserved. Tash blotted it out, doubling her doorway vigil, craning her neck, making another sweep of the crowd. She checked her phone again, just in case Denise had sent up a flare.

"And highbrow, as you mentioned." Janelle's bar stray continued to talk. He must have believed himself quite clever. "Except she seems to have rolled her eyes at the mention of a documentary, which is often considered the most highbrow form of film."

Tash lost her patience—it had already been a long, terrible day.

She abandoned her manners, spinning to give the cutesy banter what it wanted. "I rolled my eyes because a documentary about burlesque sounds like a cheap excuse to look at boobs. It's like actresses who win awards for playing prostitutes, or 'important dramas' that hinge on depictions of graphic rape. You call it 'art' to make it seem legitimate and to give yourself a pretext to sit and watch."

Saying this filled Tash with a fire. She'd have to cool down for the

Braverman dinner, but in the meantime, it felt fantastic to lash out. It felt fantastic to say what her film agent wanted her to smother, fantastic to be able to sparklingly condescend: "It *isn't* art and it *isn't* highbrow. It's exploitation."

Those blue eyes blinked at where she'd driven the conversation off a cliff. "Are you serious?" He'd hardened, no longer friendly. "Do you even know anything about the film?"

"Do I need to?" How convenient, Tash had found a handsome outlet for her rage, an ideal stand-in for her Tinseltown frustrations. "Wait, let me guess—the documentary is about how it's super empowering for women to take their clothes off. It's about reclaiming our sexuality, right?" Her contempt shimmered. "Mansplain that bullshit again, *please*. The world definitely needs it in pretentious black and white."

The stranger held Tash's glare for syrup seconds, long enough for Tash to think translation should not have been his area of film. He had an actor's jaw—squarely clenched, nicely stubbled, obviously offended. He had the rugged build for executing his own stunts.

He smiled tightly at Tash, shaking his head in disbelief, turning away, which made her zing with satisfaction and back down not an inch.

Even after he stalked off, and even after Janelle rounded on her.

"What was that? I could have hooked you up!" Janelle's memories of single life were sometimes as distorted as her irrational desire to revisit them through Tash. "That guy could have been your human Valium!" She waved a swizzle stick at Tash in exasperation. "Instead, you cockblocked yourself by incorrectly monologuing a passage from my thesis!"

Tash lifted her chin, emphatically not sorry. "That wasn't from your thesis—it was from my diary." She grinned. "And that *was* like human Valium. I feel amazing."

Although she knew it would fade—telling off a random guy wouldn't save *The Colony*'s adaptation, and it would get her nowhere with Ram Braverman.

She fished around in Janelle's purse. "Call your wife again. I can't go in there without my secret weapon."

Janelle pointed after her bar stray. "Based on that, I think you can." But she took the phone anyway and pressed a button. She touched the rim of her glass to Tash's forehead in reproachful affection. "Cheers. You do just fine on your own."

Tash would have preferred Ram Braverman to look like a cartoon scoundrel. If he was going to strong-arm her beloved novel into bawdiness, a greasy comb-over should have awaited, or beady features, or a beer gut. Could the universe not throw her a bone?

Instead, just as pictured in the industry profiles she'd dug up, a rectangularly stout, prematurely gray-haired, early-fifties corporate-entertainment bully in an expensive navy polo stood to greet her from his well-located table in the middle of the piano bar's main dining room. Ram Braverman pulled Tash's chair out, his welcome easy. His cologne carried hints of vetiver and saddle leather and the *je ne sais quoi* of corporate jet.

"I'm glad you could come, Natasha." Obviously, he knew she didn't have a choice.

Insincerely and with great strength, Tash discharged an answering, high-wattage grin. "It's so nice to meet you." She endured the handshake. "Please, just call me Tash."

Tash's father, Vikram Grover, was the only older man who used her full name—and usually only in disappointment, like when Tash had quit her master's program, or realized too late the ballroom deposit for her canceled wedding could not be refunded.

"My stepdaughter made me promise to tell you she's a big fan." Ram lowered back into his seat. "She's the one who insisted I direct this series."

Tash was pretty sure she'd read that Ram Braverman had many

stepdaughters—and many stepsons and many ex-wives. But Tash did
not inquire further. She was behaving, like her agent had instructed.
Smile and nod.

Tash crossed her legs neatly, sage-green upholstery copping a feel of
the exposed skin along her back. Across an expanse of thick cloth and
mercury-glassed candle, Ram inspected a bottle offered to him by a
sommelier, the deference of pour and patience informing Tash she sat
with a Goliath. Informing her no measure of bared spine or dramatic
eyeliner could level their mismatch.

"You know, it's funny." Nose in his wine, a deep quaff, a nod to the
sommelier. "Typically, if we have an author who's too committed to
their rights, I want to blow my brains out." Ram divulged this fantastic
tidbit as if it were not an incredibly ballsy and audacious fuck-you.

As if the contract clause he referenced—the one that had forced
this dinner, Tash's right of first refusal—were a nuisance instead of an
author's only shield. Tash had ceded creative control over the series
adaptation, as was common in literary-to-film agreements, in exchange
for a small set of legal privileges. Which, even after Braverman took
possession of *The Colony*'s existing episode scripts, specified that no
one else could write changes to them, except Tash, unless the work was
offered to her and she explicitly declined.

This provision had, this past month, been the loophole within
which Tash had hidden away; Braverman's team harassed her to write
filth, and Tash was careful never to actually decline it. Instead, she'd
simply stuck her head in the sand. Where she also buried her dreams
of meaningful feminist direction, and Gayle and Oprah hosting an
all-girlfriends premiere. *The Colony* might be the only book Tash ever
authored—she'd rather watch its screen release stall in a writers' purga-
tory forever than let it be tarted up and abused.

Mr. Braverman's expression reflected none of this contentious history as he swirled an ounce of Shiraz beneath the crystal swags of a
candelabra. "Natasha, this case is different. Your project is important.

Even though it's women's television, it reminds me of the classics—for example, when you were writing, did you ever think of Noab's mother as Tina Turner in *Mad Max Beyond Thunderdome*?"

Tash gagged. Or gasped. Or both. No one had ever asked that. It was shockingly perceptive.

Ram chuckled, not noticing her fluster. "Does that sound crazy? Don't worry—we're done with casting. I'm not calling Mel."

"It doesn't sound crazy." It sounded like Braverman had cameras trained on the inside of her head. A color printout of Tina Turner in *Mad Max* had lived on Tash's mood board for four months as she visualized Noab's family tree for that first draft, trying to capture the post-apocalyptic majesty of Noab's heritage. That widow's peak mohawk and the enormous spring-hoop earrings were Tash's shortcuts into mentally conjuring the character—even though the narrative plots had nothing in common, and the women of *The Colony* didn't wear junkyard jewelry or spray their hair.

"Good. I'm glad we're on the same page." Ram's fist closed around the stem of his paper-thin goblet balloon. "I've never done a series like this before, you know."

Oh, Tash knew. Ram Braverman credits rolled at the end of disaster movies, films with an excess of explosions, vehicles for former pro wrestlers; and typically featured a combination of grumpy and wunderkind US law enforcement, drag racing, maybe a touch of martial arts. A twenty-two-year-old actress would play somebody's mother; she might also appear topless, perhaps for no reason.

Ram kept talking, sketching out his vision for Hewett, the sea captain Noab rescues from a shipwreck: "Part seaweed-bedraggled pirate—and part frightened, unmoored knave. Yes?"

Tash was baffled. "Sure." Ram had the latitude to portray characters any way he liked, and yet, unexpectedly, he seemed to be seeking her opinion, which threw her more off-balance.

Candle flicker danced across the cube of Ram's silver-fox hairline. "That's why Hewett's perfect to save the baby!"

And there—there dropped the other shoe.

Mid-gulp, Shiraz threatened to erupt from Tash's eyeballs.

"Hewett signals a new era for the island!" Ram leaned forward, animated, elbows on the table, climaxing to his own idea.

Tash couldn't weigh her words before they rioted and grabbed their pitchforks. Her syllables lit torches, rushing to burn his village to the ground. "What? No! Absolutely not. The baby dies." *The Colony*'s finale wasn't a casual plot twist; it was Tash's sticking point. She'd bled for that last chapter, its pain a point of fan pride. "Hewett isn't even on the island when Noab has the baby. The *colony* is the new era." And in case he missed this detail the first time: "The baby dies—that's the whole point."

One of Ram's eyes twitched, perhaps because Tash had interrupted his monologue. The rest of his boxy visage remained unaltered. "That might be the whole point of *the book*, but we're making a television series. And ideally, a series has more than one season."

The statement seesawed between them. Tash's circuit board began to fry. Beneath her pulled-together shell, an adjunct professor at a backwater college cowered, wearing half a dress and feeling helpless in a cheesy piano bar.

But Ram broke away from their conversation before Tash could respond.

"Speaking of knaves!" He cast a salute to someone over Tash's head. Rising from the table, Ram thumped a canvas-jacketed man on the back. "We could have waited, but we didn't."

In slow motion, Tash fought a dry heave as the sommelier filled a third glass. The scalloped arm of the brass-legged dining chair beside her scraped back, then shuffled forward. Sitting in it now was a man with blue eyes, tortoiseshell glasses, and a collarbone tattoo.

"Natasha, this is Caleb Rafferty." Ram ping-ponged a second in-troduction. "Caleb, our scripts are adapted from Natasha's book." To Tash, matter-of-factly: "Caleb will be arranging our coitus. He's a sex designer—the best working today. You'll be collaborating with him on the new scenes you'll be writing."

In order of the things Tash was too sickened to acknowledge: coitus and sex designer, collaborating with him, and Ram's additional scenes.

Caleb pivoted to smile obnoxiously at her, milking the outrageous coincidence of their collision. "New scenes, huh? Sounds like a great excuse to look at boobs."

Tash couldn't muster the appropriate, answering churl. She reeled, defenseless, very much alone. Denise had never showed. Janelle had gone home.

She stared at Caleb blankly. "You said you worked in translation."

Ram glanced briefly between them. "Caleb and his partner con-ceive and choreograph nudity and copulation. Anything sensual our production might need." He put his post-#MeToo palms up. "My set is a safe set." Spoken like a man with an extensive team of lawyers. "But Caleb's fornication is very, very hot. We're excited to have him in the trenches with us—consider him your guide."

Despite the bizarre compliment, and in the midst of his gloating, Caleb seemed to need to clarify. To Tash, in an aside he might have offered if they were standing at the bar, if she'd never verbally attacked him: "It's called intimacy coordination. I do the physical translation and design of any on-camera intimate moments. I think your friend heard 'translation' and jumped to subtitles."

Janelle's drunken misinterpretation anchored the moment, and Tash held it like a breadcrumb, like a coordinate, like she could use it to retrace her steps.

"Now I don't want to rush this." Ram's eyes had diverted to his phone. He swiped and began typing. "But I have another dinner, up-stairs in a few. Natasha, we're very lucky." As his thumbs moved. "We want everything to run smoothly during shooting. It's rare we get a sex designer in this early to help us shape the scripts. In addition to being the best, Caleb is attached to the actress playing Noab. It's the only reason we were able to nab him during rewrites, on such short notice." Ram folded his napkin. He drained the rest of his wine.

He pushed back from the table, and Tash looked on, bewildered.

"Caleb's résumé even includes *Transtempora*." Ram proffered it to her as a shorthand. "I have the utmost confidence in his abilities to spice up the action between our leads."

Tash had seen one episode of *Transtempora*, another literary adaptation. She'd watched in glimpses, mostly covering her eyes, the show's superbly rendered time travel surpassed only by its frequent and ornate sexual violence. *Transtempora* was where commodified lady dreams were taken to be despoiled and left to die. She needed a minute. "Can we pause?"

But Ram had vacated his seat already, heading somewhere more important, somewhere else. "You two stay and get acquainted. Have dinner—they'll put it on my card." Before he walked away: "Natasha, it's your story—but with Caleb here, we can really start to *feel* Noab and Hewett's bodies."

Truly astonished by Ram's delegating, Tash glanced at Caleb, who was glancing back. His earlier affront seemed to have ceded to amusement. Probably because it wasn't his one and only opus being snuffed out.

Unfortunately, Ram moved quickly, already ascending the spiral staircase to meet his next companions. In order to be heard, Tash had to yell halfway across the dining room's plush floor. Before she knew it, she was up and shouting.

"I'm not writing tits and ass onto the screen for you!"

Ram's pristine loafers froze mid-step on the stairs. He backtracked across the dining room, his features neutral. His gaze, however, was dipped in poison darts.

"Keep your voice down. Half this restaurant plays golf with me at

Brentwood." Ram shucked his put-on niceties aside. "Unless that announcement was a decline on my script revisions? Because our legal
team tells me that would be a wonderful thing for you to screech in
public." He nodded to their many witnesses.

Tash imagined cracking her wineglass. "It wasn't a decline." She
imagined the most jagged shard. "But I won't turn my book into smut."

"It's not your book." Ram's eyes flashed. "It's my television series."

Viscerally, Tash wished to equal his monster. She wished for something barbarous and obscenely female, the bloodlust of a thousand savage harpies. "Your television series should respect its source material's
fans. There's a reason the book's sex scenes aren't explicit. The audience doesn't want crudeness—they want strength and beauty."

Ram menaced a laugh. "Look, I'm thrilled for all the lesbians at
Wellesley who came to your book signings—"

"Hey—" From the far reaches of the commotion, Caleb surfaced
to interrupt.

"—but none of them are going to watch a program about girl warriors without some tits and ass." Ram stepped flush to the table. "And by
'tits and ass,' Natasha, I mean I want the hot version. The *dirty* version."

"Ram—" Caleb shot up.

Ram remained unfazed. "I want wet spots. I want Wellesley squirm-
ing to get off. I'm the director. It's my call."

Caleb moved in front of Tash, his role changed, referee to body-
guard. "Let's stop there."

"Five weeks until rehearsals." Ram's voice jabbed at Tash from behind Caleb's blockade. "Write what I've asked for, or decline it, and
I'll get someone else to write it instead. Either way, this is going to
happen."

"Ram—" Caleb began to usher him away from the table.

"Please, decline it! Do us all a favor!" Ram called to Tash over his
shoulder. "Getting rid of you would make my fucking day!"

"Did a very beautiful, very pissed-off woman just come out here?" In the coral glow of valet signage, Caleb's tailored jacket made him look like a broader version of *Miami Vice*.

Tash might have laughed at this absurdity—under different circumstances, if her hands hadn't still been shaking. If she hadn't been holed up on the bar's covered veranda, retreating further into the shadowed dark. She watched Caleb attempt to interrogate the pimply teenager manning the cabinet of car keys from her concealed spot on a creaking rattan couch.

"Brown hair? You'd notice her. Beautiful, like I said."

The acne on the valet's chin smirked, but the valet himself disinterestedly frowned. "Dude. This is South Florida. You're describing the whole place."

Tash heard the "beautiful." It registered—even she wasn't that immune. But Caleb's notes on her aesthetics wouldn't fix what had just happened. His earnestness could keep tossing out adjectives. Tash desired only that he get lost so she could call a taxi and escape.

Her fingers fumbled on a ride app, waiting for him to evaporate.

By the rack of car keys, Caleb pressed an index finger to the top ridge of his glasses, continuing to grill the valet. "Long dress, open in the back?"

Tash set her phone aside. She was curious, despite her better judgment. She lit the cigarette she'd bummed from that very same valet.

"She kind of looks like Padma Lakshmi?"

The valet squinted. "Sorry, dude, who?"

Tash suppressed a cough, the cigarette actually kind of pathetic. She stubbed the butt out. She didn't even smoke.

She fanned the humid air around her as she followed Caleb's progress: He scanned the beach road, the small boardwalk, the parking lot of the restaurant next door.

She hated to admit it, but by purely physical standards, Janelle had chosen well—Caleb might have actually been Tash's perfect human Valium. Her animal interest mingled with her intellectual aversion: By now, the constricting outer layer of his jacket would be sweaty; beneath it, his T-shirt would be plastered to his back. June nights in South Florida simmered sticky, and Tash imagined he must be dying for his hotel room—to make quick work of that belt buckle. To free himself of those jeans.

So vivid was her visualization, she almost didn't notice him find her and sit down.

"Hey. Are you okay?" He'd dragged an ottoman over, staring at her intently, fingers steepled and knees wide. "Braverman was out of line—I'm sorry I didn't stop that sooner. I guess I walked into something I don't quite understand."

Tash prickled at his white-knight act. "We don't know each other. You should go away."

"Natasha—"

"It's Tash." She ignored his splayed thighs. She reopened the taxi app. "I'm fine. Please leave me alone."

Caleb shifted, ducking his head for her attention. "Tash. I would. But . . ." He shrugged, doing a good job of apologetic. "We have to work together."

She glanced up tersely. "We don't."

Caleb closed his mouth, his stubble caught in a passing headlight. "Okay." He nodded reasonably, a jaw rub. "But if we do—I just got this project. I need a day to get caught up. I'll read the pilot and the production team's notes and see how I can help you."

Tash glared at him fully. She attempted to dismember his savior complex with her eyes. "No, thanks." The taxi's red dot dawdled, a span of map squiggles away. "I don't want your help." She stood, deciding she'd rather wait by the road.

Caleb rose to follow.

At the porch steps, gallingly, he offered her a hand.

Tash ignored him, striding toward the sidewalk. She focused on not tripping. She focused on the Floridian coastal nightclub details: tiny sports cars with huge hubcaps, an elbow on a rolled-down window, the rustle of palm tree, the lowering lid of cicada clack. She focused on her plan to call Denise in the morning, to commandeer her attention, to address the options for legal recourse, to orchestrate a way out of this bind.

Caleb tagged along behind her. He tried again as Tash fixed on her phone: "Look, I know Ram—"

"Yes. I saw you two are friends." Tash interrupted, flicking her hair over her shoulder, laser-beaming her disdain. "Which makes me think there's probably a lap dance out there that needs you more than I do. Surely there's a topless actress somewhere who needs you to tell her where to kneel. You should get on that."

Twice in one night, Caleb's eyes darkened. "Holy shit." He'd stopped short on the sidewalk. "What is your problem?"

And again, Tash yielded to the zinging rush. "My problem is that *Transtempora* is my nightmare, and Braverman apparently thinks it's aspirational and you're some kind of savant. I don't know what your specific set of tools is, but you design amazing sexual assault. Congratulations. It must feel wonderful to set a movement back a decade."

This time Caleb stepped closer, hipster hulking, with Tash's same tinge of toxic spleen. "You have literally no idea what you're talking about."

"Right, and you do." Tash patronized him crassly, noticing the taxi's red dot announce it was near. "The fully clothed man whose job is to position the naked actress." She moved toward her getaway, her bare back throwing him the finger.

"You couldn't be more wrong!" Caleb shouted after her as Tash slid into the taxi. "I'm actually your best bet! Braverman's writers' room smells like an old jockstrap—*that's* your nightmare, trust me." He seemingly refused to be cowed. "I'm who you want on this. I'm one of the good ones."

Tash would have liked to believe that, but she'd learned the hard way. There were no good ones. Good guys didn't exist.

Chapter Three

Janelle barreled into Tash's modern duplex the next morning.

"This cannot be real!" Janelle spoke too loudly—both for the hour and for Tash's aching head. "You're *sure* he's not in subtitles? You're sure it was the same 'You will meet a tall, dark stranger' hottie you chased away before I went home?" Janelle put a sack of hangover sandwiches from the deli next to her kids' daycare into Tash's hands.

Tash's eau-de-previous-evening sagged onto a barstool at her kitchen island. "I'm sure." She opened the paper bag gratefully, inhaling a fog of bacon, egg, and cheese. "Thanks for this. I swear, I'm not really that hungover." Her frontal lobe hurt from last night's confrontation, and in anticipation of the road ahead.

"*Yet*—you're not hungover *yet*, you mean." From her tote, as if she had not imbibed an excess of Old-Fashioneds just a heap of hours earlier, Janelle unsheathed their favorite tequila. Nimbly, she unpacked tomato juice, pepperoncini, hot sauce, and lemons from the tree in her yard. A head of celery went onto a cutting board pulled from Tash's cabinet. "It's just so crazy!" Janelle gestured with a long knife. "I'll make drinks while you call Denise. Then you have to tell me everything from the beginning. Again."

Through her brain throb, Tash understood this whirlwind of grease and alcohol as an offering: Janelle felt guilty about her wife's no-show.

Booze was Janelle's love language. Breakfast sandwiches were her apology.

Even if Tash had already told her it wasn't necessary—the dinner wasn't Janelle's responsibility, and the rumble with Braverman probably would have still happened even if Denise had been there.

Still, Tash unwrapped a sandwich and bit into buttered sourdough, watching as Janelle sliced a lemon. "Don't make mine too strong. I have to go to campus and turn in grades."

Biscayne Coastal's fame and funds came from its marine biology program—and, not coincidentally, its ocean laboratory's proximity to perfect, gnarly South Florida waves. The non-ocean-science disciplines were often overlooked, and in keeping with that fond neglect, the English department's records engine ran on a backbone of 1960s vacuum tubes. Tash had to manually submit her end-of-semester marks.

Janelle halved a head of celery. "Me, too. Let's go in together."

"Okay." Tash observed Janelle's knife skills. Bloody Maria highballs had always gone hand in hand with *The Colony*; five years earlier, Tash and Janelle had devised the blueprint for the novel amid an endless pour of this very drink.

"Are those the contracts?" Janelle pointed with her chin.

Tash nodded. The reclaimed-driftwood surface of her dining table bristled with a hard-copy history of *The Colony*'s literary legalese— from its initial small-press publication to the contracts dominoing from its rights' sales. Tash had woken early to unearth them from a packing container in her utility closet, shoved there when she'd moved back into the duplex after Zachary, her ex, called off their wedding.

At the time, Tash had resolved to let her space reflect her truth— and the truth was, she sucked at paperwork and organization. Administratively, she resembled a dumpster fire. The only thing alphabetized in her apartment were her running shoes.

Also, Zach had managed to make the publication of *The Colony* feel villainous, always the thing she'd chosen over him.

And Tash would choose it again. She had no regrets in that department. She was done with machismo cloaked in a sensitive veneer.

"You know what else I found in my highly organized paperwork?" Tash started in on the second half of her sandwich, buying herself time—anxious to speak to Denise, but also scared of her verdict. "Letters my mom wrote to me when I was twelve and thirteen. She sent them when I got homesick during those summers at my aunt's house."

Janelle raised an amused eyebrow. "The Nice Indian Girl immersions?" Tash's adolescent roti-rolling failures were an eternal source of Janelle's glee.

Tash smirked back. Decades later, her rotis still were never round, she minced onions unevenly, and her Hindi broke. Tash's Caucasian mother meant well when she sent the Grover siblings to their father's sister to absorb Indian traditions she couldn't provide, but Tash always felt inadequate during those long weeks.

"The weird thing is, I don't remember if I ever wrote her back." Tash glanced to where she'd stacked the envelopes on an end table near her couch. "I didn't even realize I saved her letters."

Mary Grover had apparently written every day. In square, neat, high-school-math-teacher handwriting, on gridded paper. The letters chronicled the ordinary details of Florida summer household chores. They were actually kind of boring, but they evidenced an effort.

"That's interesting." Janelle rimmed two tumblers with several twists of coarse black pepper grind. "Stop stalling. Call Denise."

Tash gave in. She retrieved her phone from a low console beside her living room's sliding glass doors, stepping out to the best part of the duplex—the balcony that rested in the tangled shade of thatch and foxtail palms. Beyond it, down a soft-paved bike lane, through a rickety gate overrun by the gauche magenta of crepe myrtle, the blue expanse of the Atlantic Ocean surged and foamed.

It swelled out of sight but sounded close enough to soothe an insomniac through an open window; close enough to accidentally fill a driveway with wayward sea turtles, or curl an expensive salon cut with its thick air and its salt.

"Hey, Tash." Denise answered the call on her car's Bluetooth, on the highway, probably in a designer blouse. Her voice rang no-nonsense, just like the razored angles of her ash-blond bob. "I heard you two were in rare form last night. I'm sorry I missed it."

Tash sat at attention. She knew the available window for Denise to ponder non-billable literary clusterfucks would be small and short. Corporate ladder dreams swamped Denise constantly with clients and closings.

Denise plunged in. "I read the hate mail from your agency. From what I can tell, they have a solid argument—the right of first refusal doesn't mean you can block the adaptation's script changes forever. There's a time frame, and after a period of your inaction, a failure to respond to Braverman defaults to a no."

Tash stung from the swiftness of Denise's judgment.

"If that happens and the studio registers your contractual decline, you have no further recourse—especially since the series' scripts were created by other writers. The studio would be able to alter the written film property without repercussion. Then you're watching *The Colony* from your couch, just like everybody else." A horn screeched in Denise's background. "Unless the series spawns a sequel—in your case a Season Two. Then Braverman is required to come back to you and start the whole negotiation over."

Feeling ill, Tash reached across her outdoor furniture to open the balcony slider for Janelle. "Well, forget that. Season Two is moot."

"Put her on speaker." Janelle settled on the wicker couch opposite Tash, delivering a scarlet highball stilted tall with garnish. She listed toward the phone. "Babe, can you repeat whatever Season Two thing you just said? Natasha needs the money. I had to pay for drinks last night."

"What? I paid for those drinks!" Tash glared as Janelle winked. "And I don't need the money." Not entirely true—adjuncts earned next to nothing, and the book's modest proceeds were a nest egg Tash had vowed from the beginning not to touch. "Not enough to change the end, anyway—and that's their price, Jan. That's how they'd push us into another season."

Janelle furrowed. "I don't get it."

Tash point-blanked across the coffee table and the propped-up phone: "Braverman wants to save the baby. Last night he told me he thinks Hewett should do it."

Janelle coughed through her cocktail, bugging eyes at Tash as if she'd incorrectly heard. Clearing her throat, gaze tearing tequila: "Does he know the baby dies?" Janelle had read so many drafts of the novel, she could recite it in her sleep. Plus, the principles of the island's Lore were cribbed from her class notes. "That's the whole point of the book."

Denise crackled over the speaker. "Wow. Dead-baby talk is so great first thing in the morning."

Janelle shot an outraged look at the phone. "Denise! The ending is essential!"

Tash could have disintegrated into fury also—but the clock was ticking on her time with Denise. Instead, she recentered the conversation. "Denise, what about that moral clause? The right of integrity? The one you said only ever gets enforced in France?" Tash read from a page she'd pulled out from her contract: "'. . . any act in relation to the work that is harmful to the author's honor or reputation.'"

Denise boomed drolly. "It still only ever gets enforced in France. And I'm not an IP expert, but I think a plot change isn't 'derogatory treatment of the published work.' Especially if it *saves* a baby instead of throwing it off a cliff."

Tash searched the mental list of escape routes she'd calculated before the call. "What about the sex scenes Braverman wants? Does the moral clause apply there?"

"Do they constitute 'derogatory treatment'? I doubt it, unless they tried to force you to write something outrageously freaky, which they probably won't do. Braverman's movies maybe aren't intellectual, but they're also not fetish films." Denise's serrated humor bounced through the speaker. "Plus, the sex *is* in the book, Tash. It's feminist-lens or implied, I know"—before anyone could protest—"but still. You'd be splitting hairs."

Janelle drooped. Tash knew they shared the same thought: Noab *had* to cast her infant son into the ocean. The fundamentals of *The Colony* depended on it, the act both a bittersweet consequence of a fictional philosophy and a grueling example of its rules.

And in this dimension, Tash had already sacrificed so much in the same name. She hadn't adjusted the ending of the book to suit her parents or a literary formula. She hadn't softened it for her ex-fiancé or his objections—even when Zachary couldn't separate the book's fiction from their real-life facts.

Janelle grasped at a last straw: "But, Denise, don't you think it'd be bad press for Braverman to ruin the final chapter of a book that has such a devoted following?"

Denise's voice dropped dryly. "Look, guys, I support you and I support the book. But ask your film agent, Tash—I'm guessing right of integrity was thrown in as a feel-good. In actual practice, an entertainment studio would crush you in litigation."

Tash held Janelle's lamenting gaze. "Awesome." Then she held her drink out for a refill. She'd wanted clarity before this phone call, but now she longed for a blur.

Denise took them off Bluetooth, car door slamming, her heels clipping competently on concrete. "In summary, if I were your counsel, which I'm not"—her relief at this rather palpable—"I'd direct you to make nice. Braverman could have already taken action to class your dicking around as a decline, Tash. It sounds like the studio is giving you a last chance. You should probably play ball."

Tash closed her eyes against the sky and the jungle canopy above her, hauling in its cleansing breath and exhaling her own impending capitulation.

"I know you don't want to hear this—but write the scenes." Kindly, Denise's closing piece of advice. "Do it well, because we know you can, and maybe you'll win the director over. You'll have to pick your battles. If Braverman likes your sex scenes, maybe you'll convince him he *should* throw the baby out with the bathwater." Denise actually chuckled.

Janelle frowned at Tash apologetically. She reached to pull the phone off speaker. "Babe. Take it easy with the jokes."

That afternoon, Tash and Janelle kicked it old-school with the college campus mainframe. They waved a send-off to the second semester, submitting final grades. Then they resolved to reread the most recent emails from Braverman together.

They headed to Tash's favorite spot at Biscayne Coastal: the seaside, stunning-in-its-bungalow-chic-scruff, surf-shack-but-make-it-academic adjunct lounge.

Wide plank tables splayed beneath lazy fan paddles, and the side of the building facing the ocean was essentially open-air. The college's slack attitude toward its arts and letters staff could absolutely be dismaying, and Tash knew she was languishing there, rather than advancing on her career path—but the lounge's breezy gull flap almost made it okay. The fasten of a sarong knot, the grains of salt crusted on arm hair, the violence of reef break just before a sunset—the vista from the adjunct lounge had been endless inspiration for *The Colony*.

Also, the lounge had an industrial printer.

Which, when it was working and stocked with ink and paper, was a generous delight.

Tash printed out each of the adaptation's original ten episode scripts. Then she printed comments from Brian Doolittle, Braverman's head writer, who'd sent many of the marked-urgent messages she'd sidestepped. His official title was story editor, and he seemed like a total jerk.

Janelle flopped onto one of the lounge's many beanbags bordering the golden-hour sand. Boom box tunes wafted over on a breeze of portable grilling and light beer, from a squad of boisterous volleyball players bathing luminous in the fading sun. Boys on boards rode the distant sea swell beyond them. It looked like surfer centerfold, but the outlines of Noab's island lurked in those pre-dusk waves, when the murk churned fiercest, and the coral was most eager to stab.

"What exactly does this fuckwit want from you?" Janelle herself was inspiration for the story: Her love for Tash lived in the island's Sisterhood, and her wisdom resided in the island's Lore.

Tash responded flatly. "The fuckwit wants me to give him tits and ass."

Her attitude would need a lobotomy if she was going to oblige him—which, despite Denise's warnings and Tash's impressive tower of freshly printed paper, she had not fully convinced herself she was going to do.

Nevertheless, she and Janelle started reading.

The notes reiterated three priority scene additions, in Episodes One, Five, and Nine. Noab's discovery of Hewett's shipwrecked body in Episode One went first—in the novel, Noab dragged an injured Hewett from rough limestone beach shallows, before the island's savage sea-monster guardian could taste Hewett's blood in the water; and Hewett remained unconscious as Noab brought him to shelter in a sacred Prayer Grove. Noab had never seen a male body before because the island's population was wholly women.

"And in simple terms, for us laypeople, this means . . . ?" Janelle flipped back and forth through the papers, the TV-script format unfamiliar to her.

Tash rifled through her stack of corresponding comments and reported in staccato word-for-word:

"'Camera open on interior Grove hut. Hewett, unconscious, draped across prayer slab. Noab attends to his body. Peels his clothes off. What happens then? What's her reaction to seeing this unknown creature naked?'" In Tash's dry affect, it sounded like a word problem on the SATs. "'Should be extremely sensual. This is the lead-up to their explosive sexual attraction. How best to set the tone?'"

Tash dropped the paper, capsizing backward into her beanbag. "Brian Doolittle, the story editor, is contractually prevented from writing it himself—so everything Braverman wants is phrased like this, with leading questions."

Janelle had doodled a sketch of male anatomy in the margin of her printout, which she waved above Tash's face. "What I'm hearing is that they want you to show us Hewett's dick."

Tash had to laugh from where she stared up at the fan blades. "Is that what you're hearing? Because like I told you, Braverman said tits and ass—not dick and balls." She shrugged horizontally, falsely imperious: "Although. I suppose the only person who could truly decide that is the sex designer."

"The *celebrity* sex designer!" Janelle twinkled at the mention of Caleb Rafferty, whom she'd been crowing about when she wasn't cursing Ram. She'd decided Caleb was Tash's silver lining. "By far, that man is the best part of this production."

"Why? You met him for five sloppy minutes. Don't forget that he's the enemy."

Janelle's raven curls caught the lilt of dimming sun. "No—he's *working* for the enemy. Which, I agree, is problematic. But we were having such a great chat before you showed up. I liked him. He seemed funny and smart."

Tash balked. "You thought he wrote subtitles."

Janelle denied this. "No. I just wasn't listening to the details." She sighed performatively. "I got lost in those dreamy eyes."

Tash had already chided herself for a similar detour into thoughts of

Caleb's hotness and had since resolved to shutter her vision of his fine points. He could be an ogre or a knockout; either way she'd stay fixed on her book. "Wonderful. Shall we call your wife and kids to talk about him a little more?"

Janelle clucked. "I'm not attracted to Caleb sexually, Natasha. I'm just saying. Objectively, he seemed sweet and nice." She pulled Tash upright to sit properly. "His hands were also massive. Capable-looking. Probably calloused and rough." A beat passed. "Or soft, if that's how you like it."

"Jan. Please stop." Wrung out, Tash faced her friend, knee-to-knee on the floor. "Yes, he's handsome. But this is going to be miserable enough without adding in another throbbing member."

Janelle smothered her delighted expression. "But if you have to stomach these notes, you can also laugh."

"I'm not there yet." In each step of the novel's revisions, Tash had reminded herself to steady on the female point of view—to portray for her reader what a *woman* might want to know about a character, what a *woman* would find sexy.

It was a challenging exercise, and it had the added benefit of allowing Tash to skirt any writing outside her comfort zone.

She itemized her apprehension: "I've never written explicit sex for a reason—I'm afraid I won't be good at it. I feel like I'll either sound like a pervert or a prude. Also, I don't want to be responsible for asking an actress to take her clothes off."

"Those are two very different issues." Janelle slid easily into her more erudite persona. "Forget whether or not you're 'good.' You wrote a hit, so we're not debating that." She shimmied straighter, bidding Tash to pay attention. "But let's drill down on the idea of exploitation, if you want. There's nothing wrong with a female character being sexy—I just think you're associating it with shame. Which is a trap laid by misogynistic vigilantes."

Tash envied Janelle's mastery of theory. She navigated loaded ideas with a fluidity Tash couldn't begin to approach. Janelle often saw possibility where Tash only saw fraughtness.

"I'm not associating it with shame. I'm associating it with cheapness." In grad school, Tash's literary-journal-editor boyfriend liked to point out her inability to reconcile high and low—in her academic work but also in his highbrow justifications for his lowbrow sleeping with his interns. "It just seems like a dumbing-down. Throwing in nudity for the headlines it might generate negates everything I tried to message in the book. My literary fiction will become mass-market."

Janelle shook her head. "I disagree. I think you could choose to feel differently about this—maybe your literary fiction takes on another facet. Maybe making the sexuality more explicit grants the story access to a wider audience. And then the more that people choose to see it, the more they talk about its message. Which is ultimately what we're after, right?"

Tash gave up. "I don't know."

"I do." Janelle brandished her copy of Episode One. "So, like I said—let's lube it up."

Tash winced.

Janelle only laughed again, congratulating herself: "Natasha—sex can be smart. If you need a testimonial, ask my wife."

Tash's gaze went to the shirtless volleyball players ass-slapping each other on the warm sand. She sighed. "I just don't want to be a writer who says 'rigid arousal' and 'hardened shaft.' I'll feel like an idiot."

"No, totally. I get that." Janelle nodded seriously. Before she grinned again. "I guess you'll just have to ask your sex translator for some different words."

Chapter Four

Janelle forced Tash to track down Caleb's office number before they left the adjunct lounge.

Tash obtained the information easily, on a first try—Caleb Rafferty, co-founder of Scene Partners, a Hollywood consulting firm in Burbank, California. She clicked around the website, accompanied by Janelle's fascinated reading of the "About Us" highlights. Tash jotted the digits on a scrap of paper.

She closed her laptop. "I'll call him when I get home."

Janelle smacked Tash with Episode One's script. "Do it now!"

"No. I love you, but this will probably require ugly groveling, which I'd like to do in private." Tash recalled the scorched earth she'd left behind in that parking lot and the hostility that crackled between them when she slammed the taxi door in Caleb's face. "I'm probably going to have to beg him for a meeting."

Because she was out of other options.

She drew her knees up on the white shag carpet in her bedroom as she dialed. A receptionist put her on hold before Tash could blurt that all she wanted was Caleb's cell number—she didn't actually want to speak with him, she'd rather just apologize over text. Then they could begin the even worse task of tackling Braverman's edits.

"This is Stacy." Instead of the receptionist, a different woman's voice came over the line.

"Hi." Tash attempted to sound friendly and relaxed, rather than brimming with nausea. "I'm calling for Caleb Rafferty's cell phone contact, please?"

The woman shut her down smoothly. "I'm sorry, we don't give that out. But I'd be happy to pass on a message."

"Are you sure I can't just have his number? We met last night, but I forgot to take his card." Not really what happened, but Tash didn't need to get into the details.

The voice prickled with interest. "Last night?"

"Yes."

"Tell me your name, again?"

"Tash Grover."

It met with a distinct, stomach-sinking chuckle. "Ah. Well, I'd love to give you Caleb's info, but I can't. Why don't you leave a message, and I'll make sure he gets it."

Defeatedly, forebodingly, Tash closed her eyes.

She searched for the right words. "Okay. Can you please tell him I'm following up on his offer to help me with some production notes?" As if she had not ferociously spat that very offer back. "And also"—Tash breathed into the *make nice*, remembering to *play ball*—"if he could return this call, I'd like to apologize."

The woman's tone danced with amusement. "Sure thing."

Tash enunciated her own cell number, two times, before she hung up.

An hour later, her phone chimed with an incoming call from Unknown.

Tash curled in the corner of her walk-in closet, guessing it was Caleb. "Hello?"

"Hi. This is Caleb Rafferty." Indifferently, with none of the heated emotion of their last exchange. "I got a message that you rang my office."

"I did." Tash charged through her unease. She ripped off the bandage, launching rare rockets of concession. "I'd like to apologize for some of the things I said to you last night."

"Oh." A moment ticked by. "Just *some* of the things?"

Tash refused to take the bait. She focused on her desperate need to salvage her influence over the series adaptation. She inhaled through flared nostrils: "The important part is I'm sorry. If you have time to see me, I'd really like to talk through Braverman's notes."

She held on to this same, supplicating mindset the next day, on her drive to the Seashell Resort and Yachting Club. Caleb's choice of location struck her as an odd one—she'd describe the place as quintessential tourist, or exiled oligarch, or Ponzi scheme magnate cathedral-by-the-sea. It was a soaring-ceilinged, canary-yellow concrete building styled as Italian villa, its balustrades guarding not the canals of Venice, but the Florida Intracoastal Waterway.

Tash ridiculed none of this—it might not have been her natural aesthetic, but she enjoyed frozen coconut rum served in a scooped-out pineapple with a gold umbrella sometimes, too.

She discovered Caleb in the glossy marble arcade that flanked the swimming pool, where a brunch crowd in pastel boat shoes and diaphanous cover-ups made his navy turtle-patterned button-down seem restrained. He raised an expressionless hand to Tash in welcome, from a coffee nook slightly away from an extensive omelet station. His mouth remained in a straight line.

Steel drum covers of '90s pop soundtracked Tash's plank walk as she prepared to reexperience her swallowing of pride.

She arrived at the table at the same time as a waiter. Tash sat down awkwardly, ignoring the menu and ordering mint tea. The waiter barely glanced at her, seemingly unable to rip his gaze from Caleb. Tash recalled last night's bartender, who had similarly gawked, and wondered how far Caleb's looks regularly got him, what with the general chisel and the Clark Kent–climbs-Colorado vibe.

She moved a chunk of hair over her shoulder, flaunting her own charms.

There's nothing wrong with a female character being sexy—Janelle's words—and as the protagonist in this drama, and for the purposes of this meeting, Tash had decided to subscribe to the belief. Her reluctance to unclothe her characters did not mean she didn't enjoy men, or sex, or that she overlooked the value of her assets. It just meant she preferred to control the narrative in which they were seen.

The plummeting neckline of her fine white cotton sleeveless wrap dress, for example, was a strategic premeditation designed to highlight the luster of her skin. Its nipped-in side tie underscored her dedication to her yoga practice, while hinting at the fickle nature of clothing, suggesting fleshly pleasures just a drawstring pull away. The caress of its tulip hem against her mid-calf nodded to happenstance: One smooth thigh might flash unpredictably, depending on a leg-cross or a cross-breeze.

At least, Tash surmised her outfit meant all this. She had not wanted to bother Janelle, so she'd read up on third-wave feminism again, to reinforce her selection. Somewhat irritatingly, her ensemble appeared to not make Caleb even blink.

He seemed not to notice that Tash's outfit was meant to hypnotize him. His steady gaze did not dip below her chin. Once the waiter left, Caleb just sat in silence.

"Thanks for seeing me." Tash knit her fingers on the table. "As I mentioned on the phone, I don't know how long you're in town, but I'd really appreciate your help with Braverman's notes if you have the time."

She noticed a sheaf of episode scripts stacked demonstratively beside his bread plate. Tash discerned asterisks and circled passages in red and purple ink—he'd reviewed the work. She hoped this meant he was invested.

But his bedhead remained austere as Caleb sipped his espresso. He set his tiny cup down, no doubt relishing this upper hand. An ankle rested on a knee as he regarded Tash stoically, and she began to feel exposed and stupid. She groped in her bag for an extra physical layer, swathing her mild humiliation in the thin gauze of a shawl.

Caleb finally responded. "I'm contracted for prep work, which we guessed would take about two weeks, unless things progress—and in that case, Braverman might want me here for five."

Tash fingered the tent card set beside the table's clutch of sugar packets advertising Sundown Specials, feeling another surge of hope. She waved the cardstock jauntily. "Wow. Even just two weeks is a lot of Rum Runners and stone crab."

Caleb puzzled for a moment. "Oh. No." He shook his head, glancing around at all the facelifted terry cloth. "No, I'm not staying here." His mouth entertained a touch of humor. "There are only so many yachts a man can take. No, I'm staying closer to the festival."

Tash struggled to not clatter her teacup. Making her grovel was one thing, but the canal-road maze from her duplex to the Seashell had forced her to wait at raised drawbridges three separate times. She possessed the unfortunate superpower of hitting each one just as it opened to an interminable boat crossing.

"If you're not staying here, then you picked this place because . . . ?" Out of loyalty to her fellow Floridians, Tash would not outright malign the salmon-colored marble or the towering gold leaf.

Caleb's cheeks bloomed pink. "A personal commitment. Braverman's timing for this project was a surprise." He inclined his head beyond the arcade to a spa pavilion billowing with sheer curtains and trails of bougainvillea. "I'm with friends today. It's a reunion, so I couldn't bail. Meeting here was the only way I could do this." He gestured to Tash's script pile.

Curious, Tash leaned forward, letting her eyes rove. She reassessed him. "Hold on. A reunion? You went to school here?"

He seemed to find the idea funny. "Nope. LA born and bred." Then he hesitated. "It's not a school reunion. It's family. And Astrid."

Astrid Dalton—the actress playing Noab. To whom Tash now remembered Ram mentioned Caleb was "attached." Tash had not considered in which sense. From their first interaction at the bar, Tash had assumed Caleb was single.

Although the details of his personal life could go into the trash can, along with the footnote he was probably many years Astrid Dalton's senior, Tash guessed, based on the fact Astrid was best known for a laugh-tracked teenage sitcom Tash was too old to have seen.

"I'm sorry to encroach on your time then. You must be very busy." Every so often, the reality of having sold her book rights felt to Tash like shouting underwater while being forced to watch a boyfriend tongue-kiss a frenemy; her gratitude for the film option and its financial proceeds rivaled her anguish at having to surrender her story to other hands. To other writers, for example. To nubile it-girls "attached" to blue-eyed LA sex designers.

Tash stopped, glancing down at her shawl-covered cleavage. She scolded herself. Janelle would probably say passing judgment on another woman's romantic choices was antithetical to the cause.

Caleb cocked his head, oblivious to Tash's mental sidebar. "It's not encroaching. I was hired to do a job. This series also happens to be Astrid's debut in a marquee drama—so I'm on board, one hundred percent. I want to make sure it goes well."

Tash dunked her tea bag coolly, imagining Astrid's certain relief at possessing such a steadfast liege—or, depending on how one looked at it, Astrid's disempowerment at Caleb's seizure of her agency.

Tash affected ignorance: "Can you remind me exactly what you do?"

He didn't need to know she and Janelle had already completed rather thorough research into his role and his company.

Caleb pushed his empty espresso aside.

And then, with deliberate, innocent deadpan, he said: "Lap dances. That is, when I'm not looking at boobs." The unfettered joy in his false sincerity could not contain itself around his mouth. He opened his eyes widely, miming confusion at Tash's glare. "What? Come on—don't make me mansplain it!"

He delivered this as if he'd been practicing.

In return, Tash gave him a slow clap.

His straight white smile winked at her as he took a half bow.

"It's called intimacy coordination." When Caleb decided to answer her for real. "I'm half of a team. I do the script translation, which means I liaise between talent and story and direction and production in the lead-up to a shoot. My partner, Stacy Mancini, does all the front-of-camera, on-set physical coordination. Her background is combat choreography. She's awesome."

Talking about his work seemed to make Caleb relax.

He gestured to his annotated script stack for *The Colony*. "We vet and plan critical scenes. We make sure there's consensus around everybody's physical and emotional boundaries. If an actor is feeling vulnerable, we're their advocate on-set. I'd be more than happy to show you our credentials." He adjusted his glasses, appearing pleased with himself. "The practice of intimacy coordination is very feminist, you know—our values are probably more aligned than you imagine."

Indeed, the practice of intimacy coordination had apparently been adopted across the entire industry—Tash and Janelle had found scores of articles describing it as part of Hollywood's post-#MeToo reckoning, a response to decades of on-set abuse. Intimacy coordinators were to nudity and simulated sex what stunt coordinators had always been to action sequences. Caleb's partner, Stacy, popped up often in news coverage about it, her suitcase of modesty garments and private-part prosthetics in tow.

"A big part of the job is essentially to protect women." Caleb wouldn't realize Tash had already read about his status as the rare man in the field. "Which means I should be extremely offended by your slander the other night."

Tash took a deep breath. He seemed to be kidding, but she felt compelled to explain herself. "Look." She went for straight talk. "*The Colony* might be the only book I ever write." She'd only gotten serious about it when Janelle went on bed rest during her first pregnancy—Janelle claimed critiquing Tash's pages kept her sane, so Tash wrote until she finished the manuscript. "It's my sole publishing credit outside of an obscure academic essay on 'The Use of Machine Language in the American Detective Novel During the Period of Industrialization that Followed World War Two.'"

Tash had been thrilled about that paper; while her father called the magazine it appeared in *The Useless Academic Fringe*.

"And I sold it to a female showrunner. Who promised to caretake its adaptation into a streaming series." Tash cradled the bittersweet memory. "Now, instead, I find myself stuck with Ram Braverman—who, no disrespect"—actually a lot of disrespect, but she was *making nice*—"could probably do a great job of caretaking a book about rocket ejaculation. But maybe not one about a warrior island Sisterhood and the generational implications of their isolation in a hostile world." She offered Caleb what she hoped was a beseeching look. "I'm protective of my novel."

Caleb nodded, seeming to mean it. "Okay. Fair enough."

Tash savored the moment of breakthrough. "So, you understand my hesitancy."

"Not really." He didn't swerve. He folded his hands calmly.

Tash peered at him, baffled and flustered. And embarrassed. She'd just shown him the inside of her vault.

"Look, Tash—I read the specs. For a ten-episode limited series, what Braverman is asking for isn't unreasonable." Caleb referred to his stack of fucking papers. "The story team primarily wants additions to three key episodes. They're looking to add sensuality, which, in my experience, doesn't have to mean raunchy, over-the-top sex."

He'd switched modes, his manner suddenly no-nonsense—to his credit, hard to pull off in a turtle-print, biceps-straining shirt. "We could accomplish a lot by just emphasizing the warriors' physicality—Noab's musculature, her kinetic prowess. There's a fundamental rawness to her character that's appealing as a starting point for choreography."

Tash reminded herself he was talking about Astrid. Tash resented being forced to play voyeur. She found herself both uncomfortable and torn, bizarrely put out by the light in his expression and incensed at the objectification on Astrid's behalf.

"Seriously?" Tash leaned forward. "You just told me your job was feminist. Noab and her army aren't eye candy."

"Why not?" Caleb leaned in, too. "What does 'eye candy' even mean? Don't tell me you've never watched a gladiator movie just for the bare chests and the cut abs."

Tash resisted. "I didn't write that army so it could be turned into porn."

"It wouldn't be porn!" Caleb insisted. In a very spooky echo of Janelle, he added: "Do you really think your female characters can't be ruthless and honorable—and also sexual?"

Tash hadn't been able to reconcile the argument with herself or with her best friend; she very definitely would not concede anything to this guy. "Dude. Don't start. This is where you're out of your depth." The aloe-scented air around them prickled with her irritation.

"Dude—you have no idea how deep my depth is." Caleb frowned and chucked it back. "I understand you think your femininity entitles you to a superior position on the topic—but it doesn't."

Tash fought not to yell. "And I understand you think that you're woke—but the liability a woman's sexuality represents is something you can never fathom."

Caleb narrowed at her doubtfully. "I'm not sure that's true. Regardless, and no disrespect," he echoed her own phrase, "even aside from which one of us is the authority here, you have to consider the medium. This adaptation will be visual. Your viewers shouldn't have to rely on their imaginations like they do in a book. Film and television are different."

He indicated his pile of scripts. "I'm going to level with you—and this is my purely professional opinion, uncolored by the way you clearly hate my guts—the additional scenes Ram is asking for are legitimate holes in the romantic trajectory of your characters. Hewett and Noab consummate their relationship off-screen in Episode Five?" He radiated cynicism. "Story-wise, for television, that's absurd."

Tash's hackles rose even further. "But off-screen is part of the message—it's meta-commentary. We're choosing not to pander. That's what *The Colony* is about. It holds its audience in high esteem—it believes its viewers are smart enough to watch something that isn't all about the boning." She maintained her objection. "The first showrunner who bought it agreed."

"Right." Caleb's blue sparked with quip and pity. "And what happened to that studio?" He looked at her over the top rim of his glasses. "Oh, yeah. It went bankrupt."

Before Tash could lunge at him, a small shared brunch spread arrived.

Servers set fruit and muffins in the middle of the table. More hot water for Tash's teapot, Caleb's second round of bitter espresso caffeine. He and Tash glowered at each other across a battlefield of scalding drinks and jam pots and powdered-sugar ramekins.

Caleb's eyebrows continued their challenge. Tash did not back down. She watched him spear a slice of kiwi with a fork, their stares contentious as he chewed.

"Hey. Here's an idea." Once he'd swallowed. "We could spend the next two weeks like this, fighting. Or"—he threw the dare down casually—"you could let me do my job, and we could call a truce. Just for the first scene. Since *you* called *me*, right? For help with the notes?"

Tash took time with her own slice of kiwi. She spread butter on a warm round of brioche. Embarrassingly, she'd unconsciously slipped back into scuffling with him, when she'd resolved to do exactly the opposite.

"You could think about it like a trial period, if that makes the idea of collaborating with me less upsetting." Caleb stirred his espresso. "I have to give the story team weekly updates on our progress—their feedback could be our test. It'll be apparent if we can't work together." He took a small sip. "I'd even suggest you take the lead to get us started. Write Noab's rescue of Hewett's shipwrecked body as narrative bullets so I know how you want to begin. And don't worry about screenwriting format—I can handle all that."

One scene.

Narrative bullets.

Behind the guard of her hot teacup, Tash could admit she'd be relieved to pause her constant fight. "Go on."

"You could lay out the dialogue and action. It would also be helpful if you described the mood." Caleb glanced to the notes at his elbow as he paraphrased: "Noab finds Hewett washed up, all tangled and bloody. She hides him in a sacred place. She undresses him to clean his wounds."

Tash dipped a triangle of mini French toast into a pot of syrup, testing the notion that she and Caleb might harmonize. "She has to get him out of the shallows. The island is protected by a prehistoric ocean predator, called the Mother Beast." She remembered her student's pink-lettered tattoo. "She's like a cross between a demon crocodile and a monster shark. It's death for Hewett once the Mother Beast senses his blood in the water."

Caleb nodded gamely into their détente. "Great. When you write the bullets, try to paint that with adjectives. They don't have to be fancy—just list them, and do the same thing with the verbs. Imagine it as if you were watching: What does Noab look like when she saves him? How does she touch Hewett once she has him in the Grove? No euphemisms. For this kind of writing, we're never indirect. We use anatomical vocabulary and actionable specifics."

No euphemisms; it would make the task feel doubly daunting.

Tash broke off a piece of biscuit, laying it thick with ruby jam. She watched as Caleb sank his teeth into a hump of rounded strawberry. Then as two puckered blueberries drizzled with honey went into his mouth. The tattoo on his collarbone read *Calypso*—Tash could see its ebony scroll fully as he sat back, shifting the collar of his button-down. The *C* unfurled in thick-tendoned shadow, the *o* flourish trailed toward his shoulder blade. The *l* and *y* stretched, yearning to touch more skin.

He speared a chunk of melon. "Does that make sense? Description, action, and the emotion each character feels as the scene is unfolding." He waited for her answer.

Tash blinked, mentally righting herself, shooing thoughts of his collarbone away. "Well, in this scene, Hewett is unconscious. So I don't know about his emotions."

Caleb chuckled. "Perfect—one down. Just focus on Noab, then." He projected encouragement; they were teammates now. "Also, if it helps, don't think about this like you're doing it for Braverman. Think about it like you're doing it for the actors, who genuinely want to breathe life into your story. They want to do a good job, and the more insight they have into your vision, the more your characters come alive."

When they had finished, Tash left Caleb in the Seashell's grand arcade.

She shrugged off her thin shawl outside in the sunshine, righting her wrap dress and reasserting her curves.

But with each step toward the parking lot, she had the oddest sense she'd been the one hypnotized; she'd let Caleb assign her homework. She'd let him tell her to do it for the actors instead of for the fans. She'd let him pick the date and time for their next meeting, in three days. She'd achieved her goal, she'd *played ball*—but she'd let him run the court.

The closer Tash got to her car, the more she felt she was exiting a trance. The clearer her head became, the more she remembered she truly did not want to diagram Noab's bodily desire. She'd avoided the exercise quite purposefully when she'd written the book.

Because Tash's comfort zone was abstract treatises on the minutiae of modern lit; she wasn't a creative writer. She'd faked it in *The Colony*. She'd covered for her fiction inexperience by imbuing her characters' interiors with bits of external atmosphere.

She'd constructed the attraction between Noab and Hewett to transcend their known worlds, describing their connection as involuntarily magnetic, each drawn instinctively to a wisp of a past life, to the taboos of their own cultural demons, to forbidden mythology, to the shape of foreign shores.

Not euphemisms—but also not a list of unfancy adjectives and verbs. Tash hid in this kind of phrasal camouflage, behind her terrible suspicion she had no real creative fiction skills. She wouldn't know how to access the character of Noab without revealing some soft part of herself, and Tash had no urge for such a revelation.

Definitely not with Caleb Rafferty there to observe.

In retrospect, it sometimes amazed Tash that people related to Noab and Hewett's story; she thought any able critic could have scratched the surface and poked holes straight through her characters' inner lives. *The Colony*'s success was truly accidental—at first, Tash meant it only for Janelle; then, when Janelle insisted Tash submit it to an open call at a small press, it published to zero fanfare. Its good fortune came by pure luck, when a copy landed in a celebrated feminist's lecture appearance gift bag.

And now that luck had long departed.

Tash's misgivings mounted. All that tea sloshed sickly in her stomach. Caleb would be disappointed by anything she wrote.

Panic overtook her, and Tash reversed sharply, striding back up the Seashell's steps, past the tinkling fountains, into the assault of new-money faux-Italian decor, steeling herself to beg for Caleb's mercy.

Perhaps they could find a compromise.

Tash grasped for feasible alternatives. Perhaps she could offer to make things easy for him—to step aside and let him collaborate with an experienced ghostwriter. Perhaps, in return, Caleb could agree to honor certain story boundaries.

She couldn't find him in the Seashell's arcade, or where they'd been sitting in the coffee nook. She scanned the pool deck, the spa pavilion, the maze of salmon-colored marble, searching for a turtle-print shirt and a hint of sympathy. She swung in a circle, increasingly unguarded. She opened her mouth, tempted to start shouting Caleb's name.

Just in time for him to tap her shoulder.

"Tash?" He'd swapped his regular glasses for smoky aviators. He held a daiquiri, of all things.

It had only been seven minutes since they'd parted, yet his posture seemed to have completely unwound. His stack of papers had been shunted beneath a pool umbrella, next to a tube of sunblock. A loose smile played across his mouth.

And standing beside him, in a Saint-Tropez-style, wide-brimmed hat, Astrid Dalton lilted, gorgeous in a fire-engine-red bandeau swimsuit.

"You're Tash Grover?" Her opaque, Audrey Hepburn round sunglass frames bounced between Caleb and Tash. Astrid stuck a sculpted arm out for a handshake. "I'm Astrid Dalton. I've been dying to meet you!" She elbowed Caleb with a foxy smile. "This jerk said I couldn't come to your coffee."

In the presence of such a perfect creature, Tash wished herself to the bottom of the swimming pool. Kinetic prowess indeed—in person, Astrid Dalton stunned in a way her photos didn't convey. She was arresting—all burnished lithe limbs, hair in a thick plait down her back. Tash wanted to thank the universe for manifesting such a physically ideal Noab. She also wanted to stash her own dowdiness in the suffocating heat of her locked car.

"I didn't say you couldn't come." An obvious soft spot tempered Caleb's chiding retort. "I said your hero worship might distract us."

Astrid's eyebrows hoisted high on her smooth brow. "Right. And then you conveniently booked me a seaweed wrap at the same time you two were meeting." Releasing the handshake and smelling deliciously of spa, Astrid beamed at Tash again. "Anyway, it's an honor. I hope I get some time with you. I've lurked in the fan forums, but it's not enough—I have a million questions about Noab."

Caleb sipped his daiquiri. "Which is exactly why I said you couldn't come. Tash needs to concentrate. You can bug her all you want when we're finished writing." Backtracking slightly, deferring to Tash: "I mean, if that's okay."

Tash nodded, hoping to express ease while feeling impossibly awkward about interrupting their poolside frolic.

Astrid grabbed Caleb's arm mischievously. "Or maybe Tash should come with us for facials." Noab's royal bloodline glittered along Astrid's skin, the taut line of her triceps flexing, supple and persuasive. To Tash, sparkling with explanation: "I'm torturing Caleb with self-care."

Tash's plan to petition Caleb for charity vanished, and she suddenly yearned to follow. She could not sit through a facial, and she could not admit artistic defeat in front of her lead actress—not with Astrid's excitement about the role, or her possessive fingernails on Caleb, or Tash's weird curl of jealousy at their rapport. Not while Tash still clung to some semblance of self-respect.

"I can't. I'm sorry." Tash coerced her features to broadcast regret. She tried to make light: "Caleb gave me too much homework." She tried to retreat.

But a certain sex designer's courtesy wouldn't let her walk away. "Wait—did you need something?"

Tash engaged all of her smile muscles, groping for a plausible reason to have staged this encore. "Nope. I thought I left my sunglasses. They were my favorite. Very expensive. A gift." She dismissed it theatrically, continuing her fallback. "I guess they're not here."

"I guess not." Caleb stepped closer, grinning from behind the bronze rim of his own shades. His gaze dipped, lowering to Tash's mouth, to her throat, to her décolletage.

She had to tell herself her breath did not catch, her mind did not white-noise fizz, as Caleb pointed to the plunging neckline of her sundress, where drugstore frames were safely folded, tucked against the hot flush of her skin.

Chapter Five

Tash went home to submerge her body and her feelings in the bathtub.

She opened the duplex's large windows to the salty surf-song drifting over from the beach. She knew she should have embraced Astrid, author to actress. She knew she should have been excited to answer Astrid's questions.

Instead, Tash had choked on insecurity; she confessed this ashamedly to the soap and bubbles and cool porcelain of her claw-foot tub. In the moments on that Seashell pool deck, Tash had coveted the clear warmth Astrid drew from Caleb. She'd coveted their breeziness and affinity while she second-guessed herself.

She was bound to let them down. Firmly away from Caleb's red-pen asterisks and confident claims, Tash despairingly contemplated what he'd assigned her—he'd asked for mood and verbs and adjectives and specific action: Noab undressing Hewett. It sounded simple, but to write it, Tash would have to emotionally undress herself.

This was not her strong suit; she far preferred to dissect motifs in other people's literature than bare her soul in her own. She might have dropped out of her graduate program but only after she'd learned critique from a master—she'd dated Leo Rousseau at the inception of his acclaimed literary journal. They'd even cohabitated.

Their relationship was a train wreck, yes—but Tash had emerged from it with a useful set of skills.

And their intellectual intercourse still remained the best she'd ever had; Leo's cheating might have crushed her heart and her ego, but Tash never let it ruin the way he'd enlightened her mind.

Which was why she bothered to still follow his journal. It was why she'd said yes to being interviewed for his podcast's summer tour, on a panel of Florida writers, taping live from Miami in a few weeks. Leo Rousseau was a prestige ticket, and appearing in his lineup seemed an excellent way for Tash to recover the literary street cred she'd lost when Braverman's "unnamed sources" spoke for her in the press.

In fact, if she could trust him, if he weren't such a toxic, pompous douche, Leo might have been a better guide than Caleb through the writing of the new scenes. A contradiction of sex and integrity would never flummox Leo. He lived unapologetically at the intersection of base instinct and insight; of brilliant editorial work and that time he fucked an editorial assistant in Tash's bed.

Which was why she'd never ask him how to write one thing without devaluing the other, or how to handle this crossroads, or how to sepa-rate Noab's desire from Tash's own vulnerability.

Instead, she shut off the bathwater. Relying on the distant ocean sounds for help, she conjured a sea captain, shipwrecked, scraped and tumbled and bloodied on the jutting coral edging a sacred Prayer Grove. A man discovered accidentally by the heir to a female warrior crown, whose Sisterhood had banned men for generations. Whose Lore told of the latent poison carried in every XY chromosome.

But Noab's knees still collapsed on the shore beside him, despite every conscious warning. She still hauled Hewett's musculature from the dangers of the island shallows to the safety of the sacred shade. She crossed a hallowed line, laying him in an inner sanctum, drawn inexplicably to his forbidden and fabled body. Noab's hands hovered and her thoughts raced—every cell fascinated and wholly terrified.

And then Tash stalled.

In the book, the rest occurred off-screen—ostensibly, Noab un-clothed him in order to assess his injuries. Ostensibly, she experienced a male body for the first time—her fingers on his lips, perhaps. Her gaze on his lean and weather-beaten torso.

From there, Tash floundered.

She'd much rather write about the implications of the existential threat a man posed to an isolated island nation than the implications of what awaited in his pants.

The assignment gave Tash three pirate sex dreams over the course of the next two days, while she made no progress on her Noab-and-Hewett scene. She answered each of Caleb's How's it going? texts with a breezy lie: Amazing! Then she sent Janelle a screenshot of the conver-sation, adding, This is not true and I'm completely fucked.

To Tash's latest text, Janelle replied, Good thing you're on your way here to get your ass kicked. Yandra's asking for you. Come get out of your head.

Tash was late to Biscayne Coastal's annual end-of-term faculty bar brawl, formally known as Adjunct Night. Manta Ray's, the local campus beach dive, put it on at the end of every term—each department sent an adjunct to guest-bartend a subject-themed well drink. Yandra Santos, the beloved Cuban American poet who ruled English Lit with an iron, age-spotted hand, had nominated Tash as this year's cocktail slinger.

Patrons would vote, medals would be bestowed, bragging rights for the next semester would be obtained; at the birth of the tradition, there was even a cash prize.

As always, everyone expected Women's Studies to take home the gold. Other disciplines could try, but Janelle's crew usually put up the winning drink. Their cocktail was usually a Blow Job—Janelle encouraged her acolytes to take risks in every area but this one. She'd studied many esoteric human secrets, and she knew: The Blow Job was a sure thing.

Tash and Yandra had already identified the English department's biggest competition for second place—the actual Manta Ray, owner of the bar and the creator of the Asymptote, which would go head-to-head with Tash's Tequila Mockingbird. Ray had been the multivariable calculus teaching assistant for at least as long as Tash had been at Biscayne Coastal; she'd heard he was a conclusion shy of finishing his number theory dissertation. She'd also heard he had no real academic credentials—the math department just kept him in equations because they got a discount on hot wings at his bar.

Either way, Tash welcomed the excuse to leave her apartment. She'd spent too many hours staring at her blank screen, typing verbs and adjectives and then pressing delete. On the way out, she caught herself in the hallway mirror for a last glance, Boo Radley in a headlock under her bare arm. A former student had named and gifted the life-size Halloween skeleton to her for the occasion. A prop, he'd grinned, to promote the Tequila Mockingbird—revealing he'd definitely never cracked open the class reading.

Her phone trilled as Tash took the stairs down to her driveway. The name **Caleb Rafferty** splashed across the screen. For a moment, she thought about sending it to voicemail and turning off her ringer.

"Tash, hey." Caleb's voice spilled warm in the gathering dusk. "Read me your first page."

Tash frowned at his abruptness as she unlocked her car. "Right now?" She tried to shove Boo Radley into the backseat.

"Is this a bad time?"

Tash had bargained with herself about this night out: She'd take a last-ditch pass at her homework bright and early, before she and Caleb were due to meet. "Um." A skeleton leg jabbed her in the belly button. She shifted, the thrift-store pants she'd bought for Boo Radley bunching on his knobbed bones. She pinned the phone between her chin and shoulder, wrestling a fucking Halloween prop to lie flat and not give her any trouble. "I'm kind of busy."

"I won't keep you." Caleb didn't let up. "Just read me the first page."

Tash tried tugging Boo Radley into the car by his scrawny armpits. "Can I call you in the morning?"

"Tash." Caleb's tone had stopped cajoling. "I spoke to Brian Doolittle—Braverman's head writer? He said you gave him the extreme runaround for several weeks. I can't play games like that. It's important we get off on the right foot."

Boo Radley's right foot hooked on a seat belt. "Fuck." When she released it, the button on his lumbar spine depressed. His hidden speaker emitted a loop of ghoulish laughter.

Caleb sighed loudly. "Please don't tell me I gave up a night of my reunion to work on this and right now you're at Disney World on a scary ride."

"What? Disney's in Orlando—that's nowhere near here." Tash winced as Boo Radley cackled again.

"Tash." Caleb made his impatience clear. "You have to take this seriously. We're on a deadline."

"I am taking it seriously." As a last resort, she clicked her key fob. She dumped the skeleton sternly in her trunk. "Look, I'm struggling with the writing, I won't lie. But I'll get there. I have a college thing tonight—otherwise, trust me, I'd be working on it right now."

Which was how Caleb Rafferty ended up at Adjunct Night, at Manta Ray's Seaside Tavern, rubbing elbows with amateur mixologists and befriending an assortment of drunken Biscayne Coastal staff.

He ordered Russian History's Moscow Mule as Janelle excitedly waved him over from behind her velvet rope—she sat with Denise at an exclusive high-top table she'd reserved, brandishing her tenure, while Tash stood behind the sticky bar, pouring house tequila into cloudy shot glasses for Ray's less discerning clientele.

"Wait. Your original, bespoke, literature-themed cocktail is just a plain ounce of crappy tequila?" Denise narrowed in suspicion when Tash finally made her way over and thunked three Mockingbirds down.

"Yes." As Tash pointed out the obvious: "But the name." She pointed to Yandra, who had dreamed it up, and whose gray fluff and long, flowing skirt were holding court in another corner. "Tequila Mockingbird! We could win just for being clever."

She smiled a greeting at Caleb, who'd been bookended by Janelle and Denise. His hair curled slightly in the tavern's humid racket. Ray's was sawdust and peanut shells and jukebox; Tash had left the house in cutoffs. An hour of crowded adjunct bartending had dampened her with sweat.

"You won't win." Janelle smirked smugly from behind her fortress of cream-rimmed Blow Jobs, beside Caleb's rolled-up shirtsleeves, the two of them chummy as ever, picking up where they'd left off—just before Tash's verbal assault.

Caleb sniffed the Mockingbird's beigey liquid kindly, raising his shot to Mr. Radley's perch on the messy bar, where his boned hands had been cupped into a makeshift tip jar. "Is there a connection between Harper Lee and the corpse you've got there?"

Tash watched Denise taste her tequila and mime gagging. "None at all. Some freshman lit classes are sharper than others." Glancing back at the skeleton. "Maybe I should stop teaching *To Kill a Mockingbird* around Halloween."

Janelle reached helpfully for her wife's tequila, tossing it back in a sleek blur. "Were you a good student, Caleb? Did you study film?" She wasted no time shining her full spotlight on their guest of honor.

It made Tash twinge with vague annoyance. Either because she couldn't stay and listen to his answer or because Janelle seemed to have forgotten Caleb Rafferty was conspiring with the other side. Tash needed to remind her they'd be wise to stay wary.

Meanwhile, Caleb embraced her questioning. He got comfortable, heel tapping to honky-tonk surf tunes. "I was okay—nothing stellar. I didn't finish college, though. I only did three semesters at UCLA."

Tash paused where she'd been about to return to her duties, her tray of empties suspended in midair. She hadn't expected Caleb to be this kind of kindred spirit. "School not for you?" She'd aimed at teasing, but it came out weird and petty. Then weird and suggestive: "Or have you always just preferred a more hands-on approach?"

She regretted her words immediately, realizing Caleb did not know she was a higher education dropout, too. The strained, somewhat apologetic, close-lipped smile he returned to her was painful. He pushed his glasses up, a large tank watch's brown leather strap double-wrapped around his wrist.

"My stepmother was diagnosed with late-stage brain cancer when I was a sophomore." In fairness, he seemed to want to pull the stinger out of Tash's giant gaffe. "She had big plans—places she wanted to see still. I left school to travel with her."

Tash wished to be engulfed by a tornado of floor sawdust. She willed a country line dance to flash-mob, or back-bar bottles to suddenly explode. Anything to distract from this moment. "I'm an idiot." She looked at him directly. "I'm so sorry."

He smiled wistfully. "It's okay. I like talking about her—Viv was amazing. She'd just retired when she got sick. We hit the road hard to cram in everything on her bucket list." He shrugged. "Afterwards, I decided to start working. Something about her death made me need the real world."

When Tash could look again, Janelle and Denise each had sympathetic hands on his arms; Janelle might have actually been squeezing his bicep.

"Seriously." He said it to all three of them, but pointedly to Tash. "Please don't feel bad. Viv went out on her own terms. She would not want beautiful women sitting in a bar and crying for her."

Tash wavered between wanting to join the cuddle and wanting to tase herself.

"Tell us more about her." Janelle did not release him. "You said stepmom, but it sounds like you were close."

Caleb hesitated. He traced the condensation beading on the copper side of his Moscow Mule. "We were." He almost flinched as he said it, curaçao-blue eyes right on Tash: "She owned a burlesque club in Los Angeles. There's a documentary about it opening at the film festival. That's why I came, actually—I was here before I knew Braverman would be pairing me with Tash."

Tash immediately began to replay the awful things she'd said to Caleb at the piano bar when he'd mentioned the documentary. "Bullshit" was what she'd called his stepmother's life work, or at least the film about it. Forget tasing herself—Tash wanted to disappear into a bucket of Ray's shitty tequila and forget she'd been so cruel.

"Her name was Vivienne Palmer." Caleb unfastened the top button of his linen shirt, pulling the collar aside. "Her club was called Calypso." Pointing to his ink. "My dad was her set builder, that's how they met. I kind of grew up backstage." And then, not arguing it, just offering a piece of information, he added: "In certain circles, Viv's considered a pioneer."

Denise gasped. "Holy shit! I've been there. Caleb, that place is super famous."

Janelle glanced sideways at her wife's reaction. "Really? I've never heard of it."

"It isn't *super* famous." Caleb dismissed it to Janelle while winking at Denise. "Just mildly famous. At least it was, back in the day."

"Back in the day, there was a crazy lineup of guest stars—I remember." Still awestruck, Denise filled in the blanks. She tucked one side of her blond bob behind an ear, grinning at Janelle. "It was extremely sexy. We used to go in law school—way before I met you." She turned back to Caleb. "You must have a million stories."

He demurred, pretending not to recall. Throwing Denise a single teaser: "I did meet Sharon Stone once, in the dressing rooms when I was nine."

"Stop it!" Denise gasped again.

Caleb's nod was solemn. "She helped me make flash cards for a third-grade spelling test."

"That's insane." Denise's lawyerly reserve had left the building. "I want to be reincarnated as your childhood."

Caleb laughed in earnest. "It's not what you think—imagine growing up basically feral, in a theater that doubled as a boarding house, with fifteen older sisters. I had no privacy, and there was never any breakfast because everyone except for me was nocturnal."

"Fifteen *hot* older sisters." Denise verged on embarrassing herself.

"Just sisters." Caleb, all smiling chivalry. "No, but really—the community around Viv was special. A chosen family." His expression offered Tash a handful of puzzle pieces to set down. "A bunch of us are here for the documentary. Tash met one of them the other day."

Tash frowned, doing the fuzzy math. He had to be talking about Astrid, but she was twenty-five, tops—too young to have danced at Calypso. "Astrid Dalton worked for your stepmom?"

Caleb's grin was wide now. "No! She's Viv's goddaughter. Her mom was one of Viv's protégées. You couldn't tell? She's like my little sister."

Tash remembered possessive clinging, a bandeau bikini, and a girl who probably didn't want a "sibling" label on Caleb's family tree.

"I watch out for her as much as I can." He smiled. "Like on your show now."

"I love that!" Janelle joined Denise in the fawning. She raised her Blow Job to the magnificence of Caleb. "Here's to big brothers."

Caleb raised his Moscow Mule, looking at Tash, returning Janelle's hug.

In former years, out of respect for the pedagogy, Tash would have taken a full course load of cocktails at Manta Ray's. But she'd stopped drinking the moment she realized she'd impugned the legacy of Caleb's stepmom. She released him to Denise and Janelle's thrall and adulation, retreating to sling tequila behind the bar beside Boo Radley, scolding herself for behaving like an awkward jerk.

"That explains a lot, don't you think?" Janelle paused to slurrily discuss it on a trip back from the bathroom. It was late; she and Denise would have to get home to their sitter soon. "About why he's so easy to get along with. Raised in a den of women." Janelle fanned herself swooningly to underscore it. "At the center of a coven."

"He can still be an agent of the patriarchy." Tash muttered it begrudgingly, her best friend's gushing a bit much.

Janelle tilted, considering the possibility. "True. But Natasha—he really does not seem like a dickhead." Taking Tash's chin between her fingers: "I think you got lucky. The studio could have sent you a total goon."

And truly, nothing about Caleb was goon-like. Tash observed him, beyond the jukebox and the throng of adjuncts, sitting on a barstool beside Denise. He had his ear close to hear what she said over the music. He took a moment to think about it, and when he replied, Denise threw her head back in total uproar, her typically zipped-up persona thoroughly shed.

Verbs and adjectives, mood and action; if he was her assignment, Tash would write Caleb as *strapping* when he washed up on her beach.

He'd have lost his glasses in the shipwreck, there'd be wet sand matted on his cheek, there'd be castaway beard growth shading his strong jaw. His clothes would be in tatters, his salted skin a color that would burn badly. Tash would probably have to lie down right there and smother him with her hair and with her body, for sun protection; there'd be no time to drag him into a sacred shade.

The sea would lap around their tangled bodies; his eyes would open to their deep kiss.

In real life, his eyes blinked at her across Manta Ray's Seaside Tavern, dragging Tash back to her muggy sawdust reality.

He must have wondered why she was staring. She watched him stand up, bidding an indulgent good night to Janelle and Denise. He shouldered through the bar then, the closing distance to Tash practically glowing with heat.

His forearms folded next to Boo Radley as Tash wiped spilled tequila with a rag.

Caleb flattened the paltry crumple of dollar bills in the dressed-up skeleton's spindly clutches, folding the stack neatly, passing it to Tash. He leaned in over the last-call yelping. "Want some help getting this guy back in your car?"

Tash fumbled in his nearness. She felt Noab's predicament fully—drawn to a creature the legends promised tasted like poison, while most of what she sensed of him was sweet. She held Boo Radley's thrift-store-pants-clad thigh like an anchor.

"No, thanks—he belongs to Ray now." Tash was relieved to discuss something other than her recent slagging off of Caleb's stepmom. "Who hopefully will understand his fears and treat him with dignity, as Scout did—marking her progression from a child who was afraid of imaginary monsters to an adult who could recognize the real, everyday terror of existing in the world."

Caleb gave her an impressed look. "Wow. Is that what happens? I don't really remember."

Tash grabbed her bag and ducked under the service flap of the bar. "Freshman Lit 101: 'Heroes and Villains'—take my class, and you'll find out."

They found Ray smoking a joint with Engineering in the parking lot, bemoaning yet another Women's Studies' sweep. Tash waved good-bye as she and Caleb trailed from the building, the moon hazy on the roadhouse brine, Tash wondering about the protocol—if she should apologize again, if Caleb needed a ride back to his hotel. Their footsteps crunched loudly, and she realized Caleb had not once mentioned *The Colony*'s open-item workload.

"Do you want a lift?" At her car, Tash spun to face him—in time to see Caleb's eyes jerk up abruptly, from where they might have been checking her out.

He blinded both of them with his phone screen. "Calling a taxi. See you tomorrow? The conference room at my hotel at ten a.m.?"

"Let's do it at my office." Tash surprised herself with this impulse. "I have a writing studio off campus. It's quiet, with lots of natural light."

And just like Noab, she'd invited a man into a sacred chamber. Befuddled by her whim, Tash opened her car door and slid behind the steering wheel. Perhaps she'd felt moved to extend a niceness—the parking lot glimmer recalled the angry piano bar moonlight, and she still felt awful about maligning Caleb's stepmother's documentary.

"Great. Text me the address." But the cusp of something more appeared to gnaw at him. Caleb's palm hung on her car's frame. He kept the door ajar. He bent at the knees to meet her blink. "Tash." Low and close and dangerous. "Tonight was fun."

In the leather driver's seat, she stopped trying to jam the key in the ignition. "It was." She stopped breathing. The inches between them stopped pretending to not want to ignite.

They'd been combustible from the beginning. Tash could see it all now—together they'd be fiery and wrong. Once they ripped each other's clothes off, they'd never be productive; the sex would be too good. Plus, artistically speaking, they were mortal enemies.

Still, she braced for a surrender. She tipped toward him—a terrible idea. Terrible, and probably worth it.

Like rescuing a castaway.

Like discovering a hunger for him in a secluded Grove.

Caleb gazed at her meaningfully. "But we really need to buckle down now. Crafting a novel is on your own time—but screen stuff is intense. There's an entire multimillion-dollar production budget hinging on our progress. It's serious." He shifted in his squat. "I hate to be a taskmaster—but no more cocktail competitions until we finish. All right?"

Headlights swung into the parking lot.

Caleb stood, ending a thing that hadn't started. He checked the taxi's license plate. He thumped twice on Tash's hood.

He ambled off with a backlit wave, and she just sat there, gripping her steering wheel, hating the foolish creature he left behind.

Chapter Six

Caleb had said *serious*. Tash could be serious. Caleb had said they needed to *buckle down*.

And Tash awoke with this in mind, ready and resolved to thus be fully buckled. She rubbed her eyes clear, then wrestled herself into a sports bra and some running shorts. She jogged the circuit from her duplex to the ocean, along the long sandstone promenade, past the wooden surfboard racks outside the juice joint, the entire stretch balmy with the scent of pressed green apple and melting sunscreen.

She got home and marched herself into the shower. She scoured the image of Caleb in Manta Ray's parking lot from her body and from her brain. She did this properly—with a local grapefruit sugar scrub and sustainably harvested Florida sponges, sloughing off the spell of his nearness, leaving her psyche lighter. She wrung her hair in a head-dress of twisted towel, face to the magnifying mirror; in the morning light, she glowed regal and attachment-free.

She felt like Noab after a training exercise, fresh from her spear work. Except she had no spear, just sharpened pencils and her pride. Tash exited the duplex. She shut her front door with a determined slam.

By the time Caleb arrived at her studio, Tash was on her second iced masala chai, buzzing from vanilla and cardamom. She no longer kept a coffee maker in her home or in her workspace—she'd shed the habit when she shed her fiancé. She'd let Zachary keep the roaster and the grinder and returned to her roots. She'd been taught by her aunt to make chai for her father, the process both a time suck and a respite; the boil-and-stir both soothing and an obligation, like so many things about her dad.

Vikram Grover's love came always with a flip side of disappointment: Proud of Tash's success as a writer, mortified by her actual book. Thoroughly modern in his ambitions for her, throwback in his dismay at her itinerant singlehood. Critical that she dallied on at the college as just an adjunct, thrilled that the elastic nature of her schedule allowed for family dinner in West Palm on any given night.

"Hot or iced?" she called out to Caleb from the studio's tiny kitchen, straining the milky black tea mixture from a steel pot, inhaling star anise and ginger and cinnamon steam.

"Whatever you're having." He shucked his messenger bag onto the low-slung sofa, stepping to the studio's floor-to-ceiling windows, taking in the gnarled mangrove forest and the intermittent beams of filtered sun. "Tash? You might have undersold this when you said your office had 'natural light.'" His voice marveled. "This is amazing. I feel like we're in a dinosaur terrarium."

Tash filled a tumbler with ice cubes. "Easy there, Hollywood. In Florida, we just call it outside." Although, to be fair, the dry land edge of the mangrove was home to several species of large iguanas.

"Don't downplay this! Did you lure me here to feed me to your velociraptor? This place is bonkers."

The garden-apartment studio *was* 1,500 square feet of Intracoastal-facing hidden gem—which was how Tash's younger brother, Rohan, threatened to advertise it in the listings whenever he needed sibling leverage.

"I can't take credit. My parents bought it for my dadi—that means 'grandma'—to try to get her to move here, from Kentucky." Tash's dadi said it was like sleeping in a rainforest fishbowl; she spent one night, then handed Rohan the keys. "It belongs to my younger brother now. But he lives in California with his boyfriend, so he lets me use it as an office."

"Your brother lives in California?"

Tash granted him this tiny tidbit. "West Hollywood. He works at Cedars-Sinai. My dad tells people he's a doctor, because he thinks it sounds more macho, but Rohan's actually a transplant nurse."

"West Hollywood is near me. I live in Silver Lake." Caleb had turned back to the windows, his scruff and shoulder outlines reflected as he gazed. His ocean-colored eyes examined the primordial fern thicket. "Do you ever go out there?"

"To California? All the time." Tash arranged his iced chai on an end table. "Actually, if it wasn't for these scenes, I'd be visiting right now."

Caleb abandoned his ogle of the mangrove. With the driest of faux sympathies: "Oh, I'm sorry! Is the way you gave a major film studio the slip and held up their production, potentially costing them tens of thousands of dollars, ruining your summer plans? That sounds terrible! I can't imagine what that's like."

Tash suddenly was bashful. "That isn't what I meant."

But he was teasing. Caleb joined her at the coffee table, sinking into a club chair—seating Tash had added to Rohan's furniture mix, upholstered in a softened, sun-bleached jute. "That isn't what I meant, either." He thumbed to the lush, reptilian courtyard. "I was actually asking if you ever go out *there*. Into your own personal jungle."

"Oh." Tash recovered. "Sometimes."

By "sometimes," she meant all the time—but on the balcony, upstairs. She purposely didn't mention she lived in the duplex directly above where they were sitting. Or that the "jungle" Caleb referred to was basically the basement to her incredible beachside treehouse view.

"Well, Natasha." He copied Janelle's intonation, playful and austere, settling barefoot into her office's relaxed lounge. "I work with a lot of creatives. And I've met them in lots of funky places—a sweat lodge, a mountain yak yurt. But I have never"—he swept a hand at the enclosure—"been anywhere this Jurassic. So, thank you. I can't believe this is where you get to write." He was grinning.

Tash found herself grinning, too.

It boomeranged between them, and she realized he'd passed a secret test. In the same way Biscayne Coastal's adjunct-lounge sandscape inspired *The Colony*'s crushing shore, the undergrowth beyond Rohan's apartment's glass-box interior inspired the island's beating heart. To wonder at the thriving groundwork of stem and shoot and tuber was to appreciate her novel.

Buckle down.

They might have both heard the silent nudge at the same time. From her seat on the sofa, Tash reached for her laptop and her script notes. Caleb cleared his throat, unzipping his messenger bag.

Still, he asked another question. "What was the word you used for 'grandma'? I don't know it."

Tash watched him decant his supplies: two legal pads, a tin of paper clips, a wad of pink sticky notes. "'Dadi.' It means 'father's mother' in Hindi." She stirred the metal straw in her iced chai, its spice-lite mirroring her looks. Tash didn't mind offering him the explanation, if that's what he was asking: "My mother is white, and she's from Ohio—but my dad's parents moved from Mumbai to Lexington, Kentucky, when he was five." She smiled at the image of her tiny, spunky dadi in the sprawling Southern suburb. "My grandma is a widow now, but she's still ride-or-die bluegrass and bourbon, even if she doesn't drink. Think Indira Gandhi in cowboy boots. She actually wants her ashes sprinkled at Churchill Downs."

Caleb chuckled, positioning his laptop beside an array of pens. "So there's a younger brother in WeHo, a rodeo grandma in Kentucky . . ."

Tash filled in the blanks: "And an older brother an hour north of here, in West Palm. Near my parents."

"Is that where you grew up?"

She nodded.

"Are you guys close?"

The Grovers were close, but it was also not that simple. "I'm close to Rohan, the one in California. He's two years younger than me, but people always thought we were twins. Before he went through puberty and became a giant."

She could have left it there.

But maybe Tash wanted Caleb to know her family situation wasn't perfect. "Things with my parents are more complicated, though. They're conservative in a way that makes it hard for them to get on board with some of my life choices." She could have referenced her flagging teaching career, or the way she'd managed to chase Zachary away, but the day was early. Instead, she pointed to Caleb's dog-eared copy of *The Colony*. "For example, they're not huge fans of the book."

"What? Why?"

Tash's old hurt quickly resurfaced; she'd gotten used to playing it off, but deep down it pained her not to have her parents' support.

"The throwing of the baby off a cliff, into the ocean?" To explain her parents' perspective, she deliberately oversimplified the novel's final scene. "It bothers them that I could write something so radical. I think they felt it called their parenting into question." It embarrassed them in front of their bridge group, at the high school where her mom taught, at dinner with her father's colleagues—Tash had heard the long list, and could go on and on.

"But it's a plot point in a book." Caleb echoed the same rationale Tash had used in an attempt to reason with her mother. "It's not like you go around killing actual babies."

Tash gestured her agreement. "I know. But to them, the idea didn't reflect well on my upbringing, or my state of mind. They'd be happier if I could write a *nice* book." She smiled at him in self-deprecation. "And honestly, they weren't alone—my older brother felt the same. He has two kids." Tash sighed. "People have a weird way of taking fiction personally." She did not mention Zachary, her ex-fiancé. "So now we kind of just don't talk about it. It's how I keep the peace."

Caleb air-quoted his incredulity. "Wait—you 'kind of just don't talk about' your bestselling novel? The one that's going to be a television show?"

Warmth burst in Tash's chest, appreciating his objections, but she really hadn't meant to trash-talk her family. "In their defense"—she repeated what she'd often counseled herself—"the sensationalized way in which *The Colony* was sometimes marketed didn't help. Splashy dead-baby headlines were probably great for media hits but not so much for Vik and Mary Grover. Ram Braverman is not the only person in my life who wishes I would change the end."

Caleb furrowed anew. "What do you mean?"

Tash eyeballed him suspiciously. "Mr. Rafferty. Do not play dumb." Ram's exceedingly high opinion of Caleb had been clear. Tash assumed he was privy to the entirety of Braverman's cinematic wish list.

"Hey, I just got here." Caleb appeared candid, putting both hands up, mimicking backing away. "I have no idea what you're talking about."

Tash swept her hair up, clipping it all back, her view of him direct and unencumbered. "Ram hasn't told you he has big plans to save the baby? That he thinks Hewett should do it? Which, if you connect the dots, would give him the option for another season, focusing the story more on men?"

At the very least, Caleb's confusion vouched for his attention to detail: "Hewett isn't even on the island when the baby's born—how would that work?"

Tash held a long stare. "I don't know. You tell me."

"This is the first I've heard about it." He seemed genuine, invoking Ram's words from the piano bar with a smirk: "Then again, I'm mostly here for nudity and copulation."

Tash couldn't help but smile along with Caleb, and with the suggestion they were on the same side.

"I can see Braverman wanting the option to extend the series' life, though—that's the business model. They want runway for more world-building if the show does well." Caleb caught himself: "*When* it does well. No ifs."

He meant it as supportive, Tash knew. He couldn't guess the subject of a Season Two was a land mine, or that he teetered on the edge of triggering her emotional avalanche. Which was probably why she responded with an overdue apology, where she otherwise might have responded with a tirade.

"By the way, I'm sorry for what I said about Calypso and the documentary, when we first met. I feel horrible about it."

Caleb met it with kind eyes. "It's already forgotten."

Tash highly doubted this, but she allowed it as a segue to their task.

Caleb tapped his pencil, bringing them to attention. "To recap: The bulk of our scene additions take place in Episode One, Episode Five, and Episode Nine—"

"Episode Nine is a problem." Tash cut him off, aware it was poor form—but also seeking to nip Braverman's intentions in the bud. "It goes back to how I feel about certain subject matter being used for click-bait. I don't think it's necessary to represent something that graphic on-screen."

"Okay." Caleb took it in stride, seemingly unbothered by her blurt. "Right now, though, I think we should focus on the beginning—the first thing we owe Ram is blocking and dialogue for Episode One. We can cross Episode Nine's bridge when we get there."

Tash colored slightly, realizing she'd jumped the gun. She paused in her discomfort. "Can I also admit I'm not sure what 'blocking' means?"

"You can admit anything—that's part of the process. This should be a safe space." Caleb gestured between them. "Okay?"

"Okay."

He pushed up his glasses. "Blocking is working out the details of an actor's moves in relation to the camera. It's specific physical movement and defined action cues. For our purposes, it's in-scene story markers that the actors can hit with their bodies. We can also call it choreography."

He set his chai on the coffee table. "Let's find an example." He flipped through his notes, searching. He tucked the pencil behind his ear and bent his head down, long lashes magnified by the angle of the tortoiseshell-framed lens. "The great news is that your setup is already very sexy. We're already situated in the forbidden—Noab has just rescued *a man*. She brings him into what's essentially a temple. It's transgressive. She's already broken a rule."

Caleb continued to rummage. "When we talk about the mood, then, we can use words like 'illicit.'" He paused, offering her a pleased glance. "Can you see that? Temperature's rising without a single word of dialogue. All we have to do is turn the dial and ratchet up the heat."

Out of habit, Tash swiped at his description. "Wow. I'm glad you think disloyalty to other women is so hot."

She'd said it as a half joke. But the comment stopped Caleb in his tracks—the moment probably too reminiscent of Tash's history of pouncing. She hadn't necessarily meant to be back at it, three seconds after she'd just apologized.

He frowned. "All I'm doing is recapping the book, Tash. Breaking a rule *is* sexy. I hate to tell you this, but if it wasn't sexy, you wouldn't have a plot. Noab's temptation is what sets everything in motion."

In terms of story arc, Tash had to agree. But something in her gut resisted Caleb's characterization. "Yes. But if we're too flippant with the themes, *The Colony* will end up like *Transtempora*."

He blinked at her. "Why is that your go-to insult?"

Tash shrugged like it was obvious. "Because it's a spectacle of female suffering, commodified and sold back to an audience of women. It's full of graphic sexual assault, and Braverman used it as an example of why he wants you on this project."

Argumentatively, Caleb sat forward. "Let's establish something, okay? Eileen McCormack's novel is exponentially more graphic than anything I arranged for its adaptation." He repeated the author's name: "Eileen McCormack. Who is a woman. Who also was a consultant for the show."

Tash refused it. "The fact that she's a woman doesn't matter. Authorship doesn't give anyone immunity."

"Of course it matters!" Caleb threw his hands up in exasperation. "You've been telling me it matters since we met!" He ticked it off on his fingers: "You're the writer. You're a woman. Your perspective has more meaningful insight than mine. You're the one with the giant chip on her shoulder."

It was Tash's turn to blink now.

"A woman wrote those rape scenes, Tash. Female actors decided of their own free will to take those roles. I did my best with the script translation, and Stacy ran a tight set—but we don't have the ability to change the basics of a story, and I don't think the material would have been better off with someone else. At the end of the day, my responsibility first goes to the actors." He challenged her: "Ask *them* about their experience on *Transtempora*. I promise you they'll say it was safe and we were thoughtful. Those sequences are not my jam—they're gutting. *Transtempora* was the toughest job we've ever done."

The thoroughness of his pushback destabilized Tash's mental footing; she realized how many assumptions she'd made about Caleb and his craft.

After awkward moments, she could only acquiesce.

She tried to rebound with some semblance of humor. "My chip isn't giant. It's normal-sized."

But Caleb pressed on, not letting her escape. "Can I ask you something?" With elbows on his knees and blue eyes earnest. "You're angry, right? That's obvious—but lots of times, anger is really about fear. What are you afraid of?"

She scoffed, disliking his impression, even if it was fairly on point. "What, now you're a therapist?"

"Kind of." Amazingly, he embraced it. "Film is personal. Acting and directing are personal. My job is to create consensus between all our invested parties. If you're angry and scared, I want to understand so I can help you. Just get it on the table."

"Get it on the table?" At the very least, Tash admired his bravery. "You want to know what I'm afraid of?"

He point-blanked back at her. "Yes. That's why I asked."

"Okay." Tash approached the floodgates. At his own risk, she slowly unlocked the latch. "Well. I'm afraid I wrote this one great thing. It just happens to speak to a lot of women, some of whom participate in on-line forums that track this adaptation's every move. In addition, actual feminist scholars read *The Colony*. Netanya Cortez blurbed my book, Caleb—the high priestess of feminism—"

"I know who she is." His eyes narrowed.

Tash felt her words become emphatic. "Then you also know the stakes. I don't want to fail these people. I don't want to fail Janelle, who helped devise the premise—which is a love letter to every woman in my life who's sick of feeling powerless, and a flaming Yelp review of every man who's let me down. I don't want to have to compromise. This is my stamp on the world, and I want it to stay strong."

Her face had heated scarlet.

Maybe Caleb really was a therapist.

Because Tash clung to *The Colony*—maybe too much. She'd put it ahead of Zach, and ahead of her parents. She equated its virtue to her self-worth. She didn't know if that was normal, and she'd never stopped to care. But now, across the glass-walled, jungle-lit interior of her writing studio, she could also admit it made her overly defensive. She could see herself instigating conflict with Caleb, who maybe didn't even want to fight.

He just listened, absorbing her rant.

He didn't break eye contact. "Tash, this is teamwork. We'll move forward in a way that addresses your concerns." He studied her. "What does Janelle say about the scenes Braverman has asked for?"

Therapist and strategist—this guy was perceptive, roping in Janelle. He knew she was the guru and the best friend. He knew her opinion meant the world to Tash.

Tash allowed herself an exhale, feeling the defusing of her bomb. "Janelle says feminism takes all forms. She says it's important to get *The Colony* to a wider audience, where its ideas can enter a more public forum."

Actually, Janelle had said "lube it up"—but Tash was paraphrasing.

Then she apologized for the second time that morning, noting the pattern. Self-referentially: "She also says I shouldn't fuck this up by offending my intimacy translator." Tash would need to keep reminding herself not every exchange had to be a duel.

Caleb cracked a small smile, letting her slightly off the hook. "Well, that would be a nice first step. The second step might be for you to give me a real shot." He pinned her with a benchmark: "I'm willing to use everything you just said as our guidelines for working together. We can even ask Janelle to test-read our scenes before we submit."

The mangrove outside suddenly seemed filled with olive branches. Tash smelled a peace pipe. But before she could reach for it, Caleb snatched it back.

"It'd be even better if you could meet me in the middle. I meant what I said about making this a safe space, but it has to go both ways. We need to respect each other's intentions. From now on, for real—I don't want to be the target of your personal attacks."

Tash met his frank stare. She gathered up the many spears she'd thrown at him, and the evidence of his disarming patience. She glanced to the giant chip on her shoulder, considering where she might, temporarily, stash it away.

She stuck her hand out, touching him for the first time. "Okay, Rafferty. You have a deal."

Once Tash agreed to Caleb's revamped terms, they returned to dialing up sensuality, to Noab and Hewett and the forbidden, and to illicit moods.

They returned to the garden apartment for the next three days, side by side in its lounge. Tash kept it all business—she *buckled down*, she was *serious*, no more personal attacks. She gave in to Caleb's creative methodology, following his instruction. His tactics for assembling *The Colony*'s screen strokes differed vastly from the way she'd written the book.

Instead of adding words, Caleb pushed Tash to distill them, stripping the scene to its essence, identifying emotion beneath the surface, then translating it into the vocabulary of muscle and sweat and skin.

"This is our chance at stage direction—we want to spoon-feed Ram evocative physical detail. It's the closest you'll get to creative control, Tash—which is why it's so important. Braverman is always more receptive when the input is visually lush."

"'Visually lush'?" Tash took a break from her scene notes, throwing Caleb an impressed curve of her mouth. "How poetic."

He glanced up from the grid of storyboards he'd laid out on the sisal rug. "Is it? I guess that's what happens when you spend so much time behind the scenes. Every department has a different lingo—to get through to them, you have to change the way you talk." He knelt, swapping one sequence for another. "For example, right now you and I are speaking Creative Genius—but wait until you hear me talk Marketing." Caleb raised playful eyebrows. "That's the real poetry."

"I'm sure." Tash fizzed with the coltish energy bouncing off the apartment's walls. It had expanded seamlessly, filling the void her suspicions of Caleb had vacated. It seemed all the effort she'd been devoting to resenting him now flowed into repartee.

She discovered he couldn't sit still while immersed in his process—Caleb moved in the pursuit of answers, armchair to rug to standing, hands clasped in his tousled hair, eyes closed behind his glasses, deep in thought, walking them through the scene:

"The Grove hut where Noab brings Hewett's body—is it like a thatched shed? How big are we talking? And what exactly is this marble slab?"

Tash supplied answering detail:

"The slab she lays him on is like an altar table—made of coral, from the island shallows. The hut is empty otherwise. Banana-leaf roof, dirt floor, probably three hundred square feet. And most importantly"—in a display of unanimity and her grasp of Caleb's technique—"the space is divine. It's a holy inner shelter, inside a Prayer Grove, intended only for an ordained, select few. Even Noab, who's basically tribal royalty, isn't supposed to be there. And she definitely isn't allowed to bring in a man."

Caleb's eyes had opened, staring at her. "Excellent."

Tash warmed when he approved.

"What's Noab's emotion once she gets there? She has this half-drowned, unconscious dude on the table—shirt torn, pants on, bleeding from cuts on his forehead and a nasty puncture on his thigh." Handing Tash the verbal baton, he took up his whiteboard. "Word association. Go."

Her turn to close her eyes, then. In earlier rounds, Caleb had suggested she say whatever came to mind. "Fear. Apprehension. Curiosity. Dread. Lust." Tash enjoyed the linguistic salad. "Desire. Doubt. Wonder. Hunger. Panic."

"Great." Caleb steered the exercise. "Now put those things against a backdrop of Noab's inexperience. It amplifies her transgression, right?"

His pause was careful. "That's what I was getting at, when I mentioned it last time."

And Tash nodded, careful also; indicating it was safe to proceed.

"Knowing she has zero experience—that being together there is completely off-limits—makes the situation *hotter*." Caleb's grin was self-effacing. "Which is the very scientific word Ram would also use to describe the mechanics of maximizing the erotic—so we can just make it our shorthand." In deference to his deal with Tash: "While also abiding by our own principals."

Tash smiled. "Got it."

"Now we put it all together—and this is still a spitball, okay? We just say everything in our head until we get it right. In terms of visually explicit physicality—while Noab is tending to Hewett's body, what is the most innocent yet hottest thing she can do?"

Tash jumped in with something entry-level. "She could trail a finger down his body."

Caleb nodded. "Be more specific. Like"—he scrawled it on his whiteboard—"she could trail. Her pointer finger. Down the center. Of his bare sternum." Caleb added his own line: "She could cradle. His jaw with her palm."

"She could bite her lip as she does it." Tash bit her own lip, in illustration. "She could give a sharp intake of breath. She could heave her bosom." Grinning at him over the cliché, having fun now. "She could tilt her head back and gasp." Tash figured Noab wouldn't be caught dead doing such a thing, but it was fun to roll with the drama. "She could feel her pulse race." Tilting her own neck back, accidentally knocking the clip out of her hair, tossing the unleashed mane behind her shoulder. One hand to her throat, tracing the beat there as it fluttered.

"Um." Caleb's marker hovered, forgotten, by his whiteboard. His eyes dazed a bit, maybe even caught on Tash's neck and hand. He gestured between her and his paperback copy of her novel. "Do you want me to leave you two alone?"

Since they'd been at it for a while, and in a safe space, the blocking exercises had removed all shame. Tash grabbed Caleb's felt eraser and chucked it at him, grinning wide and not embarrassed. "You said this was a spitball!"

He chucked it back at her. "No. You're right." Still laughing. "By all means. Do go on."

And it went on.

In a nonstop stream of descriptive arousal, mixed with easy humor, the scene presenting challenges Tash had not known would await. Hewett's lack of consciousness turned most of the conventionally sexy ways Noab could touch him into something creepy. Each move Tash and Caleb brainstormed had to be gut-checked against the idea of consent.

"Which brings us to this puncture wound—upper thigh, correct? Are we talking inner or outer?" Caleb stood from the sofa, extending one cargo-shorts-clad leg. "He's lying on his back, so I assume it's bleeding from the front. Is this an inner-thigh, full-on groin situation?" Caleb's hands parenthesized his hip bone to his fly.

"No." Tash stood from the club chair, mirroring his posture, forming her own brackets. "Absolutely not. It's an outer-thigh, curve-of-butt-cheek situation." Highlighting the front pocket to the side seam of her cutoffs. "Which has the advantage of bringing Noab's attention to Hewett's groin, but with a tangential elegance. That way, she doesn't get a face-full of his balls." Remembering that Caleb had instructed her to use anatomically correct language, she added: "I mean testicles."

She sparkled, fully aware of an outrageous shift—in a blur of mere days, they'd gone from arguing feminist theory to talking testicles, surely a sign of true collaboration. They floated giddily on their progress, now near a finish line. They splashed each other with offhand vulgarity, aware it was unseemly. Tash would have yelled at herself about it, but she was having too much fun.

"Oh, right! Tangential elegance. Of course." Caleb smiled sarcastically as he sat back down on the sofa.

"Don't you think so?" Tash continued to dissect it. "The outside curve of a man's hip could be equally suggestive—think of it like the male version of side boob."

"Sure. Let's get it down correctly, then." He opened his laptop, beginning to type. "'Ship-mast splinter, stab wound. Hewett's outer thigh.'" He made a show of adding: "'Male version of side boob. Tangential elegance. No face-full of testicles.'"

By some unspoken agreement each day, they'd worked through lunch. By the afternoons, Tash found herself starving. Her insides growled each evening when Caleb left the garden apartment; she woke up hungry every morning upstairs in her bed.

Having dreamed again of pirates, and shipwrecked blue heat, and the printed collars a certain hipster buttoned over a scroll of ink. She dragged herself outside for another run each morning, another shower, another hard look in the mirror. She remembered Caleb's rebuke in the Manta Ray's moonlight: They had a deadline. She reminded herself she was there to *buckle down*.

Not a belt buckle, and not buckling knees, and not buckling a sex designer to her upholstered headboard.

Every morning, Tash locked her upstairs apartment and went downstairs to make chai. She became a professional, with a production budget waiting and a reader fan base and an internet reaction and a film adaptation on the line. She straightened sofa pillows and her script stacks. She righted a tower of sticky notes. She weeded out the dry pens and wiped smudges from her laptop screen.

In the kitchen alcove, she added water and masala mix and black tea to a pot. Sugar and milk. She reminded herself: The only things to stir up were her characters and caffeine.

She and Caleb polished their blocking proposal in the fading sun of a fourth day. Caleb would package it into a shot list for the Braverman story team in the morning. Hewett's unconscious state ruled out the need for dialogue.

Tash dubbed the approach they'd taken to Hewett's injured pelvis area "chiaroscuro"; she was quite pleased with the term. The scene sizzled with the juxtaposition of light and a shading—of primal instinct in a place of sacral worship, of raunch and holy. It read both racier and more subtle than any film foreplay she ever thought she'd pen.

Most importantly, it didn't feel cheap—it felt elevated, and Tash actually felt proud.

"You realize that's burlesque, right?" Caleb collected his storyboards. "The idea of what you choose not to show? I don't want to I-told-you-so—"

"So don't." Tash ferried empty tumblers to the kitchen.

"—but when Noab tugs Hewett's pants down to rub salve into his wound," Caleb continued, "while very much deciding *not* to look at his crotch—that's burlesque. That's 'The Tease.' The visual withholding of his manhood. Or, you might say, his foreign member."

Tash stuck her head back into the hallway. "Why do I have a feeling you just wanted a reason to list more penis words?"

They'd already curated a catalog of genteelisms for Hewett's length and girth; for the erection that would involuntarily arise as Noab soothed and sponged water on his body.

Caleb slung his messenger bag across his wide chest. His wink was dangerous. "Anyway. I know Ram and Doolittle are going to love this. Reggie in executive production, too."

"And now you're just listing Hollywood cartoon names."

Caleb smiled at her from the apartment's front hall. "Or, you know, the people on the story team who decide our fate." He put his hand on the doorknob, seeming to weigh an option. "Hey. You know the boardwalk I drive by on my way here?"

"I do." Tash's stomach grumbled. She needed to go upstairs and order pizza.

"Are any of those restaurants good?"

Her appetite clamored, and Tash held it purposefully at a distance. "The Mexican is." She called it out, blasé. "Order the fish tacos."

"Want to join me? Celebrate writing your first rigid phallus?" Caleb sounded casual, and then a little sheepish: "I've been eating by myself at the hotel most nights. It's extremely sad."

She'd turned back to the kitchen sink, cold water spurting on her wrists. Tash took her time shutting off the faucet. She let her pulse slow, reminding herself of Manta Ray's midnight parking lot, and Caleb's succinct hood thump as he stood and strode away.

She had no desire to revisit that sense of bumbling miscalculation. But Caleb was lonely. His overture was definitely garden-variety.

Her breathing evened. "Sure." She summoned her very professional composure as she dried her hands on a towel. "Let me grab my bag."

Chapter Seven

Tash chose the scenic route to the cantina to let the local landscape show itself off for Caleb: They strolled down the soft-paved bike lane, toward the myrtle- and azalea-choked beach gate, which led to a private stretch of boardwalk and Tash's special slice of sea.

"Dinner alone, huh? Every night?" She snuck a sideways glance at his profile. "What happened to your reunion?"

He'd matched her relaxed gait, both their flip-flops padding on pressed sand. Dusk teemed as the palms swayed, the hedge on either side of them a quake of tiny, iridescent insect wings, the coastal glade readying itself to slide into sun-drown.

"My friends took a side trip for a few days." Caleb's posture telegraphed abandoned puppy dog. "They went north to take lessons at a surf school in Vesper Beach."

Tash had always thought Vesper Beach the perfect setting for detective fiction—very underground-dogfight and counterfeit-ring neon. "I hope one of them gets to wrestle a gator or comes back married to a tidal shaman." She played at scandalized. "I want that for the plot of my next book."

"What's a tidal shaman?" Caleb had stopped walking, confused behind his smoked-mirror aviators. "Who's wrestling a gator? Should I be worried?"

Tash immediately regretted what she'd said. "No! Vesper Beach is great for surfing. It's a nice place for them to learn." She began to stroll again.

But Caleb remained unmoved—he only crossed arms, not buying it, the sunset squawk around them growing dimmer.

"You don't need to worry. I love Vesper Beach." Tash turned to face him, thinking about the way she discussed literary settings with her students. "It's just— It has this quintessential Florida shameless-ness. Sin and swamp and sweat and shoreline, our unique underbelly. There's actually a whole genre of crime fiction called Florida Noir, set in 'a sunny place for shady people.'"

Caleb's mouth bent. "Where Astrid took my aunt Ilsa."

Tash wasn't sure about Aunt Ilsa, but Caleb's swell of protectiveness was not an unattractive look. All that brainstorming closely with him had briefed Tash on his tells: He raked his hair when he was troubled. Now he stubbornly set his hands on the waistband of his cargos, clearly not budging until Tash assuaged his concern.

"Vesper Beach can also be very pretty. I swear. Seriously, Caleb— what I was talking about is right here, too." She turned in a circle, opening her palms to the tall saltwater overgrowth on either side of the lane. To the green walls of hedgerow vibrating thickly, all common beach shrubs with perfectly Florida names: fiddlewood and sea grape and varnish leaf and black torch, bird pepper, swamp privet, horizontal cocoplum.

Neck-high on both sides, blade and needle and leaf, the bike path swath a dry strip of land in a plant sea.

"Look, anything can be happening in there, right?" Tash trod backward in her cutoffs, pointing into the dense bush. "Rattlesnakes could be hatching right now, and you and I would never know it. An airboat filled with cocaine could be sinking. Alligators could be tear-ing off a corrupt prosecutor's limbs. That's all I meant—Florida is the perfect backdrop for stylized mysteries." Self-consciously: "I teach a class called 'Heroes and Villains,' okay? I can't help it—that's where my mind goes."

He peered at her over the top of his sunglasses. "You know what? You're dark." But he said it like praise. He recommenced the walking, making a show of checking over his shoulder. "I'm a little scared now."

"You should be." Tash took his response as license to elaborate. "The feminine earth here isn't wholesome, Rafferty. She isn't your California fruit. She's destructive, like a hurricane." Tash trailed her fingers deferentially along the texture of the shrubs, digging into her mental bag of class notes. "She's wise, like the roots of a banyan, and she's mystic. She has the power of wetland abundance, but she's also the undertow." Tash windmilled her arms in two directions—back toward the Intracoastal and forward toward the sea. "And we're these dumb humans who pave over her heart. We just don't get it. So now and then, she rises to smite us."

Caleb smiled. "When you talk like that, you sound just like you write."

"Well." Tash faltered slightly in his spotlight. "The vicious female protector-predator is both my favorite Hero and my favorite Villain. I'd be happy to give you a semester's worth of lectures."

"You might have to." Caleb unhinged the flower swarm of the beach gate, holding it open. "Really, Tash. You're great at what you do."

They chose a table by the cantina's rear gallery of open windows, where sunset lanterns rested on narrow ledges, welcoming the dunes. Sand dusted the floor, ranchera music competing with the salt spray. Tash and Caleb squeezed lime into the long necks of their beer bottles and descended on avocado salsa and fresh chips.

They ordered fish tacos, street corn, spicy jalapeño rice. Caleb admitted he was ravenous, and Tash scolded herself for not feeding him sooner. Starvation was no way to treat a visitor, a blocking playmate, a lonely castaway.

"Don't think I didn't notice that you said 'next book' back there." Once they were settled, once the mango pico de gallo nachos had come and gone, Caleb sprawled low in a carved, wooden chair, a Mexican-blanketed cushion at his back.

Tash took a long swallow of her second beer, wishing she hadn't been so glib when they were walking; she'd never mentioned writing another novel to anyone—not even Janelle.

He watched her hesitation. "How about this: Did you go to school for creative writing? Start there."

That, Tash could answer. "I went to school for English literature. I thought I'd be a scholar, get my PhD."

Caleb red-penned her with his eyes. "You *are* a scholar."

She broke a chip in half, shaking her head. "I never finished grad school."

"Why not?"

"New York winters." Her usual line, and then Tash caught herself. They'd just shared four days of safe space—Caleb could probably handle something truer. "And a very unpleasant breakup." She tried to make it punchy: "With my master's program, my thesis adviser, and my boyfriend, all at the same time. I was naive and young, and I let a bad relationship ruin my academics. I took a leave of absence"—Tash mimed looking at a watch—"approximately nine years ago."

Caleb appeared to accept this without passing judgment. "Do you think you'll ever go back?"

Tash toyed with a coaster, knowing she would not. "Not to the same program. The guy I had been dating launched a journal, and it's still affiliated with the school." A bit of self-help diagnosis: "It would be unhealthy for me to reengage with that dynamic." She lifted her beer ironically, impugning the very thing she'd just said: "Although. I'm going on his podcast in two weeks."

Caleb lifted his beer, too. He lifted an eyebrow. "What's the podcast about?"

"Literary critique." She offered it bashfully, knowing it had the potential to sound ridiculous. She'd already gotten an earful from Rohan, who despised Leo and did not approve of Tash's plan to reclaim her narrative from Braverman by gracing Leo's stage. "During the summer, he interviews his subjects live, like on a tour—just with book nerds instead of rock stars. It'll be me and two other Florida writers."

"That's cool." Their food arrived, and Caleb surveyed the spread. Over yellow rice and grilled fish tacos and pomegranate-sprinkled corn, he lit with the idea: "Are there any tickets left? Can I come? Maybe I'll bring Astrid."

Tash stalled, hedging, unsure if she'd want Caleb to watch. The podcast would be snooty. She also intended to use it as a clearing of her name—to balance out the besmirch of Braverman Productions, who'd taken the liberty of speaking for her in the entertainment press.

She would speak for herself with Leo. "You might think it's really boring."

Caleb laughed. "Is that your way of saying it'll be over my head?"

"No!"

He passed Tash a sharing plate. "Good. Because I'd like to come. Astrid's been begging me for time with you anyway. This sounds like it could be great background." He spooned rice, glancing at her slyly. "Actually. Maybe then you'll come with *us* to the reception for *Vaudeville Striptease*. That might be great background for you." He smirked. "Since you're already putting burlesque into our blocking."

Tash shook too much hot sauce on a taco. Caleb's interest burned behind her chest. It burned her lips as Mexican folk music swayed around them in the sandy shadows, convincing her to have a third beer.

And the third beer convinced her it was okay to ask: "So. Astrid's like your sister?"

Caleb rolled with the invasive question, picking up on Tash's reference to what he'd said the other night at Manta Ray's. "Yup. I was twelve when she was born. Her mom was Viv's lead, and we all spent a lot of time together at Calypso. Even after Viv and my dad split, we were always at the club. He'd use any reason to be near her. She never really let him go." Caleb's mouth had gone nostalgic, the memory seeming to jog a solemnity.

But Tash couldn't shake the image of Astrid's lacquered fingernails territorial on Caleb's bicep when they'd collided at the Seashell. "And you and Astrid never dated?"

Caleb evaluated her. "Have you ever dated one of your students?"

"No!"

He smiled. "Right, because it would trash your reputation. It's the same for me. The ethics of intimacy work have to be completely above-board. My job depends entirely on my reputation. Even if Astrid wasn't literally like family, Stacy and I don't date people in the industry."

Tash suddenly felt very stupid. "I'm sorry. I shouldn't have asked."

"No, ask whatever you like." Caleb shrugged, seemingly not irritated. "Being a man in the business is complicated—it's a selling point with bros like Braverman, but it comes with its own set of fine print. That's why I would never want to do it without Stacy."

He pushed his plate away, as if entitled to his own interrogation now. "So. No students. But that doesn't explain why you're single."

"Who said I'm single?"

"Janelle."

Tash laughed out loud then. "You go first. Why is Hollywood's foremost designer of nudity and copulation single? And forget the work excuse. There's a whole world outside 'the industry.'"

Caleb disputed this. "It doesn't always feel that way when you live in LA. But my real reason is cliché: My mother left when I was two. I have mommy issues, even though my stepmom was amazing. Or maybe I have commitment issues. Viv and my dad flamed out, and he never recovered. I don't want any part of what that looked like."

He'd made the first move—in a game of vulnerability, or damage, or bravery, or truth.

Now it was Tash's turn.

She stared at him across the table. "My reason is that men suck."

She lit up a little when Caleb laughed. "I have the track record to prove it: My grad school boyfriend cheated on me, and the guy I got engaged to afterward called our wedding off—*in the middle of my press tour* for *The Colony*." She nodded when Caleb winced. If nothing else, Zachary demanding his diamond ring back outside a public radio sound booth made an entertaining anecdote. "He couldn't be the pediatrician who was married to the baby-killer. Not a good look for him, apparently."

Caleb's mouth opened. Before it closed again. "I don't know what to ask first. You were engaged to a pediatrician?"

"A pediatric resident."

"And just to be clear, again"—not masking his incredulity—"he knew the baby wasn't real?"

Tash's arguments with Zach remained vivid. "In retrospect, I don't really know if it was the baby-killing or the book's success. There's a chance he never expected me to sell it, or he never really understood what the book was about, but the minute it gained traction, he took the plot personally." Tash waved a palm widely around her aura. "This all became too much. He was embarrassed." Just like her parents.

Which Tash mourned sometimes—in the forlorn corners unreached by her feminist bonfire light. For a while there, Zach had seemed the ideal medicine for Tash's other wounds—he was not artistic, he was sweet and stable, their spheres didn't overlap. He appeased Vik and Mary Grover. His aesthetic could border on doctor kink when he wore rubber-duckie scrubs.

"For the record, he sounds like a wuss." As he looked at her, Caleb's eyes were just shades lighter than the sleeping sky. He finished off his beer. "Please excuse my toxic masculinity."

But Tash thought there was more to it; she'd learned even supposedly evolved men couldn't rise to the occasion. Zachary couldn't get past his outsized sense of self. She'd wanted to believe he was an exception, but instead he fit the rule.

Quietly, almost to herself as Caleb signaled to the waitress for their check, Tash shook her head. "He was actually one of the good ones. That's the disappointing thing."

Tash drifted into her duplex alone, warm from the beachside dinner. She glanced to a wall clock. She had the urge to call her mom.

She dialed, starfished on her bed, woozy with cantina conversation and blocking-bootcamp afterglow, hoping this was the perfect frame of mind for dealing pleasantly with Mary Grover—as Caleb's talk of mothers had fortified Tash's gratitude. Her mom was healthy and still living; she was present in Tash's life. She was well-meaning, despite her often antiquated opinions.

Plus, alcohol and the drowsy hour; Tash did not feel combative at all.

In recent years, Mary Grover had even made an effort to shy from topics that caused the two of them to clash. She'd stopped asking if Tash planned to apply for a more prestigious teaching position, for example. It'd been months since she last mentioned the sure decline in quality of Tash's eggs.

Now Mary's matter-of-fact inflection postmortemed an evening of bridge game drama into Tash's ear, the code indecipherable, as Tash and her brothers had never learned how to play, even though Vik and Mary's cards night had commanded a spot on the family calendar for as long as anyone could remember.

Her mother recounted a particularly fearsome duo she and Tash's father had just beat, and Tash rolled over on her bedspread, stretching to her nightstand for the letters she'd discovered in her utility closet beside *The Colony*'s legalese.

"Yes." Mary affirmed their provenance once Tash seized the chance to ask. "I wrote each of you. Every day. But I think you're the only one who read those letters." Tash's mother reported this without a trace of bitterness. "Rohan and Neel usually came home with theirs, still sealed, at the bottom of their bags."

Unsurprising, as Rohan and Neel hadn't been desperately homesick during those Seema Auntie stays. Rohan and Neel hadn't been cooped up in the kitchen, chopping onions for chaat. Rohan and Neel had been playing soccer outside with their male cousins, joyous and free.

Tash shuffled through the heap of aging envelopes, scanning her mother's tidy penmanship. "Everything you wrote in here is true, Mom?" She unfolded sheets of crosshatched math-teacher paper, Mary's trademark. Tash chuckled confusedly as she read a particularly strange line aloud. "This one says you spent 'a long day plucking chickens.'"

She noticed the flatness of her mother's unelaborated phrasing—Caleb would love it. Mary Grover *also* sounded in person just like she did on the page.

"Yes. One hundred percent true. I got a bargain at the butcher shop, fifty raw birds. I was so proud of myself until a van showed up and all the chickens still had their feathers." Her mother laughed softly, beads sliding on an abacus, smooth and measured. "You should have seen your father's face."

"Wait—" Tash could not imagine her father helping. Vik Grover usually just got home from a day at his busy dental practice and sat at the head of the table. He never cleared a single plate. "Dad *also* spent 'a long day plucking chickens'?"

"Goodness, no! Grandma Sally flew down—and trust me, we spent more than one long day." Without a whiff of resentment: "It was awful, actually. We wore nose clips and rubber gloves."

For the entirety of Tash's childhood, a square meal awaited every night—in addition to teaching high school math full-time and doing all the housework, Tash's mother also cooked. She spent her vacations restocking the deep freeze in the garage with casserole dishes, labeled and tightly sealed. Mary ran a military, oven-ready operation: orange chicken, lemon chicken, cherry chicken, coq au vin.

Over the summers, her mother would have only had a quiet house for a short time, while Tash and her brothers were away at Seema Auntie's. Mary Grover got three weeks without the early-morning tutoring of failing algebra students, or Neel's hairy teenage body odor, or Rohan's endless pile of grass-stained tube socks. Or Tash's emo poetry. Or Tash's misanthropic huffing off.

Through Tash's adult eyes, it seemed tragic, a waste of precious peace. "Mom, how come you never traveled while we went to Seema Auntie's?" Tash asked it with a relaxed openness that, without the booze and exhaustion, might otherwise have been tempted to judge. "You had time to yourself." The contents of the envelopes fanned across her bed. "These letters make it seem like all you did was chores."

"Your father was working." As if this were self-explanatory.

Tash frowned, glad her mother couldn't see her expression. "Okay. But wasn't there anywhere you would have wanted to go alone?"

"Without your father?" As if the very notion was ridiculous. "Who would have taken care of him while I was gone?"

Tash tried to make her tone teasing, rather than deliver a treatise on her mother's generational, internalized patriarchy. "Mom. That might be the most old-fashioned thing you've ever said." She tried to make it gentle: "You were working really hard. Dad could have taken care of himself, and you know it."

Mary's voice sharpened, marking the overstep. "Don't lecture me, Natasha. I do what I like. I'm not old-fashioned—I'm the proud parent of a gay son." Her clip became imperious, a mathematician's absolute: "I'm one-half of an interracial couple in the South, I'll remind you, before anyone thought that was 'cool.' You have no right to impose your values on my decisions." And then she hung up.

Tash's beer warmth receded under her mother's cold verbal slap. Her stomach sank as she let go of the letters. She closed her eyes into her pillow, pulling the phone away from her ear.

She chided herself for the souring—after all, her mother's hierarchy of social progressiveness had always been clear:

Gay son, fine; mixed race, okay. But feminism—or rather, a made-up tale of feminism on a pretend island—caused Mary to struggle, either with the storyline or with its author. Probably just with Tash.

The botched call with her mom became feathers in Tash's dream.

It became REM chicken-plucking, Seema Auntie's cackles echoing from another room. It became an enormous tray of tandoori drumsticks Tash could not balance upright. It became Caleb zigzagging his plate away as Tash tried to serve him, sending cascades of cilantro-cucumber yogurt crashing wetly to a tiled floor.

Tash woke just as the dream narrowed only to Caleb, one last image, white teeth sinking into golden-skinned tandoori thigh, blue eyes blissed out on Tash's skillful and well-spiced marination.

She couldn't shake the mental picture.

Even a day later, as she sat cross-legged in her regular Saturday yoga class, her mind swam with the ridiculous impression of Caleb wantonly biting moist flesh.

It could've been the contentious conversation she'd had with her mother; it could've been the letters still scattered in her room; it could've been a legitimate, sudden craving for Punjabi flavor.

It could have been that right then, somewhere on a videoconference stream between South Florida and a production office in Los Angeles, Caleb was unveiling their maiden Noab-and-Hewett scene.

Tash grounded on her mat, in the yoga studio's Zen, flowing through a sequence of poses set to rhythmic electro-sitar vibing. She followed the instructor and balanced on her hands and knees. She twisted left and right slowly, the movement meant as a wringing out. Instead of emptying, however, Tash just gathered thoughts of Caleb:

piano bar to parking lot to Seashell to Manta Ray's; laughing on Rohan's sofa, whiteboard and blue eyes and tattoo scroll and large hands; inviting Tash to burlesque for some background.

Even straightforwardly confessing his mommy issues.

That last one stoked a solitude the yoga couldn't cleanse: the idea of a little boy, abandoned and alone, even in a gaggle of his foster sisters. Tash had tasted drops of that rejection from her own mom, on the phone. It left her stinging, and she was supposedly an adult.

The summer Saturday stretched ahead as Tash ambled home along the beach, pondering an indistinct sense of isolation. Ordinarily, she would have been more occupied—she would have gone to visit Rohan. She would have spent time with Janelle—but her kids had summer activities, and music class, and newfound playgroup friends.

Back on her balcony wicker, Tash sprawled out as she rang Caleb from beneath her palm tree overhang. Yoga mat tossed aside, ponytail undone, the bare soles of her feet pressed together in a butterfly pose. In her stomach, more butterflies.

"How'd it go?" She bypassed a greeting in case he thought she'd called to gab.

"Tash! Hey."

"Did they like it?"

Caleb had assumed the role of middleman, buffering Tash from the Executive Production team, shielding her from Ram and Doolittle and Reggie and protecting them from Tash.

Even if she loathed Braverman, Tash knew this first Story Edit meeting was an important test. Of her partnership with Caleb, and Caleb's talent, and the blocking they'd put to page. They would need to pass this gauntlet if she wanted to retain any bit of control over the adaptation.

Caleb's voice dropped. "Well." Audibly, an intake of breath. Low and grave: "Ram and Reggie hated where we put Hewett's stab wound. They think it's too nuanced. They want to move it inward, closer to his groin."

Tash fumed. Instantly, she was up, out of her yoga legs, stomping across the balcony. "Are you fucking serious? Braverman has no taste. That guy wouldn't know nuance if it slapped him with its dick." She collapsed back into the sofa irately. "What do we do now? Revise it? What else did they say?"

But Caleb had exploded into laughter.

"What's so funny?"

"'If it slapped him with its dick'? Jesus, Tash. I was joking. You really think they'd want to move a stab wound closer to his crotch? It hurt me just to say that." His laughter became a guffaw. "Remind me not to cross you."

Tash had to smile. "Don't cross me." Begrudging. "And don't do that! I was already writing testicle stage direction in my head."

"Please don't." Still chuckling: "No. They loved what we submitted. Executive Production gave us the green light. They're extending me. I mean, if you still want to work together."

The thought of registering her decline with the studio didn't even peek its head around the bend. "I want to work together." Tash said it definitively. Her film agent would be thrilled.

Janelle would be thrilled.

Tash might have thrilled a little also.

"Okay, then." Caleb sounded pleased. "The first thing we need to do in order to continue this partnership is to find a way to thank my dad for taking care of Iggy."

"Who's Iggy?" She slouched back, aware she was looser now than she'd been after yoga class.

"My dog!" Suddenly indignant. "Haven't you ever looked at my screensaver? He's at my dad's while I'm away."

"I don't spy on your laptop, Caleb." Only because she hadn't had the chance. Now Tash cradled this new crumb of information. She grinned fully while she closed her eyes and spitballed his life in LA: "Let me guess—Iggy is a rescue Chihuahua. You carry him from your boho-modern home in Silver Lake to the farmers' market every week-end in an artisanal murse."

"Excuse me?" Caleb's fake offense bounded across the line.

"A man-purse. A murse." Tash happily offered the glossary.

"No, I got that." His voice affectedly miffed. "Iggy's a Lab, Tash. He never fit into a murse. I *walk* him to the farmers' market on the weekends."

"From your boho-modern home in Silver Lake."

"Don't profile me!" But Caleb didn't correct her. "You just finished yoga. You're sitting somewhere outside, drinking a green juice."

Tash glanced to the green juice idling on her balcony coffee table. "Are you stalking me, Rafferty?" She glanced over the wooden railing, down into the driveway—before she remembered Caleb didn't know about the duplex or where she lived. "Are you following me with hidden cameras?"

"Yes. I'm following you with hidden cameras. It's definitely not the bird yapping in your background. Or the juice bar loyalty card on your key chain. Or that you've mentioned yoga a zillion times."

Tash played at unconvinced. "That's a suspiciously high amount of attention to detail." She fully enjoyed the scrutiny.

"It's my job. Plus, it makes sense—a revolutionary feminist writer should be recharging on her day off." And then his discipline reemerged: "Her *last* day off. Because we start again, tomorrow. Bright and early." He chuckled when Tash exaggeratedly groaned. "We can't let one win make us complacent. Episode Five's lagoon sex is going to be hard."

"Is it?" Tash only smiled at the unwitting innuendo.

"Yes. It's going to be rough." Caleb joined in the immaturity for a moment, before his voice grew serious again. "For real, though—Episode Five is going to be a slog. We've got dialogue. We've got fore-play. We've got epic intercourse. This is A-game territory, and we're going to have to bring it."

"Wonderful." Her reluctance was half feigned. "Now I'm terrified."
But she really wasn't—Caleb had made the first bout so much fun.

His competence was apparent even through the phone: "I'm not
trying to scare you. I just know from experience these climax scenes
are work. They require tons of creativity—four episodes of tension will
have been building. When Noab and Hewett finally get together, we
want it to be good."

Tash couldn't help but taunt him. "Is that a technical term? Is 'good'
the same as 'hot'?"

Caleb huffed long-sufferingly. "We want it to be *inspired*, Natasha.
We want it to live up to your book."

The words hit her somewhere beneath the neck and above the
knees. Somewhere that had nothing to do with the mechanics of physical blocking, somewhere that wasn't sexual, somewhere that relished
this collaboration. Somewhere that made her stomach flip.

Somewhere that reminded Tash she was lonely, and that the day
stretched companionless ahead. "Hey. Speaking of inspired—are you
free? I have something I can show you to help us make it good."

Chapter Eight

The landscape that inspired the backdrop to Noab and Hewett's earth-shattering alfresco beachside sex could be reached through a parting in the sand dunes, outside a restricted-access back door, which opened with a certain type of Biscayne Coastal key card, tapped against a wall sensor inside Ocean Science Research Laboratory Three.

During the regular school term, Tash knew the Marine Ecology adjuncts who supervised the study of this rare, limestone-rimmed lagoon—its razor-sharp rock base the result of tens of thousands of years of shell and coral and fossil accumulation, the largest sedimentary formation of its kind. Between it and the shoreline, wind and water erosion had chiseled the terrain. At high tide, in hurricane season, Tash had seen vertical spouts and jagged valleys force seawater plumes through its carved-out chimneys like blowholes, sending sea geysers fifty feet into the air.

At low tide, in calm weather, however—the preserve sunbathed stark white and bone-dry, as lazy afternoon waves half-heartedly lapped the sanctuary stretch of coast.

Tash's faculty friends were all away for the summer. There was no one there to ask to tap their card. Instead, Tash and Caleb had to park near the adjunct lounge and hike up the beach, approaching the lagoon from the sand side.

"I like your campus." Caleb's flip-flops dangled from one finger, his bare footprints dissolving in the dune, his baseball cap low and his aviators mirroring the sun's glare.

Beneath her own cap, Tash inhaled the scent of surf verbena and tide. She'd never attempted to reach the passage this way, and up ahead, she spied the coral climb—ocean to the left, modern lab roofs screened by thatch palms on the right side. In the middle, an alabaster range of pock-marked mini mountains cupping Noab and Hewett's secret sex lagoon.

"I like this campus, too."

Gulls screeched as Tash tipped her face up to the cloudless yonder. "Although, honestly—the beach is the best part. My humanities block would not impress you. They stash us by the sports fields, near where Fishery Conservation dumps their tanks."

Caleb glanced at her sideways. "But you still stay here." Both statement and an inquiry.

The breeze tangled sea salt in the low knot of Tash's hair. "Yes. I like my colleagues. I love the chair of my department—she's seventy-five and still producing poems." Yandra Santos's lyrical legend kept the entire English department afloat. "She lets me teach as much as I want, and she let me write the curriculum for 'Heroes and Villains,' which is unusual since I'm not permanent staff."

"I'm guessing she also doesn't pay you like you're permanent staff." The comment came out of nowhere—as if Caleb had just been commiserating with Tash's father about the sad state of her career.

She slowed her pace, puzzled by the change of subject, sliding her sunglasses down her nose.

Caleb put his hands up. "Sorry, it's none of my business! Stacy's brother teaches physics at Pasadena, and she's always saying he's ridiculously underpaid. I think he might even have tenure. I'm guessing adjuncts get an even shorter end of the stick."

Admittedly, Caleb's concern felt different from Vikram Grover's judgment. "Yandra would pay me if she had the budget." She slid her sunglasses back into place, starting the trudge up their first limestone knoll. "I could also make it easier for her and finish my master's. In the meantime, the adjunct rate is fine. And I have the flexibility to work on other projects." Like *The Colony*.

Like if she wrote something else.

Coral jutted from beneath the sand, and Tash and Caleb paused for a moment to slide their feet back into the flip-flops they'd been holding so they could scale the jumble of life-size sandcastle stairs. They ascended to the preserve's highest point. From there, sharp crags sloped downward, fenced by ocean and trees.

They surveyed the descent, sandpipers hopping between cratered puddles, the lagoon's water level demure and low, though Tash knew, in a few hours, the same shoals would be flooded, the spiny decline made impassable by the influx of the tide.

The spiny decline made impassable . . .

Tash stopped, staring at the helpless bare skin on their rubber-thonged feet. She grit her teeth, taking one tentative step forward. She'd completely forgotten she and Caleb would need protective shoes.

A quarter inch of flimsy foam bowed beneath her arches.

"Shit. I never come this way. Ugh, Caleb, I'm really sorry." She airplaned her arms for balance. "They give you knee boots when you enter from the labs." Another step, and Tash felt barbed coral catch on the bottom of her flip-flop. She glanced back at him. "If this is stupid, we can turn around."

"It isn't stupid." He'd already begun to follow, his gaze trained on a dipping angle of thorned ground. "I mean. It might be a *little* stupid." Beneath his baseball cap, his mouth curved. "I like how you made me go back to my car and put on more sunscreen, though. It'll definitely help when I bleed out from my feet."

Tash laughed, not daring to look up. They proceeded downhill slowly. In her peripheral vision, she saw him edge alongside her, board shorts stretched across athletic thighs.

His T-shirt hung threadbare, molded to his chest. He teased her: "Just so you know—when the Mother Beast comes, you get eaten first."

Out on the water, rainbow-colored sails ballooned. Far off, in a clearing, tufts of Bermuda grass rippled on the palm-lined side of the lagoon. Saw palmetto hedged the open dell.

Tash pointed to it. "That's where we're going. It doesn't look like anything right now, but wait until we get there."

"Don't worry. I trust you. Kind of." Caleb's visual attention stayed on his feet. "Hey—you know what I was thinking about after our dinner the other night?"

Tash did not know, but she was going to fall over if he said, *Tandoori chicken, in a bizarrely sexual way.*

"You must have written *The Colony* while you were with the pediatrician."

Tash paused, recognizing the trick of salt-spray triangulation: limbs too occupied with the danger of their scramble, brain too busy to guard words, the brined narcotic of the ocean too strong a truth serum, suggesting a confidence between Tash and Caleb and the sea.

Still, she answered. "When I met him, I'd just finalized a draft. Why?"

Caleb picked his way carefully beside her. "I don't know. I was just thinking it's the kind of book you could imagine being fueled by a breakup—not written in the throes of a romance." He steadied on a spurred ridge. "I mean, I'm guessing. I'm not a writer of literary fiction."

Tash smiled. "And yet you just said 'in the throes.'"

He chuckled, aviators opaque. Sunscreen streaked his forearms, where he'd been lazy about rubbing it in. His calves flexed.

Tash kept deflecting. "Also, as we've established, nothing in the book is true. It's fiction. I could have written it during the happiest period of my life. There doesn't have to be a connection."

Caleb straddled two calcified outcroppings. "I know."

However. Safe space and seaside truth serum. And Tash would be baring other inspiration anyway. She told herself Caleb had grown up in a coven—all those chosen-family sisters.

"But you're right, kind of. The impetus came from a bad date. It happened at a bar right down the street from where we met Ram that first night, actually." She half smirked. "Maybe that's why I came at you, guns blazing. I have a bad association with that whole zip code."

Caleb half smirked right back. "I don't think that was the only reason." He softened. "You don't have to talk about it. It was just a random thought."

She realized she wanted him to understand her. "No, I don't mind."

She continued down the ragged bluffs, ripping holes in the rubber of her flip-flops. Caleb's shins were scratched, but he didn't complain. He just waited for Tash to talk.

"After I moved back to Florida, after I started teaching at Biscayne, I swiped right on someone who seemed nice, and I went to meet him." Tash could barely picture the male in question—with time, the memory had grown blessedly faint. "Yandra needed me at school early the next morning to set up for some conference with the dean. Which is funny, because otherwise I wouldn't have been trying to cut the date short. The guy was actually very charming."

Caleb nodded, clouds already gathering on his face.

"When it was time for me to leave, he wasn't ready to let me go. He yanked me back into our booth by my hair." Tash mimed a reenactment. "He pulled a whole chunk out."

Sometimes, in grim moments, Tash could feel the skid of unfamiliar palm against her scalp and a split second of metallic taste in her molars. "He did it with this perfectly blank smile. Then he dropped his hand and ordered me another drink. He kept on with the conversation like nothing had happened, but there was violence in his eyes, like he was daring me to try again. The bar was crowded, and I was so confused. I didn't know how to react. I didn't even realize I was bleeding until after, when I got to Janelle's."

Tash had given Hewett's men that same vein of brutality, when they attacked Noab at the end of the book—it had been horrendous, and heavy to write, and Tash had been fortunate to be able to leave it on her pages.

"I was afraid if I tried to get up again, he'd do something worse. When the waitress came back, I pretended to recognize her. Luckily, she went with it. She sent another group of women over to say hi. One of them drove me to Janelle's." Tash had never been more grateful for the Sisterhood.

Caleb stopped, mid-stride, legs split between two rocks. "Tash."

She tucked her hair back into her cap. "It could have been way worse, and it happens all the time. It's why I get upset about *Transtempora*, or Braverman's Episode Nine notes—which I can't really bring myself to read yet, by the way. Gender violence exists, or sexual violence, or relationship violence, and we should absolutely talk about it—but it isn't 'for your viewing pleasure.' It isn't for other people to exploit. It's not entertainment." Tash paused. "Do you know what I mean?"

Caleb stared at her intently. "I do. I'm sorry that happened."

Suddenly too raw, wanting to wrap it up, Tash continued their downhill journey. "Anyway. After that, I changed my number. I got off all the apps."

"Did he bother you again?"

She shook her head. "He didn't have any of my information. But I slept at Janelle's for a while anyway. She and Denise also happened to be in a bad place—their sperm donor, who'd been a good friend, suddenly wanted parental rights. It was a shit show, and we went on a bender. We sat around in pajamas drinking Bloody Marias and fantasizing about a world without men—where we'd never need them for reproduction, where we'd never feel physically at risk." She jumped to the epilogue: "Basically, we got super drunk and brainstormed a feminist dystopian quasi-bildungsroman I later called *The Colony*. The End."

She finished her answer to Caleb's question once they finally reached the bottom of the descent. "Then, one day, I met a seemingly sweet pediatrician. Just as I polished the manuscript for a book about how men completely sucked."

Tash heard Caleb laugh as she led him away from the ocean, toward the clearing, around the rim of the low-tide lagoon.

Crystal clear seawater pooled shallow in its uneven rock basin, tiny fish darting, crab-scamper and silt-swirl in impossible blue. Ahead, now that Tash and Caleb had reached level ground, the dell's carpet of beach grass beckoned like an oasis. Ribbon palms towered, throwing a ring of shade.

"You know what's so embarrassing, though?" Apparently, the ocean's truth serum continued to work its magic—Tash kept on spilling her guts. "By the time the book was published, I'd secretly changed my tune. I was so sure Zachary was different. I was so smug about how I'd found a good one." She turned, kicking off her flip-flops and setting her backpack against a tree trunk. "But there are no good ones." She sealed it with a grin to Caleb. "I'm sorry to break that to you, Rafferty. Because you really do write a nice penis scene."

Caleb heaved himself down to the grass, dropping beneath the palm-frond cover, pushing the brim of his cap back. Smiling faintly at her: "You really believe that? There are no good men?"

"Yes."

"What's the reason, do you think?" More curiosity than argument. "Same as *The Colony*—males are inherently flawed?"

Tash let him bridge the reality-fiction divide. "Yes. Men can't escape their biology."

He pushed her on it. "And there's not a single good man in your whole life?"

Tash unzipped her provisions, offering him a bottle of water. She lowered beside him, taking her time to think. "Well. I hate to knock my dad." She recalled the way her mother had ended their last phone call.

"But he and my mom have a very traditionally gendered relationship." She brushed sand from her ankles. "My brother Rohan happens to be amazing—but he's also gay."

Caleb pulled his hat off, hair matted and damp. "I take issue with your sweeping generalizations. And the rules of this game."

"It's not a game." Tash retrieved two rolled-up towels from her pack. "But I'll beat you later. For now, do this."

She stretched her legs out, knees flat in the cordgrass, gesturing for Caleb to follow suit. She leaned back, head resting on a towel propped against the tree trunk. She gazed over her midline, over her belly button, over her cutoffs and bare legs. She looked to the lagoon and, beyond it, to the sea and the horizon.

She made her hands into a rectangular picture frame, blocking out the BISCAYNE COASTAL OCEAN SCIENCE: NO TRESPASSING sign. The tableau glimmered: green tapestry, white bowl, endless smashing blue. Grass, lagoon, sea, sky. Scruff and bone and sweat and breath.

She waited for Caleb to copy her position. "Marine Ecology runs a sea turtle rescue here during hatching season—that's how I know what it looks like at night. The eggs get laid there"—breaking her finger frame to indicate the nearby dunes—"but sometimes the hatchlings get turned around or get stuck in the rocks. You can volunteer to come out with a flashlight and help them find the water."

Caleb sat up abruptly on his elbows. "Seriously?" He made a show of revelation. "Babies into the sea? Natasha—this whole time, you've been talking about turtles!"

She strained to reach for one of her ruined flip-flops. She tossed it at his head. "No, I've been talking about forsaken human love." She tossed the other at him, not mad at all. "Good thing *I'm* taking this seriously." She struggled in her shorts pocket, pulling out a folded sheet. "I even brought the mock-up from my mood board when I was outlining the book. I thought it would help us with *inspiration*. Since you said that was key."

Tash hadn't been sure she'd want to share it; she'd torn the prep work from an old planning notebook on a whim before she left the duplex. Now, as she read it out loud, she rather pleased herself—the word illustration still struck her as compelling. Even if it was fragmented and unrefined.

Midnight. The moon reflects off the silver lagoon, its perimeter roughened and knifelike, coral banks still warm from the day's sun. The scent of night-blooming jasmine is everywhere— mixing with gardenia and lemongrass and arousal. The only sound is wave-lap. The wind is silent, suspending time. The impenetrable, luminous limestone creates a moat, separating the lagoon and its cool grass from the ocean. It's a private planet. Hewett and Noab are completely alone.

If it had been anyone else, Tash might not have plunged in that fast, but with Caleb, at this point in their collaboration, she somehow didn't mind.

And in response, he took the torn-out notebook paper from Tash's fingers, his contemplation shifting from the lagoon panorama to her scrawl. He'd stopped joking; caught, perhaps, in the visualization. After a minute, he turned his musing gaze on Tash.

He stared a beat too long. "Is it too late for me to apply for next semester?"

She flushed, staring back. "Biscayne doesn't have a film department."

Caleb just shook his head, aviator smoke opacity remaining fixed on her face. "I'd go back and study psych. I'd investigate the very curious way you marry an obvious, deep love of place with both sex and menace."

"Is that what you think I do?" Tash pushed herself to sit up all the way, retrieving the notebook paper from his fingers.

"Yes. It's great. Very intriguing."

She began to feel exposed. More exposed than when she'd shown him her unvarnished string of syllables. "Really? I think it's straightforward." She crossed her legs, tucking the draft notes into a zipped section of her backpack. "I wanted Noab to have her island armor nearby when she finally bared herself to him. The lagoon is a protective setting—she has sharp rock and the Mother Beast."

Caleb's bemused attention loitered on her. "You're assuming *she's* the one that's vulnerable. Which, if you think about it, doesn't make any sense. Noab and Hewett are on *her* turf. She's the island warrior. She's royalty, and he's just some shipwrecked dude."

Tash returned to the backbone of her argument. "But he can physically overpower her."

Caleb nodded. "And I would never discount that. But there are other ways to think about sex and power." His gaze held something secret.

Then he folded his hands behind his head and lay back in the tall grass. Loftily: "This was very educational, though. I like it. It's a good thing you're coming with me to go see some burlesque."

Chapter Nine

Tash's brother Rohan called to video-chat as she readied herself for the film festival's *Vaudeville Striptease* event.

She balanced her phone on the bathroom marble as she assessed her makeup, Rohan's easy smile wedged between a flickering dark-rum candle and a half-drunk glass of red wine. The setup stirred Tash's memories of high school weekends—that hour before she'd go out on a Saturday night, when Rohan would sit on the ledge of the bathtub and shoot silly jabs as Tash flat-ironed her hair. The sight of his tired eyes and West Hollywood man-bun, now slightly askew from a long nursing shift, panged in the hollow carved by their distance—Rohan's affectionate insults so close, and still so far away.

After several wardrobe conferences with Janelle, Tash had selected skimming tuxedo pants and a filmy, sheer black shirt for the evening— the top's fabric a contradiction, both covering and exposed. Her silhouette apparent, but only in relief—against the right light, in her chosen arrangement. Janelle assured Tash it read "courageous and carefree."

She left her hair loose and wavy, thin gold bangles on both wrists. She fashion-showed Rohan her earrings—a birthday gift to her from his boyfriend, Wesley. The tourmaline and gold spangles caught the glint of candle as she spoke.

"They're a talisman." Tash patted a subtle highlighter beneath her brow bone. "I'm bringing you two with me."

"Where—to your 'work event' at a 'burlesque club'?" Rohan gave her taunting air quotes as he swapped his scrubs top for a T-shirt. "Just admit you're on the pole, Trash"—invoking his favorite, most horrid teenage nickname for her. "I get it—the TV money's running out."

The soft tip of her eyeliner pen stuttered. Tash narrowed at her brother on the screen. "It's research, idiot. Caleb thought it would be good scene prep—we're working on something where the physical choreography needs to be more than just plain humping." She gave him a rude look. "Which I'm sure is something you don't understand."

Rohan's thick eyebrows furrowed. He pretended to squint into the camera. "Oh. This must be the wrong number—I'm looking for my sister? She drives a hatchback and wore headgear? She doesn't say pretentious screenwriting shit?"

Tash laughed. "Tonight is work. That's all I mean."

Rohan's tall frame lumbered through his sun-drenched 1920s bungalow, his phone camera catching wisps of bright, basil-hued cabinetry and a collection of hanging copper pots. Tash watched him assemble a post-work vodka tonic in his spotless kitchen, then rustle around for snacks. Wesley must have been out; Rohan put his legs up in a leather armchair in their library alcove.

"You're not allowed to eat there!" Tash loved taking Wes's side.

Rohan's middle finger filled the phone screen as he gulped half his drink. "Now back to tonight's orgy—is the studio guy still being a douchebag? How many orgasms have you had to fake so far?"

It took Tash a moment to decrypt Rohan's teasing and realize he meant Caleb—the last time she'd spoken to her brother, she'd painted Caleb as a foe.

She dredged a powder brush through iridescent shadow, tapping away the excess, considering her near-complete reversal: The few days they'd already spent on new Episode Five development had been nothing short of great.

"Actually." She figured she could be completely honest with Rohan, maybe even more so than Janelle. He was less invested in the book's themes. Tash could unguardedly unpack. "Working with him has been kind of amazing."

From an armchair in West Hollywood, Rohan coughed. "You're kidding."

"I'm not." Tash finished her mascara. "I know. I thought it would be sleazy, but Caleb's approach to intimacy is really thoughtful. It's getting me to consider character dynamics in a totally different way. It might change the way I write." Her eyes flicked to watch her brother, who visibly did not buy it. "I know I said a ton of horrible things about him when we started—but he's gotten me to keep an open mind."

Rohan repeated it, disbelievingly: "He's gotten you to keep an open mind?" He set down his glass, extremely suspicious. "Hold on. What does he look like? Is he cute?"

Tash tossed her brother a close-lipped, lash-fluttering shrug. She left it to his imagination. To her imagination.

She wouldn't even know where to begin the rundown.

She ducked coquettishly away from the camera, hunting in her wardrobe for a clutch.

"Ho! Loose woman!" Rohan shouted from the screen at her back. "I don't even believe you! There are no thoughtful, cute guys in LA! I had to import Wesley from Nevada!"

Tash returned after a moment, slim black calfskin clutch in hand. "It doesn't matter what he looks like." Even though her face gave it away. "Not only does Caleb not date people he works with—but how dumb would I have to be to mess around with someone who reports in to the studio?"

All true. And even as Tash said it, she didn't believe her own words. Or at least she couldn't believe Caleb would be that complicit.

"I'm already compromising on the parameters of the adaptation—legally, I have to." Sparing Rohan the rest of the details. "But come on, I'm not going to get involved with him, Rohan. I'm not stupid."

"Um." Rohan's little brother's ragging begged to differ.

"Go fuck yourself." She smiled, smoothing her hair one last time.

"I don't know what to say. I'm speechless." Rohan kept talking as Tash retrieved her shoes. "Does this mean you decided not to do that podcast? Now that you're in bed with Hollywood, New York can kiss your ass?"

"I'm not 'in bed' with Hollywood." Tash sat down to slip her heels on. "I'm still doing the podcast."

He grimaced. "Trash! We hate that fucking guy!" Rohan had hated Leo Rousseau firsthand—he'd driven to New York with his fraternity brothers, after the breakup, to help bundle Tash back home. "Have you actually spoken to him?"

"No." She shook her head. "Just to his guest outreach." Her admittedly self-justifying reasoning met her brother's frown: "Look—it's an opportunity to align myself with a broadcast that's more in keeping with my sensibilities. I can remind the fans the book is predicated on feminist tenets that I haven't forgotten."

"You're joking."

"I'm serious! And they definitely only invited me on because Leo's on a tour. If they weren't in Florida and looking for local writers, I'd never make their short list."

"That's bullshit." Rohan maintained his legs-up chagrin. "They asked you because that super-nerd wants to see if he can get back in your pants. Your fans won't be paying attention. No one listens to that podcast or reads that loser's zine."

"It's a journal."

Her brother persisted. "It's academic splooge. All you're doing is giving that jackass another chance to hurt you."

Tash checked the clock, realizing she had to leave or she'd be late to meet Caleb. She knelt on her carpet, trying to locate her keys. Letters from her mother still sat in a pile at the foot of her bed.

"Speaking of hurt feelings." Glad to shift the conversation. "Mom hung up on me last week."

"Yeah. I heard you asked about plucking chicken." Rohan, the baby, was definitely Mary Grover's favorite. His voice muffled against the headboard as Tash groped under her nightstand. "I don't know why you poke that bear."

She palmed blindly at assorted dust balls, quoting an essay from one of Janelle's reading lists: "Because mothers are the wall against which daughters bash themselves, Rohan." Not adding that she still grappled with the bruises; ever since her called-off wedding, when her mom empathized a bit too much with Zach, Tash had been picking at the scabs of their angry exchanges. "And because sometimes I don't understand how Mom and I could be related."

She remembered: The keys were on her balcony.

"She thinks I'm selfish, and I think she makes herself a patriarchal sacrifice." Tash checked her reflection in the hallway full-length mirror. "I was looking through those letters for something to explain it. I just don't get her."

Rohan might have always received special treatment from their mother, but to his credit, he could also be generous with the sibling sympathy. "I don't have an answer for you. But if you come to WeHo, I'll make you her Ohio chicken special." Rohan smiled out from the screen. "No plucking—I promise! I'll even serve it without the side of judgment."

Tash deadpanned into the camera. "Are you suggesting that opening a can of cream of mushroom and dumping it into a slow cooker will help heal my deep philosophical divide with Mom?"

Her little brother laughed. "Yes! And if that doesn't fix you, we'll go clubbing. You know, we have burlesque in LA, too."

Tash did know—she'd spent her bath time with a profile of a certain burlesque nightclub, dug up from the LA Magazine online archive, circa 1998—featuring Vivienne Palmer in pin curls, straddling a backwards cane chair in the middle of Calypso's main stage, wearing the hot pants version of a navy-sequined sailor suit, her amused gaze smoldering directly into the lens.

Draped at the foot of her fishnets was a squadron of Calypso's leather-and-feather, rhinestone-retro girls. But Viv clearly commanded the photographer's attention. The profile's boldface dubbed her "a pioneer of the neo-burlesque renaissance," "responsible for corseting the zeitgeist." It claimed "Calypso's chorus-line seduction set a new standard for modern-dance striptease."

To Tash, it evoked a definite pop-culture moment—when the revival of Cabaret won Tony Awards on Broadway, and pole-dancing for exercise emerged as all the rage. Calypso began as an unknown Sunset Strip revue—but by the time LA Magazine ran their feature, Viv's vision had become a sold-out ticket. The show spawned a residence in Las Vegas. Both up-and-coming and established starlets vied for a guest spot, "harnessing their sexuality and bedazzling their curriculum vitae."

Tash had rolled her eyes at that part.

Viv retired from dancing in her thirties, remaining a "sexy mother hen." She also remained the proprietor of an LA nightclub landmark. The article's text repeated popular legends about her love life: Viv was rumored to have dated a mobster, a South American dictator, the oil-magnate owner of Texas's largest cattle ranch.

"Or, you know, my dad," Caleb laughed when Tash told him about the profile. "Natasha, come on. You know better than to believe everything you read."

He'd greeted her in a sky-blue, slim-fitting chambray blazer—white cotton button-down beneath it—with full-hipster, topstitched lapels. His hair had been domesticated. His eyes shone bright behind his glasses. He guided her into the venue's ambient jazz warble, his hand on her lower back.

Miami Arts' black box theater had been dolled up as a burlesque club for the night, complete with tufted, chesterfield sofa seating, shirt-less and suspendered male waiters, and an ebony-paneled stage. Ruby light filtered through candelabras. Champagne circulated in old-school, wide-bowled crystal stems.

A woman with a silver pixie cut lifted one from a passing tray and latched herself to Caleb.

"Tash, this is Ilsa Hines." Caleb grinned down at the graceful sixty-something tucked into his bicep. "One of my stepmom's closest friends and Calypso's longtime choreographer." He reversed the introduction. "Aunt Ilsa, this is Tash Grover. Astrid's series—the one I'm chaperon-ing? It's based on Tash's book."

"'Chaperoning'?" Tash delighted at Caleb's choice of word before turning her attention to his aunt Ilsa, who swanned forward in a chic black jumpsuit and a double strand of pearls. "Caleb told me you went surfing up at Vesper Beach." As Ilsa kissed her on both cheeks. "How was it? Shoot any gnarly curl?"

Ilsa smiled at Tash, all gray radiance and cheekbones. "I drank Ba-hama Mamas and flirted with the instructor—does that count?" She assessed Tash openly, holding out an arm for a once-over. "You're too supple to be a writer." A step closer. "You look like you should dance."

Caleb huffed dotingly at Tash over the older woman's head, reining her in. "Tash is a professor of literature, Aunt Ilsa. A connoisseur of stories. She was just asking about Viv and my father."

"Shane Rafferty?" Ilsa's bright eyes widened, lifting her dramati-cally plucked brows. Conspiratorially, to Tash: "I'll tell you everything." She handed Caleb her glass and then covered his ears, exaggeratedly loud-whispering: "He's fucking delicious!"

Then she fanned herself, giggling when Caleb groaned.

She retrieved her drink, still sparkling, affecting placid respectabil-ity. "Also, I must add that Shane Rafferty is the most gentlemanly set de-signer in the history of West Coast cabaret. When Calypso set up shop in Vegas, he came on-site with us—and a hundred showgirls went into heat every time that man strapped on his tool belt." Ilsa's hand blocked out Caleb's renewed protests. She continued telling Tash: "Shane pretended not to notice. Pure chivalry. He only ever had eyes for Vivienne."

Ilsa gestured toward the stage then, sipping her champagne. "I'm sure you'll see him on the screen tonight."

It hadn't occurred to Tash that Caleb's father might be included in the film. "Wait—is he here, too?" She looked around, puzzling at Caleb, who just sad-smiled and shook his head.

"No. It would have been too much. He barely got through the documentarian's interviews. Viv's picture is still sitting on his dresser." Caleb gestured around the low-lit room. "There's no way he could take this."

Ilsa's expression became somber and far away. "It's true. Those two wrecked each other." She smiled wistfully at Caleb, tilting her head. "The best, most stable thing Viv got from Shane was this handsome one right here."

Caleb's cheeks flushed. Tash's vision of a younger Caleb reappeared. Ilsa went watery—she sniffed, the edge of one long finger pressing at the inner corner of her eye.

"Ilsa, I don't know a lot about burlesque." Awkwardly, Tash grabbed the conversational wheel. "Caleb's given me some insight, but do *you* think burlesque is feminist? As an art form?" She grabbed another shallow goblet of champagne.

Caleb seemed relieved, and Ilsa swiveled as if she hadn't just been on the verge of crying.

"Oh, without a doubt! There's a saying in classical burlesque that the performer never plays to the audience—rather, the audience plays into the performer's hands. That's very feminist, I think." Ilsa continued to reflect out loud, listing burlesque's merits: "It's shape-positive, which in dance culture is quite uncommon. Burlesque can also be used to help women reinhabit their bodies again, after a trauma." She turned to Caleb. "But I'm sure Caleb has already told you all of this."

Tash cast a contrary glance to Caleb. Then she smiled placidly at Ilsa. "Actually. He hasn't."

As Caleb jumped back into the joust. "In my defense." Guileless in his topstitch. "Tash is an extremely difficult student."

She gasped. "I am not!" She met his evil grinning, smacking the hard muscle beneath his crisply tailored blazer.

Ilsa just watched them, slipping a card out from her wallet, passing it to Tash. "Next time, come to me for the girl talk, dear. Our darling boy means well"—Ilsa winked—"but in this case, I wonder if he's out of his league."

"Excuse me?" Caleb mimed outrage.

Tash beamed back at Ilsa, snapping the card into her clutch. She noticed guests milling toward the chesterfield sofas on the theater floor. She made one last play for a question.

"But while we're here, just quickly." Tash hushed Caleb when he laughed. "What about commodification? Like, what about when a man takes the images of you onstage and passes them around a locker room?"

Ilsa steadied on Caleb's arm. "Well. Context is important, you're absolutely right. I was lucky enough to spend the best parts of my career at Calypso, which was a haven from that kind of thing." She pointed to the stage. "That's why they made this movie—Viv was a trailblazer. The only female entrepreneur on that entire Sunset Strip, and we told the boys' club where to shove it."

The house lights flickered, and Ilsa toodled fingers at Tash over Caleb's shoulder. "To be continued! Enjoy!"

Caleb escorted Ilsa to a section of inner-circle theater seats—a horseshoe of couches framing low cocktail tables up front, near the center of the stage. He left her there, in the care of the documentary's director, waving for Tash to join him on a different set of sofas, nestled at stage right. He flagged down a passing waiter and got Tash a fresh glass of champagne.

She gestured toward the VIPs. "Don't you have to sit there, too?"

"Nope." Caleb relaxed, arms wide across the sofa's back.

Tash fit herself against the chesterfield's curve, surveying the outrageous degree of female beauty in the theater. "Wow. It must have been nuts to grow up around these women."

"It was something." Caleb, ever modest. His gaze caught on a woman on the other side of the room. "Hey, see the lady in the blue dress? Right there. She taught me how to samba for my junior prom."

Tash peeked, discreetly. "'Samba'? Is that code?"

"For what?" Caleb gave her mystified. "I was fifteen. The only thing it's code for is 'Hi, I'm awkward. Watch my terrible ballroom moves.'"

She imagined him as teenage gawky. "Did you actually samba?"

He switched his grin to naughty. "Only after the dance." He upped the ante. "Want to know another secret?"

"Sure."

"Viv and Ilsa met at choir practice—they were church girls. Viv's first showbiz dream was evangelical hymns."

Tash plunked her glass down. "No way."

Caleb nodded at her disbelief. "Way. Viv sang on Christian records. That's where she got the seed money for the club. My dad has the vinyl. I can play them for you."

Tash craned, hoping to reevaluate Caleb's aunt Ilsa through this newfound lens.

But when she turned to find her, mile-long legs belted underneath a satin boudoir robe were in Tash's way. She followed a line of pale-pink feather trim upward to find Astrid Dalton in a platinum flapper's wig. Astrid's smooth, luminous familiarity zeroed in on Caleb.

She didn't clock Tash's presence. "Hey! Scooch over. I have a surprise."

Caleb glanced up mildly at the interruption. "Ilsa was looking for you." He pointed as the theater's lights dimmed to half-mast. "She's over there."

But Astrid's twenty-something flawlessness intercepted the gesture, grabbing Caleb's hand. "I was looking for you, though." Her satin robe swished against his legs as she began to slink down onto the couch—butt perked, lithe figure saucy—just as she spied Tash. "Tash!" Astrid blinked, her switch flipped from private to professional ingénue. Unconvincingly: "How great to see you! I didn't know you'd be here!" Astrid straightened her knees, suddenly upright again.

Her tight smile rang clear in an instant—at least to Tash, who could very palpably sense Astrid's uncloaked want. For someone like Astrid, Caleb's older-brother vibe could launch a thousand little-sister heartbreak ships. *Of course* Astrid was in love with him—they made a gorgeous, no-brainer match.

Meanwhile, Tash suddenly felt frumpy. She smiled, attempting to dispatch warmth. She hoped the low light masked her urge to bludgeon Astrid's intrusion with a nearby candelabra; she hoped her teeth looked friendly, and not like savagely possessive fangs.

"Astrid, dear!" Across the room, Ilsa fluttered silver in the stage glow. "Come! Let me squeeze you for good luck."

The stage lights blackened completely.

Astrid and her bad timing thankfully flitted off.

Tash stared straight ahead, grateful for the darkness, grateful to let it smother the war drum of her pulse. There was no time to examine her reaction. A pink spotlight hit the stage.

It illuminated two sets of snapping fingers, attached to wrists poking through the velvet curtain. This became a twisting snake of limbs as three, then four pairs of arms joined the choreography. Then a ballet barre rolled in from the left, led on a short leash by a voluptuous redhead dancer in a tartan micromini. Her stride pitched exactly to the backdrop finger-clacks.

She struck a pose at center stage, her retro push-up bra and gartered fishnets bumping to the beat.

She hooked one knee-high, heeled boot defiantly over the wood barre, its steel base held in place by the disembodied hands behind. One of her arms went overhead, thumb to middle finger splitting out the sound of friction. Her hips canted forward, miniskirt lifting with each snap.

She stayed like that, a throbbing statue—head stock-still, torso an undulating drum. The hands that weren't hers took turns flossing a feather boa over her clavicle, sliding it under her rib cage, around her waist, the swell of her bottom, in a dirty spiral that reached its finish line between her thighs. All the while, the dancer's eyes stared out into the theater rebelliously.

Mesmerized, Tash leaned over to Caleb. She whispered: "I thought this was a movie screening."

Caleb shook his head, bending to whisper close to Tash's ear in a way that obliterated any lingering traces of Astrid. "It's a movie *teaser.*" His rasp covered her in goosebumps. "This is burlesque, Natasha. I told you—we like to draw it out."

The stage blurred, which was either Caleb's nearness, or the champagne, or the theater's general state of increasing musk. The floating hands rearranged the woman, turning her around, folding her over the barre. Her cheeky knickers were exposed to the audience, her derriere up; all the while, the snapping rhythm never stopped.

No clothing was shed, and yet. When the white glissade of projection screen dropped to spank the dancer's upturned bottom, the entire theater flinched and squeezed its knees together. The room erupted in appreciative hoots.

Which only quieted when footage of a dance rehearsal began to whir, sepia and burnt-out at first, across the screen. The camera zoomed in on a cane, tapping counts out on hardwood flooring. It skipped to fingers on ragtime piano keys, then the glitter of a faceted Vegas headdress.

The sepia celluloid bloomed into color—what seemed like B-roll from Calypso's dressing room. The camera panned along a wall of sequined and bejeweled pasties. Then a rack of burlesque baseball-team uniforms: hot pants and balconette bras with player numbers poking up over the half cups. It swung to mannequins in leather cinch-belts, a patent police cap pinned jauntily to a tumbling bouffant wig.

Then a man—on a simple stool against a pointedly empty backdrop. He had a full head of salt-and-pepper hair and a Tom Selleck pornstache. He began speaking to the camera about a month-long "family values" protest outside Calypso; and how every day, he would bodyguard-piggyback Viv across the Sunset Strip picket line.

Tash could not contain herself; she leaned over, her whisper more a delighted hiss: "Caleb! Tell me that's your father!"

There was no question—on the screen, the elder Rafferty had the same ocean-blue eyes, sans glasses; the same hair rumple and strong jaw, his carpenter shirt rolled up and showcasing muscular forearms.

Caleb hissed back. "Not you, too!"

"Oh, me, too." Tash grinned her whisper when Caleb growled. "I'm sorry, but that man's a stone-cold fox."

Then Shane Rafferty's testimonial transitioned to silent footage of a woman who had to be Vivienne Palmer—she dazzled from atop a parade-float-size papier-mâché cake, bright and joking with whoever was behind the camera. The footage resembled a home movie, with voice-overs from the Calypso crew. Moving images of Viv onstage, in a spotlight, roughing steps out in a simple dancer's leotard; holding a giant white feather fan; lifting a whiskey to someone in the footlights. Viv backstage, a cadre of makeup-free dancers of all shapes and sizes hanging on her every word; then the same women later, costumed and clasping hands in a circle right before a show.

At Tash's elbow, Caleb had gone still.

His breath held, his eyes glistening the reflection of his stepmother's laughter, her vibrance caught in the projector flicker, unmistakably alive.

And Tash didn't even think about it—on an instinct, she reached out and grabbed Caleb's hand, squeezing, acknowledging the moment.

He squeezed back.

Then he intertwined their fingers instead of letting go.

He kept his chin up, gaze fixed on the film teaser—a little boy in tor-toiseshell glasses, a stepson with a tattoo, a grown man in hunky chambray trying to hold it together in a darkened theater, his grip hitching him to Tash.

She leaned her head against his shoulder—in solidarity, in comfort. But as soon as she got there, she smelled him—husk and cedar and California wild grass, rock canyon and morning sex, easy laughter and unruffled patience. Solid and strong and so potently *Caleb*, Tash's vi-sion blurred again.

He trapped the gesture, dropping his temple to Tash's crown.

Every molecule in her body reared up, bucking against the harness of her better judgment, begging her to twist ever so slightly; to part his shirt buttons with her mouth and press her face there and just give in.

Just as the film teaser ended.

Just as Caleb didn't move.

Just as their hands stayed clasped, and the projection screen lifted, and Tash and Caleb remained side by side together in the fragile, glim-mering dark.

Then a bathtub-size martini glass pushed through the curtains.

The water sparkled with tiny, gilded bubbles. A crystal ladder tilted carefully against its rim. An emcee's voice boomed, announcing none other than the lithe and lovely Astrid Dalton, in a surprise tribute to Calypso, and to her godmother, Vivienne.

Astrid sailed onstage, burlesque her birthright, flinging her satin robe aside. The room exploded with applause as she posed in an elaborate nude gown, dusted head to toe in diamante. At the sight of her, Tash wanted to shrivel up and die.

But she endeavored to live—because a breath later, Caleb chuckled.

He'd turned his face into Tash's hair.

In a rumble only Tash could hear: "I can't look. I used to pack her lunch box." With his free hand, he removed his eyeglass frames. "Tell me when it's over."

Tash had struggled to believe him when he'd told her, "She's like my little sister"—but now it actually seemed true.

Tash anchored herself to the sturdy rope of his upper arm. She felt his breath in her hair. She sank into the delicious backfire of Astrid's seduction—which would have worked on any other man. Tash barely noticed as Astrid began a slow peel, timed to Jazz Age snare swells. A languorous striptease unfolded, but Tash's mind glazed over, too busy memorizing Caleb's closeness.

When Astrid's garments had been reduced to just a flesh-colored body stocking with rhinestone nipple tassels and a crystal thong, she scaled the martini bathtub's shining ladder, perching on the rim of the wet glass, sending a flirty wink beyond the blinding spotlight in Caleb and Tash's direction. She pointed her toes, pinup posing along the edge, scooping an oversized bath sponge meant to look like an olive from the water's surface. She arched her back, wringing out a downpour over the peaks of her breasts. The action was so jarringly erotic, it startled Tash slightly from her Caleb haze.

She watched the slow slide of Astrid's thong-clad bottom as it piked to the base of the glass, water sloshing between her legs and brushing the tips of her pasties. Astrid spun, lifting back onto the rim, skimming down skillfully into the water again, head thrown back, thighs spread, a rush of liquid up her belly and through the valley of her breasts. She raised the sponge brazenly overhead again—another rush of water, drizzling diamond suds over her long neck, splattering her pasties, drenching the glittering apex of her thong.

The theater cheered. Astrid beamed. She swirled, articulated toes kicking a crest of water across the stage, playfully misting the front clutch of chesterfields. The house lights illuminated softly, just for a moment, accenting the audience's delighted squeal.

The brightness lasted only seconds, but it was long enough for Astrid to blink beyond the spotlight, searching for Caleb—and instead meeting Tash's gaze.

Long enough for Astrid to see where Caleb's effort to avoid watching her had become a rather intimate cling; and Tash saw Astrid's flicker of dejection.

The house lights extinguished.

Astrid extended her legs again, kicking with a sunny flair, punting a stream of water directly at Tash and Caleb.

It doused them both.

The act continued.

Caleb jumped off the couch. But no one else seemed bothered. No one else around them had gotten wet.

Caleb bent to gasp at Tash's running mascara.

"Come with me." He crouched, ducking them out a side door.

He led Tash through a fluorescent-lit passageway, past rolling wardrobes heavy with embellishment, to a dim hall that must have run behind the stage.

He pulled her along, fingers still tangled, peeking into small side room after side room, each lined with supply-closet metal shelving. He tugged her past a row of mops and buckets, past two trolleys of lighting equipment. He continued past a bank of folding chairs.

"There have to be towels back here somewhere." Caleb stopped at a cinder block linen closet, its door anchored open, starched catering tablecloths and banquet bunting piled in neat stacks.

Against a far wall, they found a cache of bubblegum-pink bath sheets.

"Ha!" He released Tash's hand to pilfer from a top shelf. "We had a bathtub number at Calypso. You have no idea how long I spent on towel duty." Caleb's blazer stretched dry across the wide range of his back.

He turned, victorious, brandishing the bath sheet—revealing the front of his white button-down, transparent and soaked through. It plastered to his chest, every plane of torso and ridge of stomach showing, everything he'd been hiding for no good reason. Tash's irritation with Astrid's hijinks suddenly disappeared.

Tash shivered, her blouse also saturated, the once-subtle burgundy lace bra beneath it now flamboyant and pronounced.

"Cold?" Caleb stepped forward, the bare lightbulb above him casting a mood. He wrapped the towel around her shoulders. He gathered the corners, pulling her close.

Tash's heart beat like a hammer, her shirt a topographic map. She stared at Caleb's throat. Egyptian cotton fibers had never felt more obscene. "Towel duty? Is that what this is? Rubbing down wet girls?"

His chuckle vibrated. Caleb released her from the pink cinch, shifting to drape the towel like a veil over her head. "No. Towel duty is *folding towels*." He began a scalp-scrunch, both ludicrous and exceptionally hot. "This is something else."

It *was* something else, and Tash swayed with the movement, eyes closed, face half shrouded, until terry cloth became her kink.

Caleb hummed. "Interesting. The lady likes a scalp massage."

He leaned her shoulder blades back against the soft wall of shelving. He moved the towel, collecting one side of her hair's long, still-dripping ends. She felt him shift to grab another bath sheet from behind her, and Tash knew if she opened her eyes, he'd be *right there*.

She twisted slightly to give him better access. She didn't know which elephant in the room to address first. "That must have been hard."

He squeezed her hair gently. "The scalp massage? Or towel duty?"

Tash huffed. "The movie teaser."

But Caleb continued to joke. "Please—you're not the first girl to ditch me for my father."

"I was talking about seeing your stepmom." She blinked her eyes to half-mast.

Caleb shifted to the other side, giving the strands there the same pink-towel caress, becoming serious. "It wasn't hard. Just concentrated, maybe. Sometimes I forget how much that club felt like home."

Pulled heartstrings must have made Tash do it—or the way Caleb had intertwined their fingers in the theater, or the aphrodisiac of his towel-dry in this linen-closet private universe. Emboldened, Tash reached for the letters on his collarbone. She traced his ink scroll through the translucence of his shirt.

The world reduced to wet broadcloth and her trembling fingers.

Caleb took a step closer, perhaps so Tash could see. "We each got one when Viv sold Calypso. We didn't know she was sick yet—only that we'd been happy, and it was ending."

Tash held still. She held her breath. "Who's 'we'?"

Caleb covered her fingers with his whole palm, pushing the collar of his shirt aside. The bare script was cool under her touch. "Well. There's me, right here. Then Viv"—sliding Tash's hand over his shirt buttons, to the depression between his pectoral muscles—"Right over her heart. Which was pretty sentimental for such a hard-ass."

Tash's own heart was racing.

Caleb moved her fingers over his jacket to the outer curve of his bicep. "My dad got his here."

Dazedly, Tash still managed to taunt him. "Do you have any pictures? Just so I can get a sense of scale."

Caleb snorted quietly and ignored her, slipping her hand around to his shoulder blade. "Ilsa has one on each side, like fairy wings." Then he adjusted, repositioning to coast Tash's palm to the center of his lower back, bringing their bodies closer. "Last one, right here. Astrid's mom."

The tour he'd offered drew Tash into a rather clever bit of blocking. They hovered a half inch from each other, almost in a dance. His mouth was well within striking distance.

"That's kind of awesome." She meant the family tattoos, the tactile expedition, her hand pressed to his back over his chambray. "I don't have any ink."

He glanced down hotly. "Good to know."

Far away—down a long, dim hallway; beyond folding chairs and rolling wardrobes and burnt-out, fluorescent light—a one-night-only LA revival roared boisterous with clapping. The show had apparently gone on without them. Caleb prowled a step closer to Tash.

He caged her firmly against the towel-shelving wall. "Do you remember, at the lagoon, when we were talking about power?" His eyes had begun to blaze. "About who has the upper hand?"

He'd mixed his words up—in real life, the lagoon was an ocean lab—but Tash nodded anyway.

"You said you needed sea monsters." Purposefully, with one fingertip, Caleb tucked damp hair behind her ear. "And I said you have so many other weapons."

"Did you say that?" Tash had lost coherent thought. "Are we talking about work?"

"We're talking about how you hold all the cards, Tash." Almost a whisper. "Burlesque. This audience is at your mercy."

More applause boomed from the theater.

And less distantly, a slamming door.

Exploratory heel-clicks resounded on the backstage concrete.

"Caleb?" Mops and buckets scuttled in the corridor. "Caleb! Are you back here?"

He stared at Tash mutely, his expression paused. He kept his back to the doorway. He kept his eyes on Tash's face.

"Caleb?" The heel-clicks near now. Outside, in the hall.

He took a step backward, away from Tash, dropping his hands from where she'd willingly been trapped, and turning just as Astrid stopped short in the doorway.

She'd wrapped up in her own terry cloth. She still wore her blond wig and rhinestoned stage paint. From behind the squared-off block of Caleb's body, Tash glimpsed Astrid vacuum up the evidence—the used pink towels, Tash and Caleb's general disarray.

"You left." Astrid's words came out as allegation. "During a tribute I've been practicing for weeks."

Caleb sighed, exuding undisguised irritation. "Astrid, can we talk about this later?"

She blanched at his dismissal, her death stare only upping its beams. "I came to get you because Ilsa's tired. She wants to go back to her hotel."

"Okay." He said it flatly.

"She wants you to take her. She's emotional and overwhelmed."

Tash sensed Astrid's mounting tantrum. She had no desire to be struck by a stray bullet. She took a clammy step out of Caleb's shelter, moving toward the door.

Astrid bristled, tucking her towel tighter under her arms—and Tash would have liked to remind her they weren't rivals.

Although that felt false as Caleb reached for Tash's hand.

He shot her a private headshake. "Don't go."

It thinned Astrid's mouth into a hard line. "You know what? Don't worry, Caleb—I'll just tell Ilsa you're *working*." She waved at them sarcastically. "Because this seems super professional, and we all know how important that is to you."

Tash had to get out of there. She pulled away from Caleb. She bolted.

She'd claimed to have written a Sisterhood; she'd claimed to put it first.

And yet, as she darted down an echoing corridor in a streak of embarrassment and wet clothing, she swore the lead actress in her book's adaptation would quite like to push her in front of a bus.

Chapter Ten

Tash had already agreed to meet Caleb at his hotel's conference room the next morning. They'd moved their Episode Five work there before the *Vaudeville Striptease* event, for a change of scenery, and because they could put lunch on the Braverman tab. And because the hotel advertised a poolside happy hour they could reward themselves with each time they met a scene milestone.

The idea of which soured in Tash's stomach as she dragged herself out to her balcony, thoughts of Caleb in that linen closet still muddling her head.

She'd slept poorly and woken humiliated, Astrid's *this seems super professional* haunting her dream. Just one day ago, Tash had boasted to her brother that she wasn't dumb enough to put herself at risk. She'd flippantly told Rohan she was too smart to get involved with Caleb—but if Astrid had walked in on them ten seconds later, *involved* is exactly what she would have found.

Tash muffled the mental replay by opening her laptop. She and Caleb still had scenes to complete. He'd forwarded the "blue" version of Episode Five's script and explained the way the paper color changed with each revision—they'd begun with white and were on blue now; pink came next, then yellow, and then green. The color differentiation kept Braverman's production departments literally all on the same page.

Tash's screen filled. Light blue, as promised, with highlighted comments in the margins, official communique between Caleb and the writers' room. Tash paused at the very first notation, a general greeting from @BrianDoolittle:

Good work on Episode One @CalebRafferty! Nice job getting the author to loosen up.

"The author" read this and immediately stiffened.

And then the author's hostility toward @BrianDoolittle came rushing back. Tash fantasized about setting fire to the pile of phrases he would have used for a male writer who'd put up her same resistance: *Brave*, he would have proclaimed loudly. *Principled. Daring. Tour de force.*

She stewed about this the entire drive to La Playa, Caleb's very fashionable boutique hotel. She stalked through its turquoise, pop-art-infested lobby, around an ironic large-scale installation of sculpted flamingos, beneath a massive ceiling mobile meant to mimic the sunset. She found the conference room he'd reserved, appreciating its white-on-white-on-white domed space, soft with slices of skylight, textured by florets of ivory stucco, a contrast to the rest of the hotel.

Tash's head filled with thunder in the room styled like a cloud. Her anger bloomed, unchecked and easy. It scalded away subtleties, concentrating her emotion, chasing off the sheepish traces of last night's near miss—with the man seated at the whitewashed-wood conference table, wearing a T-shirt and board shorts, as if he actually intended to follow through with their post-work plans and invite her for a two-for-one drink by the pool.

Tash marched past him, dumping her bag on an ivory chenille ergonomic chair. "In the interest of today's tasks, I should tell you I was upset by the comments in the blue version of the script I read this morning." She announced it evenly, proud of the personal growth she'd demonstrated by keeping her voice to less than a yell.

She stood beside the seat farthest away from Caleb. At the other end of the table, he'd startled and looked up from his screen. He closed his laptop, dropping his espresso to its tiny saucer.

"'*Nice job getting the author to loosen up*'?" Tash continued, her gall hoisting offended air quotes. "I don't know what's worse, Caleb—the insinuation that I'm a frigid shrew or the way you get full credit for our work."

Long, frowning moments passed, his face never shaking its confusion. "Shit. You don't have the software, do you?" Caleb reopened his laptop. "You only have the email attachment, which is a static copy of the script."

He busied as Tash stood in fuming silence.

"Your docs aren't dynamic because you don't have the screenwriting software. If you look at the script on my computer, all the comments click through. They drill down. That's how Story and I resolve changes, and how production keeps track." He spoke very deliberately, as if negotiating a hostage scene. He rose, bringing Tash his laptop. "Before you look, though—please remember that I know you don't need me to fight your battles."

Tash's outrage wavered. Somehow his kid-glove handling hinted that he'd addressed this days ago. She could tell from just the angle of his shoulders, which made her even madder—mostly because fury would be better than relenting. Fury would be simpler and safer than setting the controversy aside and having to acknowledge how they'd left off last night.

Grudgingly, Tash looked to where the blue pages were open in a program she didn't recognize. She clicked on Doolittle's first comment, spawning a waterfall of margin dialogue boxes. From @CalebRafferty:

Thank you @BrianDoolittle. I'm enjoying this collaboration. Natasha Grover is a pleasure to work with, and her source material is already very rich. Btw, thanks for your notes on the python. I'm sure you'll love our future pages.

Tash kept her head down, rereading Caleb's response. She tapped her lips, taking time to weigh his words. Just a handful, but in a tone she'd come to recognize—direct and dauntless and on her side.

"I give it a B-plus." Tash forced her expression stoic, even if her outrage had begun to fall away. "You would have gotten an A if you'd asked how often he implies that male authors are uptight, rigid hags." This seemed a compromise—a few spikes on the drawbridge as she lowered the gate.

Caleb met her mixed frequency. "I agree with you. But I also know it's not productive for me to correct him. Doolittle is touchy. He's resentful because the polishes have to go through you." Before Tash could argue: "Which doesn't mean I'm defending him—I'm not. I'm just explaining where he's coming from."

"Doolittle is a jackass." Her temperature cooled as she said it. "And that's me being nice."

"Doolittle *is* a jackass. But he's also the head writer on your show. Part of my job is to humor him—just like part of *your* job is to ignore him." Now Caleb wore the beginnings of a grin. "Remember when I told you each department has its own language? Scroll down and click on Doolittle's comment about the python. He thinks it symbolizes the penis."

The idea of following that thread was exhausting. Tash shook her head and closed Caleb's laptop. She made a show of pushing the computer toward him with a single finger, as if she wouldn't touch it again without a hazmat suit.

She flew her white flag: "From now on, all script comments are yours. I don't want to see them. I'll work from your notes."

Caleb's grin grew. "You sure? Because Reggie thinks Doolittle's wrong, and the python isn't phallic, but it does have biblical overtones—something about Moses and parting the Red Sea. Executive Production likes to connect content to viewer data mining. They like to make sure their projects are 'on trend.'"

She sighed. "The python is nothing." A tea service had been set up on the conference room's credenza. Tash saw Caleb had requested fresh mint leaves for her, because the hotel's kitchen didn't carry chai. "I promise, it's just a snake. I couldn't think of anything scarier when I was writing. I'd already used up prehistoric-shark-slash-crocodile on the Mother Beast."

"Well, keep that secret to yourself. It's more useful to me and you if we let them duke it out." Caleb's reflection fixed Tash in the sideboard's hanging mirror, swinging back to serious. "But don't let it get inside your head, Tash. Concentrate on what *we* put on the page. You know that's what Janelle would say."

Tash loaded a fancy mesh infuser with dark-green mint chiffonade. "Oh, now you think you can just name-check Janelle?" She poured steaming water, marveling at how reflexively she'd bounced back into their banter.

"She said I could. She told me to refer to her as often and as flatteringly as I like." Caleb met Tash's smile in the mirror before he withdrew it again. "For real, though—ignore them. I'm careful with my bullets because if I give Braverman's team a hard time, all I do is make things difficult for us. And for Astrid."

Whose mention immediately killed Tash's enjoyment of the repartee.

"And on that note, in the interest of today's tasks"—Caleb appropriated Tash's opening words—"I want to apologize for last night. For Astrid, if she was rude to you, but also, mainly . . . for me."

Caleb paused uncomfortably. "My behavior was profoundly unprofessional, and I shouldn't have needed Astrid to point that out. She and I had a long talk, and we cleared up a bunch of things—but none of them excuse my extreme lapse in judgment. I'm sorry. I got carried away."

Only Caleb Rafferty could make rejection look that good. His penitence nailed Tash to the credenza, while blistering mint water burned her tongue. She didn't dare lower her teacup, or he'd see her hopeless disappointment—she didn't even know what she had expected from the conversation, but it was not this.

"I thought the burlesque would be useful, and I knew you and Ilsa would hit it off. But Stacy would have killed me if she'd been there." Caleb radiated self-disgust. "I'm supposed to be an experienced professional. I have a responsibility to you, and to this project. It won't happen again."

Tash swallowed her boiling water dumbly, rooted there until her cup was drained.

She knew he was right, the evidence as recent as Doolittle's comment—"Shrew" could swap for "slut" too easily. The studio discounted Tash already. Braverman hardly needed further fuel. But Tash resented being termed a "lapse in judgment." She remembered his hand in that darkened theater, his hands in the linen closet, the feel of his tattoo.

"It's fine." Tash smoothed her sundress, smoothing the awkwardness, smoothing her internal tempest until she could parse it out at home. "Let's just forget it." As if that were possible. "Let's just rewind and start over."

Incredibly, unbelievably, Caleb took it as a cue.

He actually got to work—which, of course, Tash had just suggested. Although she hadn't really meant it. Surely the fire of their chemistry was not that easy to put out.

But he'd sat back down, already scrawling on his collection of whiteboards. "Don't rewind too far, though—I thought we could use last night's teaser, and look at our new sequences through the lens of burlesque."

Tash sank into a chair. She waited for the cracking of the joke. The undercurrent of Caleb's meaning swirled around her ankles.

He uncapped a marker. "It would be great to take Noab's seed of emotion and express it in dialogue and movement that allows her to retain her sense of power."

Tash felt powerless. Caleb had to have amnesia. He had to willfully be messing with her, if he couldn't discern the parallel between his present words and the previous evening.

He prattled at his keyboard. "As always, this is just a spitball—but I think it's worth a try. To start, why don't you recap where we are at the beginning of Episode Five?"

Tash tried not to say it like a jilted lover: "Do you not remember what happened?" She couldn't understand his need for a rehash, or why he'd want to put her through these paces. He'd whispered, *This audience is at your mercy.*

Tash wanted to scream.

"I remember." Caleb answered with sincerity. "But I'm asking because I would never squander the opportunity to hear directly from a creator." He glanced up. "I'm asking because we're a good team, Tash. I can't do this alone."

His earnestness made her crazy.

"From the top." As if he'd never pressed her to the precipice, or a wall of pink towels. "Tell me what happens right before Noab and Hewett engage in the unbelievably fulfilling and well-choreographed copulation we have yet to craft."

Tash wanted to crawl under the table and cry.

She yoga-breathed with her eyes closed, just to get this over with: "In the lead-up to this episode, Hewett has become Noab's ultimate risk. She's breaking all kinds of ancient laws for him—she's even set him up with refuge in the lagoon. She's skimping on her duties, like perimeter patrol, and sneaking off to see him. She's stopped protecting her island. She's shown him too many secrets."

Caleb interjected. "All of which, we've established, is very sexy."

Tash flashed with irritation, struggling to respond only for her characters, to free her answer of personal overtones. "It was sexy *before*, when Hewett was unconscious and she was only flirting with an idea. But now she's in too deep—now he's awake and gathering intel. The allure is laced with self-destruction. Noab is compromised by her desire, and it puts the entire island at risk."

Caleb tapped at his computer. "I like it—heightened stakes. Good stuff."

Tash imagined pelting him with sugar cubes from the credenza in frustration. "The real terror is that the more time Noab spends with Hewett, the less she believes the Lore. It's devastating for her to suspect her beliefs have been lies. All she can do is cling to the certainty he's a monster, as a last defense."

Tash kept her eyes closed. Caleb had to hear the subtext—Tash had just delivered a verbal striptease. All for an audience of one bespectacled gentleman, whose keyboard kept on tapping.

"But even then, his goodness disarms her—she's drawn to him on a level she doesn't understand." Tash flung the words at him. "That's where Episode Five opens. With Noab dropping her guard, because she's desperate for him. Which is when the python attacks."

No, the python wasn't a penis—the python was Astrid, barging into a linen closet, destroying a mood. "Noab enters the clearing and the snake strikes. Hewett jumps in to save her with his bare hands, like a total barbarian, surprising even himself." Not that Tash wished Caleb had *murdered* Astrid; that seemed too far. "Hewett's slaying of the python is transformative—something new and different has taken hold between them. They're covered in the blood of a brutal communal slaughter. It's mythologic. The air is thick with adrenaline."

The intensity of it blinked Tash's eyes open, to Caleb mildly typing, clueless, aloof as a courtroom stenographer.

"Great. Let's sketch some basics." Wholly absorbed by his screen. "Give me the who, what, when, where, why, and how of it."

"Are you serious?" Forget burlesque; Tash had just metaphorically given this guy a private dance. He needed to be throwing dollar bills at her, not listing investigative basics.

"Of course I'm serious." From the other end of the table, Caleb glanced up. "Don't knock the exercise, Tash. These are good entry points. Who initiates their physical contact?"

Tash dissolved into pink terry toweling, a velvet stage curtain, a Bermuda-grass-carpeted clearing, a razor-edged lagoon. She willed herself to get through his questions. "Noab. The hunger's been building for too long."

"When does it happen?"

"After dark. After Hewett's saved her, and they've washed off the python's blood in the lagoon." She had to add it, weary: "That part *is* meant to be biblical. It's baptismal. Everything before that moment is washed away."

"Where does it happen?"

It made Tash lose control of her facial muscles, sure he was being purposely obtuse. "*In the lagoon.* I showed you." She took umbrage on behalf of the moonlight wave-lap and the night-blooming jasmine, the cruelly barbed moat and the entire luminous dream. She reached for her mental trench coat, retying it with a mad knot.

"And how would you characterize their coupling? One word."

"Frenzied." House lights up. Tash glanced around and saw the scraps of story she'd strewn across the stage. "Nothing else matters—not reason, not her Sisters, not the place that he's from. They have no loyalties to anyone but themselves. There's no world outside the hot slap of their bodies. She offers herself to him like a sacrifice." Tash glared and Caleb didn't notice. "You forgot to ask me why."

"I'm getting there." He made her wait for it, before lifting his gaze. "Why, Tash?"

She gathered up her precious bits and pieces. "Because she knows there's something inherently right about the two of them together. It's fumbling and authentic. It fuels them. It's special, even while she wishes that it wasn't. It's out of bounds, but she doesn't care."

Tash clutched this to her chest, fists shaking, determined not to throw herself off the cliff until she got home.

Chapter Eleven

Tash woke up early the morning after she'd left La Playa. She texted Caleb to cancel their work session. Twenty minutes later, her phone rang.

"You can't cancel." His voice barely masked its irritation.

"I can." She'd already quite decisively skipped her beach run. "I have to." She'd poured whiskey straight into her tea. She'd hauled the rest of the bottle and a fluffy blanket out onto the palm hideaway of her balcony. "There's a scheduling meeting at Biscayne Coastal I can't miss." Tash was proud of her made-up, erudite obligation. "Fall classes go up for registration soon. I've got to be there."

Caleb persisted: "You said you were iffy about teaching in the fall."

Tash buried her face in the blanket, muffling a silent howl, realizing yet another of her mistakes. She'd confided to him that she'd been toying with taking a semester off, to explore the possibility of perhaps writing another book. She hadn't even processed the idea with Janelle yet—she hadn't had the opportunity, what with the constant Caleb and *The Colony*.

Tash swigged spiked chai, clinging to her story. "That's what Yandra wants to talk about. She's pushing me to decide."

"Come on. You told me your department head was traveling. You showed me pictures of her in Cuba."

"She's back now." Yandra would be away until the end of the month.

But Tash couldn't spend another minute near Caleb. She wouldn't survive another pass at illuminating her thesaurus, only to watch him not be able to read. His redoubled professionalism was insufferable, and the prim face of his rejection bothered Tash even more—along with her own willingness to relinquish every wisp of self-preservation, if he'd let her.

Meanwhile, if she had any sense, she'd be celebrating his restraint.

Because for the first time, a man was prioritizing her work over his own stake; Caleb cared more about his duty to *The Colony* than sleeping with its author. This was a revelation. Tash should have been ecstatic. She should have welcomed his prudence and circumspection.

"I know you're avoiding Episode Five's dialogue, Tash. I'm not going to let you sabotage our work. We have to stick with it."

She stifled the urge to throw her phone into the trees.

"We're on a deadline. You can't cancel, sorry." Caleb's aggravation scalded her ear. "I'll come to you. I'll be at the dinosaur den in an hour."

He left her with no choice. She waited downstairs, resentfully—flushed from a shower, in cutoffs and a tank top, still a complete mess. Caleb kicked his flip-flops off and made himself at home on Rohan's sun-bleached club chair.

"But before we get to dialogue, I think we need to know their movement." He'd dropped his messenger bag on the sisal-covered floor.

Tash had presented him no tea.

Caleb didn't deserve it.

She sat, braced on the sofa, knuckles white, evading his stare.

"I reread my notes from yesterday before I came here." He leaned forward on jute cushions. "I think we got off track."

"Did we?" She skirted her gaze from the threadbare neckline of his T-shirt to his wrinkled cargos. Caleb seemed a little messy, too.

"Yes. We have pages of language we can't use. We can't block figuratives. We need literals—explicit action verbs." Forearms resting on his knees now. "We need specific words and movement. Body mechanics, like what we cooked up for Episode One. Then we can move on to the dialogue."

But Noab and Hewett's pre-intercourse syllables would be too intimate, too revealing, too much of an exposé of the inside of Tash's head. The prospect returned her apprehensions to their original state, before Caleb became her ally. Before she'd had a glimpse behind his curtain.

"Or, if it's easier, we'll write the dialogue first. Your call. Either way, we need to nail the scene to its details. No more hiding behind wordplay."

Tash could have shrieked at the unwitting irony. She hadn't been hiding. The pages of yesterday's language that he deemed useless were her version of emotional nudity.

"Look—I know you hate this." Caleb raked his fingers through his bedhead as he misconstrued her fugue state. "I wish we could go back to where we were before *Vaudeville Striptease*. Because Noab and Hewett have to talk, Tash. Then they have to touch each other. It would be great if you could help me write it."

Tash booted back his agitation, her mind stalled out on his interpretation of her attitude. It struck her somewhere tender, someplace where Caleb valued their connection. "Fine."

"'Fine'? Is that today's plan? One-word answers?" He stood from the club chair, stalking to the window and the green snarl beyond. "Why do you have to make everything so difficult?"

Tash rose sharply also. "Are you sure that's what I do? Because yesterday you said I was 'a pleasure to work with.'"

"Yesterday you left me with a hill of metaphors." Caleb yanked a spiral notebook out of his messenger bag. "None of which are useful." Rifling until he found his page, brandishing it at her like evidence of her obstruction. "'Transformative' isn't helpful, Tash." He flipped. He pointed. "'Mythologic' doesn't tell me where the actors put their hands."

He chucked the notebook on the sofa bitterly. "We said we'd be a team, but then you give me nine pages of deflection. What am I supposed to do with that?"

"I don't know." Tash steadied herself beside her desk, one hand on the trestle table lamp. Her fire chilled, a glacial freeze creeping across the phrases in his discarded notebook—each of them ripped directly from her heart.

She grabbed her tote bag icily. "Write the scene yourself, maybe. You're the expert. Since all I contribute are useless figures of speech." Recalling her favorite from yesterday, which Tash believed was abundantly clear: "Like how 'she offers herself to him like a sacrifice.' Start there. Block that one however you like."

Caleb's incredulity followed as Tash made her way to the front door. "You're leaving?"

Her hand turned on the knob.

His incomprehension wore a fading sunburn and a shin scratch from their lagoon trek, trailing her to the opened door with a wide-eyed, flabbergasted look on his face. "You'd just hand me your main characters? To position however I want?"

All frost, Tash swiveled on the walkway. "Is there a reason that I shouldn't? You're a good guy, right?" She cast cold contempt back at his daftness, her spine straight with pride. "Everyone says you're the best—especially our lead actress. Whose feelings are apparently your priority." Tash cursed herself for mentioning Astrid.

She moved before she could incriminate herself further, flinging Rohan's house keys in Caleb's general direction. "Lock up when you're finished. Leave the keys under the mat."

Tash's footsteps faltered once she turned the corner on the stone path, the entrance to Rohan's apartment disappearing behind the bend.

She slumped against a honeysuckled trellis scaling the building's outer wall. She worried Caleb might come chasing after her, then was disappointed when he didn't show. She coaxed herself upright again, pulling it together, marching toward the hedge of beach sunflowers lining the shared drive.

The shared drive—the driveway shared by her duplex and Rohan's apartment.

Tash halted by her oakleaf hydrangea, contemplating the flight of stairs to her front door, reluctant to be hemmed in so soon after fleeing.

She began the walk to the ocean.

Just as she registered the black clouds darkening the sky above her, and the faint thunder rumbling from the coast.

Tash reversed course, slipping cautiously back past her mailbox; beneath the buttonwood branches, around the wild cactus, breath held the whole time. She skittered up her duplex stairs, quietly closing the door behind her. She abandoned her bag somewhere by the kitchen, then crumbled onto the white shag beneath a bedroom window overlooking Rohan's front door.

She settled in full-blown sniper mode. She kept her gaze fixed on the outside. She grabbed her phone from her pocket, dialing Janelle to fill her in.

"Why are we whispering?" Janelle's summer backdrop clanged with toddler playground.

"I don't want Caleb to hear me." Tash cupped her palm around her hushed tone, which definitely made no sense. "I tried to go to the beach, but it looks like it's going to rain here. Now I'm trapped in my apartment, waiting for him to leave."

"You have to speak up, babe. Hold on." The connection rustled. When Janelle returned, her voice was close and low. "I'm under a seesaw." Distant sandbox laughter filtered through the phone. "Are we whispering because you need me to talk you through some cunnilingus?"

"What? Are you insane?" As Tash herself rocked back and forth on the carpet like a lunatic, eyes on Rohan's front door. "Why would you ask that?"

"Because I'm a lesbian." Janelle said it plainly. "And you're suppos-edly writing good sex. At some point, you'll need my guidance."

Tash did take a moment to file it away as a resource. "No. I just walked out on Caleb. I left him at Rohan's. He doesn't know I live here."

"Natasha!" Janelle seemed to guffaw. "You continue to be my favor-ite prickly creature. You actually ran away? What are you, one of my children?"

Tash thought over her enraged exit; perhaps it had been juvenile. Perhaps it also had been extremely adult. Perhaps she'd wisely left be-fore she said too much.

"Where'd you hide your car, then?"

The car. Caleb would see it. The car was a dead giveaway.

"Why'd you walk out in the first place?"

"He didn't like my metaphors." Tash heard the absurdity of it; for Janelle, she added the real truth. "Also—something almost happened between us the other night. I'm rebounding poorly."

"Something like sexual relations?!" Janelle's excitement bounced off a jungle gym. "Why didn't you call me?"

Tash quit her surveillance for the moment, falling back to lie prone on the rug, staring at the ceiling and wishing to be chopped up by the slowly spinning fan blades. "No. Something like Astrid Dalton interrupt-ing what might have been a moment." Tash threw her bicep over her eyes. "Or a whole night. I don't know. He changed his mind. He said it wouldn't be professional, and that he has a responsibility to the project."

"Ha! I told you he wasn't your usual dickhead! That sounds so sweet."

Tash denounced it lividly: "Are you kidding?" Her phone bleeped; she pulled it from her ear as Caleb's name lit up the display. "Oh, shit. He's calling me." She panicked. She swiped the button to ignore.

"Answer it!" Janelle was no help. "No! Let him leave a message!"

The screen returned to idling in Tash's shaking fingers. "I sent it to voicemail."

Minutes passed while they waited to see if he'd left a message, or if the phone would ring again. No notifications arrived. Tash might have wailed if she could do it without her fear of Caleb hearing.

"Hey. You freaked out on him, babe. He probably doesn't know what to say."

Tash dismissed the explanation; she didn't know what she would say, either, but she still wanted Caleb to call again. She'd returned to her stalking station, eyes peeled. "Do you think I should call him back?"

Swing set noises indicated Janelle might have resumed caring for her children. "Sure. Can I stay on conference?"

"No." Before Tash hung up: "I love you, though. Thanks for doing this with me."

And then there was no time to dial because below, outside the window, Rohan's front door unsealed.

Caleb emerged. He locked up. He very responsibly lifted the mat to hide the key.

He paused on Tash's same stone-path footfalls, staring at his phone.

Then he took off for the driveway. Tash lost her visual. She popped up, following alongside, running to her living room, plastering herself to her balcony's sliding glass doors.

She didn't open them to step out—it was too near, she'd be right above him, the trees obscuring her, Caleb beside his rental, Tash hovering like the fast-approaching storm.

Her phone vibrated: Hey. Can you come back, please?

The sky crackled as Tash's beachfront struggled to reconcile its uneven distribution of temperature between land and sea. Damp air lifted over the ocean. Electric charges banged.

Another text: It's your book. I need your input on these scenes.

She fogged up the sliding glass with expectation, her gut a completely confused curl. Her phone rang. Tash hesitated, roiling with indecision.

"Hey." Caleb sighed into her ear.

Apparently, her body had decided to answer. She retreated from the sliders. "Hi."

"Can you please come back here?"

Tash backed up nearly to her bedroom. "I don't think so, Caleb. Not today."

"Look, I didn't mean to push you. I value our partnership." Point-blank everywhere she'd been baroquely ciphered. "If you can't tell, I feel shitty about the other night. I'm just trying to get us back on track, Tash."

She breathed. "Because we have a deadline."

"Yes. Because we have a deadline." Caleb's exasperation lived on. "And because I want this project to succeed. I was being stupid about the language, and I'm sorry—I'm not an English professor. There's stuff I don't understand." Blunt and beseeching, he pleaded: "Come back. I'll listen. Break it down for me."

Outside, thunder growled; broad leaves swayed in the gathering wind.

And beneath the trees, the translator standing in her driveway had asked Tash for basic paraphrasing.

She slid down to the floor, needing the grounding. She fortified herself. "Caleb, do you realize you never asked me how *I* felt about the other night? You just woke up and decided it was reckless."

"No. I knew it was reckless as it was happening." Of course he had to correct her. "It didn't stop me, which is worse. It's bad for both of us. I never should have crossed the line."

Tash hunted for more courage, ignoring his nice-guy repentance. "But what if there's no line? What if we're a safe space?"

Another split of thunder. "Tash. You're doing the metaphor thing again."

She *was* doing the metaphor thing again. Because the starkness underneath it terrified her; the simplicity of what she wanted, and what she wanted to say. She hugged her knees, hearing Caleb waiting. She distilled the ember of her aching down to a glowing seed.

Before she could examine it too much, Tash reached for ordinary words. "I'm saying I want to trust you. Being close to you didn't feel reckless. It felt right."

Rain fell. Tash heard the fat drops plunging past the palm cover, splattering the wicker couches on her balcony. She died a thousand times in the space of Caleb's silence.

Finally, he exhaled. "I want to trust you, too. Very fucking badly."

It sounded like a promise. It sounded like unfinished business. Tash could not hear what else it sounded like over the rush of her own relief.

She was out her front door, barefoot, halfway down the stairs before she realized she should probably clarify, since they were going for candor:

"Caleb—you know *trust* is a euphemisim, right?"

She grinned at the exasperated sound of his head banging against automotive metal.

Which was how she found him: hair matted by the rain, messenger bag discarded in his front seat, smiling into the side of his rental car.

In both her ears as she approached: "Really? For what, Tash?"

She reached for him. "I guess we're going to find out."

The front door to Tash's duplex thudded shut behind them. Caleb slipped his shoes off. His damp T-shirt clung to his chest.

It was a repeat of the linen closet, just without the pretense. He moved deeper into the open-plan space, his gaze sweeping through the living room. He took in the balcony, dim beneath the shuddering sky.

"You live here." He turned in a circle, shorts slick to his thighs. He cataloged the dining table, the barstools at the kitchen island beyond it, the jars of seashells crowning Tash's wall of floor-to-ceiling bookcase.

She perched lightly on the curved arm of her living room sofa, resolved to be explicit. "I do."

"This whole time?" Behind rain-spotted glasses, his eyes threatened retribution. "You've just been coming upstairs, while I have to break a land-speed record getting back to my hotel room for a cold shower?"

She followed his movements. "Is that what you've been doing?"

"Do you really want to know?" The air around him hung dangerous, diffuse with delicious squall, the argument from the garden apartment wiped out. All their arguments wiped out.

Tash nodded, and suddenly, she found herself in the bracket of his knees.

"Then yes, Natasha, that's what I've been doing. While we could have been right here, *trusting* each other." Caleb slipped a finger under the strap of her tank top, pulling her to stand. "We could have trusted each other that first night, at the piano bar." His fingers mapped a trail from her earlobe to the point of her chin.

Tash arched her neck, letting his touch trail down the slope of her throat. "First of all, that's presumptuous." With one hand, she pulled off his rain-streaked glasses, examining the espresso fringe of lashes, dark hem to the blue heat in his eyes. "There was no way I was going to trust you then. I didn't even like you."

He lowered his face into the cove above her shoulder. "I didn't like you, either." It came out muffled, his mouth beneath her waterfall of hair.

Tash felt him take a deep breath in, running his nose along her skin. She felt him smile; she felt him know he made her dizzy. Her palm went to the muggy cotton covering his sternum, to the warmth beneath the humid fabric, the rise and fall of his chest.

She crooked a finger into his belt loop, the hand over his heartbeat grabbing cold shirt in her fist. He kissed her like a man with faith in his vocation, invested in specific physical movement, who tasted like a thirsty shipwreck, like peeling her fate off and casting it eagerly into the sea. He tasted like adult male, and she was the restless, devouring female of the species. Outside, the storm lashed leaves against her windows; petals everywhere gasping and open, begging to be ruined.

She pulled him closer, his palms in the back pockets of her cut-offs. She tried to steer him toward her bedroom. They backed into the kitchen marble, fumbling into the hall.

At some point, Caleb caught her wrists.

"Tash." Pausing their pilgrimage, pinning their lower halves against the wall. "Safe space, right?" Both of them panting, forehead-to-forehead, wound up. "Let's just have one more conversation."

Through a lust fog, Tash laughed: "About what?"

"About the fact that this could get in the way of work. You should care about that."

"I do care." She pulled one wrist from his grip. She wove her freed fingers through his now completely wild hair. Falsely, with a teasing smile: "I just think this could be great research."

He chuckled. "We could get distracted." As he proceeded to get distracted. "We could miss a deadline."

"We won't."

Not really a conversation, then; Caleb hitched her legs up to lock around his waist.

She stripped him of his shirt the moment her bare feet touched down in the bedroom, walking him backward until he tipped onto her mattress, shrugging off her own top and tossing it into the sea of white shag to join other discarded garments; mementos of a strange world, where people needed clothes.

She feasted on the moment, kneeling above where Caleb splayed, his inked collarbone a lone contradiction to a fair expanse of muscle and freckled skin; his body broad and lean and rugged, as if Angeleno hipsters had declared push-ups the next big thing.

Frenzied, she'd predicted—and yet there suddenly seemed no rush. The rain outside seemed certain of its brunt and potence, and of its stamina. Without his glasses, Caleb's gaze glowed molten and unleashed.

"Research, you say?" He locked her in place with a hooked ankle.

"Research." Tash lowered leisurely into the straddle. "I mean. Doesn't the great Caleb Rafferty block all his scenes this way?"

He retracted. "No." He lifted to his elbows to underscore it. "No, Tash—I really don't. Ever. That's what I've been trying to tell you."

Her heart tripped, just a tiny bit. She pushed him back down, huffing the pheromones of a man raised by a coven, who wanted to protect her story, who couldn't help but break his own rules. She nodded. "Okay."

"Okay?" He searched her gaze for further acknowledgment.

"Okay." Tash smiled. *Fumbling and authentic.* "Yes. I hear you."

Caleb flipped their positions. "Good."

She let her hands roam then, collecting raunchy, man-candy adjectives. She deferred to Caleb's skill set. They began the rough outlines of their blocking with hard verbs and raw nouns.

She tried to stick to literals but couldn't resist the imagery—the bluffs and crests and flat plains and wingspan of his shoulders; the flex and clench of thighs. She rolled the syllables in her mouth. The brainstorm lit her body.

And this time, legitimately, she felt no need for further dialogue.

Chapter Twelve

Caleb had said he worried the research would distract them. So Tash delighted when, quite conversely, the venture of their professional relationship into new territory added a unique synergy to their adaptation work. Once she'd tasted trust with Caleb, she wanted it for Noab and Hewett, too.

"Let's just try it as the genesis for this sequence—I really do think it's 'trust' more than 'danger.' More than 'survival.'" Tash squiggled the last two words through with a marker, Caleb's whiteboard bolstered by her bent knees. "Even more than 'risk,' actually." She squiggled that out, too, Caleb's too-big T-shirt sliding off her shoulder. "I know you don't like figuratives—"

"I do now." He interrupted, grinning and bare-chested, propped against her pillows, rumpled with bed-warmed skin. "You've convinced me metaphoric phrasing can be instructive." He reached loftily beside him to Tash's night table, raising an eyebrow and his double chai. "Please. Continue."

She smiled back, lingering on his relaxed, muscled appeal: on the sex-hair that was now her doing; on the big feet poking out from covers draped across his bottom half; on the intimacy collaboration made so much clearer, now that she'd worked through their real-life scene.

She refocused and started over. "The emotional core of Episode Five ties to trust." She felt sure. "That's the backbone of the story when you scrape everything else away. We're at the midpoint of the series"—she put her hand up, preempting Caleb's inevitable quip, laughing when he batted her palm away—"yes, also known as the climax—where she suspends her beliefs. She'll trust him; then it'll all be downhill until the very end, when he betrays her."

Caleb's expression tested her theory, arms crossed over rugged freckles. "One thing, though. They've just survived the python and their adrenaline is high. Their emotions could easily tie to lust or hunger. You said it was 'building for too long.'" He referenced this without his notes. "Animal instinct would be easier to cinematically block than trust. Trust is kind of abstract." Acknowledging the freshest iteration of their teamwork: "Even though you know I'm in favor of the idea."

Tash thought about it, turning toward him, leaning sideways against her headboard. "Hunger is more obvious, and it'd be easier, agreed. But I think I was wrong the other day. Instinct and lust play some part, sure"—eyeing the whiskers darkening the line of Caleb's jaw—"and the sex wouldn't happen if there wasn't some level of attraction—"

"Or an insane level of attraction." He cut her off again, raking her with his gaze.

"Or an insane level of attraction." Tash repeated it, conceding to his correction. "Either way, I'd like to revise my earlier characterization: I think Noab makes a deliberate decision. I think the sex goes slow."

"Okay." Caleb unfolded his arms. He leaned close, unhurriedly dragging his fingers over the whiteboard pressing against Tash's naked thighs. He multitasked, rubbing out the letters of the dismissed words, his mouth lazing in the hollow of her neck: the scrawl of *danger, survival, risk, lust, hunger* all disappearing until only *trust* remained.

Tash swam in the hot rock canyon of his two-days-in-her-sheets scent, which suddenly evoked Silver Lake farmers' market Sundays and dog-walk conversations about character motivation, and sprinting home to fall right back into bed. None of which she'd even consciously considered—the picture of it all simply arrived, parading across the front of her mind, as Caleb slid the whiteboard from where it'd lodged between them, one-handing his glasses to drop beside it on the rug. He kissed her, and for a searing moment the sequence escalated alarmingly into West Hollywood brunches with Rohan and Wes.

Until Tash caught herself, tucking that particular craving back into its hidden place.

She pushed him away gently, camouflaging her swerve into hipster picket fence visions by wriggling out of his T-shirt and throwing it at him; it landed where she'd left him face down and chuckling on the bed. "Put some clothes on, Rafferty. We have work to do. An entire production budget depends on your professionalism—show the process some respect."

She ducked into her closet and emerged in a Florida-winter hoodie and track pants, upping the bedroom air-conditioning. Caleb laughed at her in earnest as Tash chose the overstuffed armchair beside her window this time—far away from him but still facing the bed. She sat on her hands and waited for Caleb to collect himself.

"Apologies." He kept smiling, definitely not sorry, retrieving the whiteboard from the carpet and balancing it against her reading lamp. He put his shirt on. He opened his laptop, using one of Tash's pillows as a desk. He stared at her over his screen and through the mist of bedroom afterglow. "So. Tell me how 'trust' moves."

It took Tash a moment to remember this was where they'd left off—at midnight, in the minutes following a brutal python slaying.

In a private, coral-ringed grass oasis, beneath the swaying palms.

She took the prompt and heard ocean moonlight in the near distance. She felt for the jagged limestone lip of a lagoon. She closed her eyes and painted Noab's racing pulse at python fangs and the breathlessness of being rescued. She painted the awestruck shock at Hewett's protective, ferocious savagery.

"I think it begins as an awareness that he's saved her—which is crazy, because *she's* the warrior, not Hewett. No one's ever stepped in to shield *her* before." Tash kept her eyes shut, sitting up straight and letting a warm sense of security wash her from head to toe. "I think she stands tall under a female moon, and lets her armor fall away. Literally and also figuratively—she looks right at him, dismantling her defenses willingly, dropping them beside her on the grass. But it's not coy. It's a baring—like, 'This is me, and I trust you with it.' Zero artifice."

Caleb's keyboard continued to tap softly. "You're good at this."

"I have a good teacher." Her eyes remained closed, guessing at his smile.

"I like it. It's different from the power I originally had in mind, because she's not setting out to seduce him."

"Definitely not." Tash shook her head.

"But she's still on a stage, in a way." The sound of Caleb typing filled the bedroom. "What if they haven't touched at all, yet? What if they're so shaken by the python, they're silent and shivering as they wash the blood off in the lagoon. Then Hewett staggers to the grass, stunned by his own actions—and that's when Noab rises from the water. She bares herself to him, but it's not a power exchange—it's more like a mirroring. Then Hewett's in the same place as the audience, vibrating with the will-they-or-won't-they tension as she walks toward him. It's perfect. Because at this point, we owe our viewers a show."

"Come on, Rafferty—let's not call it a show." Tash smiled in her sweatshirt, teasing and also the truth. "You know I'm still getting my head around being this flagrant."

"Oh, it's a show. Don't kid yourself, Natasha."

She heard him close his laptop. She blinked open to see him toss the pillow aside. Caleb grinned wickedly, once he had her up and out of the armchair.

"Every time he had to pretend he didn't notice her body? Every time they argued, and she was so smart? Every time he had to wonder what that fire would be like?" Caleb hovered over her in the wreckage of her bed. "Your audience has waited a long time to get right here. We're absolutely going to give them a show."

Later that evening, as a reward for work well done, Tash led Caleb past Rohan's front door toward the mangrove's Intracoastal-facing boat dock—a sleepy little jetty too bound by buttonwoods for active use, but perfect for the coconut-granita stall set up by a local bar during the summers.

From her duplex, it was only a few minutes on foot. But the stone path wound through the tree-root forest Caleb had so admired from inside Rohan's living room, and at night, without the window barrier, Caleb seemed less sure. Tash walked ahead to guide him, their fingers tangled, laughing every time he jumped at the encroaching chorus of croaking frogs.

"Rafferty. They're tiny, harmless amphibians."

Caleb tugged her back to his strapping shadow, shushing her mocking with a hard kiss. "Are you kidding? You said anything could be happening out here, and we'd never know it. You have to protect me."

But then they emerged from the vine-choked coppice onto the fairy-lit wooden dock, and Caleb paused, taking in the waterway's idyllic tropical scenery. They leaned their elbows on the pier's tall railing, the Intracoastal's surface a tranquil chop, the canal's opposite shoreline dotted with lanterns on patios and lamps in bedrooms. They shared a frozen coconut blended with candied ginger and key lime as small skiffs motored up to place their orders.

"This reminds me of the slushies we made for my stepmom when she was sick." Caleb licked his spoon, bumping Tash's hip when he could tell she didn't quite know how to respond. "In a good way." He smiled. "We used ginger ale and orange-juice ice cubes. Viv kept me busy, trying to re-create a drink we'd had in Hawaii."

Tash turned to face him, interested and careful, alert to fragile memories. "You went together?"

He nodded, his eyes reflecting the luster of tiny bulbs strung up overhead. "At the very end of our last trip, which was a pilgrimage to see her favorite ballet companies. We went to Paris, Copenhagen, Sydney, and Milan—not in that order. I couldn't tell you which productions we watched, but Viv was happy. Afterward, my dad met us in Kauai."

"For ballet?"

"No." Caleb's expression clouded, poignant. "For a sand ceremony. It's part of a Hawaiian wedding—you mix your grains of sand together. It was kind of like the two of them renewing their vows. Which was sweet and also torture—at that point they'd been on and off for years."

Tash examined his angles. "But they were 'on' when she passed away?"

Caleb confirmed it. "It's what they both wanted. And maybe also"—his nose wrinkled—"not super fair to my dad."

They wrecked each other, Ilsa had said.

Tash set the coconut aside. "I've never been to Hawaii." Then she yanked him closer, lightening the mood.

Caleb came willingly.

His granita-cold mouth found her just outside the ring of fairy light, before they strolled back to the duplex, before the swallow of jungle overgrowth, while they could still feel the water's wide-open gale. "You'd love it. Lots of places like your lagoon."

Eventually, Caleb needed clean clothes.

"I mean, do I, though?" He pulled Tash into his lap on her living room sofa, after they'd made it as far as the oceanside cantina for lunch. "I just figured out how to use your washing machine."

Tash buried her face in the scent of her laundry detergent, her hands already plucking at his cargo shorts and cotton shirt. She removed his aviators. "Don't you think the people on the boardwalk are suspicious you keep wearing the same thing?"

Caleb rasped his beard scruff across her cheekbone. "You give your stoners at the surf shop too much credit. You're right, though." Shifting, roguishly dumping her backward on the sofa cushions. "You need to brush up for your podcast panel tomorrow. I'll give you space and head back to the hotel."

Tash laughed from where he'd tossed her, preventing his escape by locking her feet behind his calves. "I didn't say you had to leave!"

He reached around to resituate her ankles on his shoulders, kneeling over her, blocking out the streaming daylight and birdsong warbling from her balcony. "I need to get away from you." He twinkled, lowering until he murmured it into her mouth: "Plus, Story Edit just moved up their meeting. They're done with Episode Five notes. I have the call later today."

"That's fast." Too fast, Tash suspected—Caleb had only sent the pages the day before. She felt him nod distractedly against her bra strap. "Is that a good thing or a bad thing?"

He shrugged. "Can't tell."

"Can you take the call here?" She skimmed her hands up Caleb's back. "Or take it from downstairs—Rohan's is all yours. I'll do podcast prep while you're gone."

"If you insist, I'll stay. I have some emails to answer while I'm down there. Stacy gets mad when I don't immediately write back." He rolled them over, smoothing Tash's hair behind her ear. "How dumb is it that I didn't realize you lived upstairs?"

She smiled quietly. "You had other things to think about." Tash propped her chin on her knuckles, resting on his sternum. "Hey. How did you and Stacy end up together?"

Caleb fixed a couch pillow behind his head. "She was the assistant stunt coordinator on a show my dad designed the sets for. We just hit it off. The business was her idea, because there was a huge demand, and

Stacy's amazing with on-camera physical choreography—but she hates production negotiations and risk assessments and contract riders." He gestured like it was no big deal: "And I'm good at all that stuff."

She deadpanned. "Because you spent a lot of time on towel duty."

"Because I'm used to being the glue between headstrong performers, tightly wound producers, and a visionary director." Caleb poked Tash's ribs as he edited her rationale. "I grew up on the daily clash of Ilsa and Viv. Viv and my dad. Viv and her dancers. A childhood in a burlesque bar has to be worth something. That's why I don't mind working with Braverman—they want me involved fully. Not every production company lets me into the creative process like this."

Tash pushed up on her elbows teasingly. "Like this?"

Caleb narrowed. "Like this." He waggled his phone in her face.

She laughed. "It's worth it, is what you're saying."

"It's Hollywood. I've worked on worse. I also happen to like my current project." He smiled softly, shifting the subject sideways: "Did you know our office has a yoga studio? It doubles as a mat room. Stacy meditates with actors before and after scenes." Meaningfully: "She's even taught me a few tricks for staying calm when I'm dealing with certain personality types."

"I cannot imagine what you refer to." Tash laid her cheek to the amused sound in his chest. In the contented silence that followed: "Stacy sounds cool." Tash's thoughts non sequitured to her own work wife. "If I really do take time off next semester, I don't know how I'll function without Janelle. We eat lunch together every day we're both on campus."

"You couldn't still go in to meet her?"

Tash shook her head under his frown. "The whole point of a sabbatical would be for me to write. I'd need to sit around in my pajamas, no other obligations."

His fingers played along her spine. "Am I allowed to ask what the next book is about now?"

Tash considered for a moment. She didn't answer. Instead, she disappeared into her bedroom to retrieve her mother's letters.

"I don't know if it's a next book. I found these in my closet when I went searching for my contracts." She plunked the carton on her coffee table.

"What am I looking at?" Caleb righted himself, straightening his glasses, already peering over the box's worn cardboard flap.

"Letters from my mom, from when Rohan and Neel and I used to get sent away in the summers."

Carefully, he riffled through the tattered envelopes. "You make it sound like the Grover siblings did hard time."

"Well, we did get shipped off to New Jersey." She smiled wryly. "To my dad's sister, who ran a proper Indian household. We were supposed to learn all the things my dad was too busy to teach us and my mother didn't know. But instead, what really happened was the boys were allowed to run around outside in the backyard in the nice weather, and I had to stay inside and chop vegetables with the disapproving aunties."

Caleb's mouth went tender. "Baby Tash!" He pulled her into his lap again. "You're killing me—no wonder you don't need a man! They stuck you in the kitchen."

Tash indulged his sympathy. "Funny thing is, Rohan and Neel can actually cook. The only traditional thing I make is tea."

"Is that what the next book's about, then? Mean New Jersey summers?"

"I don't think so." Tash shook her head. "But finding an old trove of letters has the potential to be very dramatic, right? They should at least be a jumping-off point—I just don't know for what."

Caleb studied the carton. "That's a lot of correspondence. Is your mom a writer, too?"

The notion made Tash laugh. "No, she's the opposite. She taught high school math. She's extremely analytic. We have almost nothing in common. It's hard for us to get along."

"And yet." Caleb pointed at the evidence.

"And yet." Tash couldn't help but agree. "She wrote us every day."

"That's kind of incredible." Caleb murmured into her hair. "Sometimes I wonder what it must have been like to have that."

Tash gasped at her own tone-deafness. She trapped him in a tight hug. "Baby Caleb! Now you're killing me!"

Tash sat outside on her balcony relistening to an episode of Leo Rousseau's podcast while Caleb called in to Story Edit from Rohan's apartment downstairs. In the gathering dusk, the Eurogeek lilting of Leo's consonants flowed through Tash's headphones, his upper-crust accent dead sexy. Most people would never guess he grew up in rural Indiana.

Leo Rousseau had asked her out the second time he guest-lectured for her graduate requirement in critical theory. Tash was shocked Leo even noticed her presence—she hadn't engaged in his classroom discussions at all. At the time, Leo's young-professor enthusiasm for dissecting Modernity and Dialectics far exceeded Tash's ability to make sense of it; if he'd mistaken her for attentive, it was probably because she'd been pondering his sideburns. Beneath showy, too-long-to-be-a-stodgy-academic blond hair, Leo wore them like muttonchops.

After two ninety-minute lectures, Tash still hadn't been able to decide if he was coolly handsome or slightly gross. Leo convinced her of the former—over drinks, in a bar near his faculty apartment on Washington Square. Leo also eventually convinced Tash he loved her, but that monogamy was unenlightened, and any failure to see it that way was her fault.

Leo convinced Tash to help him launch his journal, but her name couldn't go on the masthead—because the teacher-student taboo was silly, and it could also cost him his grant.

Leo Rousseau had convinced a younger, foolish Tash Grover of a lot of things she regretted now, although she suddenly found it difficult to care about past grudges with Caleb Rafferty in her present.

With Caleb Rafferty dropping his bag by her front door again and smiling at her through the balcony's sliding glass.

He was on the wicker sofa with her a moment later, under an umbrella of fading beach light and rustling fronds. He wasted no time, his enthusiasm tipping Tash laughingly horizontal. "They loved Episode Five. Like, *loved* it—Reggie, Doolittle, everyone." Caleb pressed their foreheads together. "The story team came back with zero notes. That never happens. They thought our intercourse was flawless."

Tash smiled into the close-up of his triumph. "That's great news."

"It is great news." He levered them both up from the couch, raising their joint fists overhead in victory; before wrapping Tash's arms around his waist. "However, it accelerates the schedule. Preproduction needs Astrid in LA now. It means I have to miss your podcast taping."

"You're going back to California?" Tash's gut lurched involuntarily.

"What? No." He cocked his head at her in confusion. "I have to head to the hotel. I have calls all day tomorrow." He took a literal rewind as he stared at her expression. "Sorry. I got excited. Let's do that again."

Tash's reflexes loosened as he manhandled her back onto the outdoor sofa, repositioning her face and penning her with his forearms.

He took off his glasses and set them on the coffee table. "Hi." He pantomimed a starting over. "I'm finished downstairs. Braverman really liked our sex. The production schedule moved up, and tomorrow I have to be on calls." Regret shadowed Caleb's unshaven jawline. "I'm bummed to miss your podcast taping."

"It's okay." Tash dismissed it easily, simply relieved he could stay. She'd have to process that, and all its implications—what would happen once one of them exited their bubble of fiction.

Caleb wasn't finished. "Lastly, now Astrid can't come to the party Sweetwater is throwing for Ram's *Big Gun* anniversary. She wants you to have her ticket and her VIP pass."

Tash didn't try to hide her doubt. The only thing Astrid Dalton probably wanted to give her was a giant fuck-you—despite Caleb's insistence they'd "had a talk" and "cleared things up." Tash had seen that unrequited little-sister heartbreak with her own eyes.

She wrinkled skepticism at Caleb's grin. "Don't you think that ticket should go to someone who doesn't get hives when Braverman's around?" She counteroffered: "You should take it."

"Natasha," Caleb reprimanded, nose-to-nose, "I *have* a ticket. I want you to take Astrid's. So you can be my date."

"Oh." The swooping in her stomach flitted to Caleb in red-carpet formalwear. Then to "date," then to worry about the studio's impression. "Is that smart?"

He shrugged. "What, for writing buddies to attend a celebration of their director's work? It could be a show of unity. Preproduction is so busy, no one from *The Colony* will be there anyway, aside from Ram." He feigned more indifference. "Plus, we're in the homestretch—pretty soon, we won't be colleagues anymore."

Hope joined her uncertainty. "You've thought about this."

"I've thought about it." Caleb's eyes went earnest. "I cleared it with Stacy."

"You cleared it with Stacy." Tash parroted the revelation, the disclosure fizzing in her chest.

He floated over her with set-back shoulders, seemingly ready to make his case. "She's my business partner. I had to come clean—I hope that's okay with you. She'll keep it confidential."

"It's okay." Tash lifted her mouth to meet his concern. "When's the party?"

At this, Caleb fully braced: "Thursday night."

Tash gasped in outrage, palms pushing him away, as Caleb laughed and pinned her struggle. "*This* Thursday? As in, two days from now? Rafferty, that is *not* how you ask a girl out! What if I don't have the right dress?"

He gleamingly resisted. "Come on—I read your best friend's paper on female costume semiotics. You have the right dress."

She paused her skirmish. "You really read that?"

From where he'd dropped his face onto her stomach, Caleb peeked up bashfully. "Not the whole thing. It got pretty complex." His mirth slid up her body. "But just listen—the party's at an estate in Coral Gables. A car will come to pick you up. I have to go back to my hotel tonight, and I won't see you until then." His blue became a pining premonition. "Two days could be a long time."

Tash stilled. She let his words sit like an unopened present, the gifting itself enough, and too new for a tearing open. She kissed him on the balcony until the tree canopy went dark.

Back inside, she made them dinner with the only things left in her fridge, toasting bread and scrambling eggs while Caleb collected his belongings.

She piped Leo's podcast through her speakers as she foraged for knives and forks and plates, pointing her spatula sarcastically at a convoluted bit of Leo's critique. "See what you'll be missing?"

Caleb came to sit on a bar stool across the countertop expanse. "Remind me why you're going on this podcast?"

Tash herself might have been no longer sure. She heaped eggs onto a square of buttered toast, sliding him the plate, rummaging for salt and pepper. "It's good press."

Neutrally: "And are you doing press at the moment?"

"No. But there's been publicity around the adaptation. Which the studio's been handling. I don't get to be involved." Because Braverman had boxed her out. "Leo's podcast came directly to me. It's an opportunity to talk about my work in my own words."

Caleb took a thoughtful bite and chewed. "Fair enough. Although it sounds a little niche. Like, I've never heard of this journal—not that I'm your benchmark."

"It *is* niche." She couldn't refute it. Leo's journal was esoteric, elitist, illuminati, self-referential, smug, and Tash had been clutching her fraught thread of connection to it ever since she'd received the panel invitation. Despite the way she'd parted with the journal's founder, Leo's opinion still carried ivory-tower weight. "Which makes it interesting."

"Okay." Caleb accepted her explanation without a trace of judgment, returning to his toast and eggs.

"And . . ." Tash sighed, because *trust*, and because she was sharing Caleb's plate and fork. "I hate who I was when I knew him—I was inexperienced and intellectually uncouth. Our relationship was the definition of a power imbalance. He manipulated me, and I dropped out of school when we broke up. This is my chance to redeem that Tash. To show us all who I've become."

Caleb stared at her intently, picking up her napkin, wiping his mouth. "That's a lot of pressure to put on a podcast appearance."

"I know." Tomorrow she'd feel like a boxer getting ready for the ring.

"Janelle will be there, right? Tell her I say hi."

Tash used the opportunity to change the subject, elbows sweetly on the counter. "Out of curiosity, do you have any male friends?"

He went with the pivot, blinking into her gibe. "Sure. I have buddies from basketball. And I'm in a poker game with my dad and his dudes."

"But all the closest people in your life are women?" She came around the kitchen island to confirm. "Except for your father?"

Caleb clamped his knees on either side of her cutoffs. "Is there something wrong with that?"

"Of course not." She looped her wrists around his neck.

"Why? Do you have male friends?"

Tash scowled playfully. "Are you kidding? Men are the worst. Have you not read my book?"

Caleb slung his messenger bag on a half hour later, the strap across clothes he'd been in and out of for days.

Before he left, he organized a parting gift, insisting on setting Tash up to meditate with Stacy. He moved throw pillows from Tash's living room couch onto the floor, opening her laptop on the coffee table. He switched off the extra lights.

He kissed Tash by the duplex's front door.

"She'll ring your screen in five minutes." He performed reluctant motions of decamping, tangling Tash by the hallway mirror. "She's great. It'll clear your head for tomorrow. I asked for the same technique she does with actors."

Tash's fingers burrowed into his back pockets. "Thank you."

"You're welcome. Okay, I'll go."

But he was still there when her computer trilled with an incoming videoconference.

"I'm leaving." He promised this to a live feed from a mat room in a Burbank warehouse, before he made buoyant introductions. "Stacy Mancini, this is Natasha Grover, the author of *The Colony*."

"I know who Tash Grover is, Caleb—she's the only reason I took this call." Stacy winked. Her head was shaved, her muscle tee showing off ripped biceps. "Tash, I've heard a lot about you. I think we spoke on the phone."

"I remember." Tash suddenly realized the importance of this interaction, and that she was desperate for Stacy to like her. She beamed warmth at the other half of Caleb's boutique consultancy. "It's nice to officially meet you."

"It's nice to meet you, too." Stacy's vitality buzzed through the cross-country pixels. "I've been following the additions you two are blocking—no comments on Episode Five? That's unheard of. Doolittle probably shat himself."

Tash's automatic bias toward this woman ballooned. She surveilled the high shelf lined with flickering pillar candles running the length of wall behind Stacy's head, dance-studio-style mirrors reflecting polished flooring, stacks of crash pads, industrial concrete. Tash absorbed every detail, tucking away another Caleb puzzle piece.

Deep male grunts and vinyl thwacking began to echo from the warehouse end of the call.

"What's that noise, Stace?" Caleb backtracked from yet another half-hearted attempt to leave.

Stacy smiled dryly. "It's the combat class I had to kick out. They're sparring in our hall. Tash, you'll have to forgive us." Ostensibly, her glare was meant for Caleb. "Someone did not give me a lot of time to prepare."

Caleb raised his chin at her affectionately. "Pros don't need time."

Stacy raised her own chin. "Sometimes they do. Especially when you abandon me for five weeks and I get so lonely, I let an MMA stunt team book our room."

"You're renting out our office?" Caleb bugged his eyes.

"Not for money, Caleb! Calm down. It's just guys from upstairs. They let me sit in on drills. It's networking, some might say." Stacy smiled in challenge. "You're not the only one who can collaborate."

Tash charmed at their dynamic, respect and fondness trafficking across the line.

"Now, Tash." Stacy got up to slide a wall panel closed, dampening the grunts. "Caleb had asked me for meditation—but if you have time, I also have another idea. There's a pranayama breathing pattern called *kapala bhati*, or skull-shine breath. Have you ever done it? Caleb said you're into yoga."

Tash had to wonder how else she'd been described. "I am. But I've never done that."

"I'll teach you—I use it all the time on-set." Stacy rolled her shoulders and folded her legs into lotus. She sat tall. "You seal your mouth and focus on the exhale, pulsing breath out through your nose." She put fingers on the lowest point of her sternum to demonstrate. "It engages the power of the diaphragm to sweep away unhelpful thoughts. Maybe we'll do that first."

Tash nodded eagerly. "Sounds great." She had to say it loudly as the fight-club volume grew.

Caleb smirked and leaned into the laptop facetiously. "Wow! This is so Zen. I hope those guys are still there when I get back."

Stacy smirked with equal sarcasm as her form broke. "Weren't you heading out? You have, like, seven calls tomorrow—I saw the Braverman agenda. You have a whole new slavery sequence to write."

The MMA barking became a full-blown ruckus, and Stacy held a finger to her ear. She muted her feed, gesturing at the camera. She got up again, striding out of the frame.

Tash turned to Caleb in confusion, certain she'd misheard. "What slavery?"

"Prelim notes on Episode Nine's script changed." Caleb reported this like happy news. "Story Edit is in favor of removing any elements of sexual violence and treating Noab's capture as if she's being sold into bondage."

He was talking about *The Colony*'s catastrophic third-act twist— when Hewett's surviving crew against-all-odds finds their way to the island to retrieve him but demand Noab as payment for his passage home. In an ultimate act of betrayal, Hewett agrees to their terms. He turns his back on Noab and stands tall at his ship's helm as she's outnumbered by his men, who drag her down the beach by her hair, violence feeding their sick zeal.

Until the Mother Beast tastes Noab's blood in the water—but doesn't come after Noab. In an act of instinctive female solidarity and vengeance, the Mother Beast rises to murder Hewett's men. Noab escapes, spared but forever broken. She watches Hewett sail away, having traded her for his own security.

"What?" Tash deflated. "Since when? That makes no sense."

Caleb's expression faltered. He glanced to the laptop, muting their feed, too. "It just happened today."

Tash tensed. "And you didn't tell me?"

He furrowed. "It's preliminary notes. We just closed Episode Five. We'll get the final direction for Nine in a day or so." He scooted closer, pushing a throw pillow out of the way. "And it *does* make sense. Hewett's men can still attack Noab on the beach, but they can do it because they want to sell her to the slave trade—"

She stiffened further. "What slave trade?"

Caleb shrugged. "It doesn't matter. What matters is there doesn't have to be any hint of sexual assault. They can march her out into the water, she can refuse to get on the boat, she can goad one of the men into slapping her with his rifle, which makes her mouth bleed. She spits into the water, summoning the Mother Beast."

Tash shook her head. "But we need the threat of sexual violence. Hewett's men have to be brutal—it's what the Lore warned Noab about." She diagrammed it for him: "If the men don't fulfill every terrible expectation the Lore instilled in Noab, she won't be justified when she kills the baby. They can't be gentle pirates, Caleb. They have to be a nightmare."

Tash's nightmare. Which was why she'd assumed Caleb would understand. Hewett's men stood in for a swerve of fate Tash by luck had avoided; they were an echo of someone she'd told Caleb about, who'd psychotically ordered another drink after he pulled her hair.

Caleb continued to look baffled. "But you hated the assault in *Transtempora*—"

"Because it was gratuitous," she finished his sentence. "It's not like I want ours to be on-screen. But Episode Nine needs disgusting male depravity. The threat has to be visceral."

"Wait." He balked, holding up his hands. "The threat has to be visceral but not on-screen?"

"Yes."

"Tash, we talked about this when we started." Caleb exhaled. "You can't have it both ways. Film is visual. What we don't show doesn't happen. If you put the assault off-screen, it's not part of the story."

"And if you put the assault *on-screen*," she countered, "it becomes a spectacle. It becomes somebody's turn-on. It becomes clickbait and entertainment. Which is not acceptable to me."

Caleb nodded. "Exactly. That's why capturing her for slavery could be better."

"No!" Tash winched up from the floor. "It's not awful enough. The audience has to feel the horror, or else they won't be with her, later on the cliff. Killing the baby won't seem justified by her experience." She sensed a snag in her rebuttal. She jumped to its conclusion, the suspicion that had dogged her all along: "Unless this is just another gateway to making us have to change the ending."

"That is *not* what this is." Caleb tightened at the accusation. "Among other things, this is Noab getting the chance to very explicitly save herself."

"At the expense of showing how rotten men are."

Caleb's comeback was stifled by Stacy's return to the frame.

She unmuted, ambient spa music now in her background instead of grunts. "Sorry about that. Where were we?"

Caleb unmuted, too. "One sec, Stace." He pressed mute again and angled the laptop away. "How about we table this until there's time to talk about it properly?"

Tash recognized him in this role—the glue between all parties, always the voice of reason.

"Like I said, the notes are just preliminary. We can't start working until after the *Big Gun* retrospective anyway." Caleb reached for Tash's hand. "Trust, right? I don't want to fight with you. We're on the same side."

But Tash worried she was maybe in his blind spot, far across an impasse; that the place she found herself was somewhere Caleb couldn't recognize.

Chapter Thirteen

Tash wondered if every venue on Leo's podcast tour was as gorgeously pretentious as the one she entered the next day—a library inside the Miami Museum of Cartography's archive, just an intimate two hundred people seated beneath soaring bookshelves and architecturally filtered light.

She told herself not to be nervous. At Biscayne Coastal, she lectured to freshman auditoriums this same size all the time. She'd addressed even bigger audiences on *The Colony*'s press tour—and even if she was a bit out of practice, her recent immersion in the book's guts with Caleb had situated all the important themes at her front of mind.

The worst, best part of the taping would be seeing Leo, after so many years. Tash resolved to rub her success in his face graciously, while hiding her insecurities. In a pinch, she could always go into a corner and do some of Stacy's breathing.

An audio tech funneled Tash into a makeshift greenroom off the library's main hall, where, among clipboards and heavy-duty mic rigs, a man without sideburns sat on a child's stool. Beside him, an unadorned woman in a slip dress. Together, they were feeding a toddler.

"Tash." Leo Rousseau glanced up pleasantly, holding a plastic forkful of chicken nugget. "Hello."

Tash's thoughts of him, up until that instant, had been primarily conjecture about his estimation of her book: Did Leo think it was brilliant? Was the invitation to the podcast his personal request? Or just the fishing of a producer who needed local talent and happened upon Tash?

Tash did also wonder if Leo still left condom wrappers he'd used with other people for his girlfriends to find, sometimes by their pillows.

Once even on her desk.

"Meet my wife, the conceptual artist Olga Horvat." Leo flourished the hand unencumbered by baby fork around his cozy circle. "And this is Digby." Leo indicated the chewing toddler. "Our extremely precocious three-year-old."

At no point had Tash considered the possibility of a married and fatherly Leo Rousseau—whose smile still oozed elbow-patched charisma, whose body stood to greet her, still lanky and fit. He half embraced her with one arm, still redolent of chlorine—in New York, he'd been a swimmer, venturing to the school's pool even on the coldest days. A sudden memory of balled-up bathing suits left repeatedly on bathroom tile streaked through Tash's mind.

"I did a double take when I saw your name on our guest list. I didn't know you were writing."

And there—not four seconds into their reunion—Leo brandished a move Tash must have willingly blocked out: first a glimpse of appeasing warmth, then a sharp jab to the solar plexus. *I didn't know you were writing*—code for *You never had any talent*. Tash's work would never show up on his intellectual radar. She was insignificant.

The conceptual artist Olga Horvat remained seated, gaze bouncing between them, the three-year-old Digby obediently masticating chicken. All while Tash attempted to parse and order her reaction—to Leo's couched insult; to his affected introduction; to the fact he'd incongruously, since she'd last seen him, become a family man.

"Yes." Tash said the one word, ever articulate. "I wrote a book." She gestured to the tech who'd escorted her inside, as if for validation.

The greenroom continued to fill, the scent of burnt coffee and stale pastry wafting from a folding-table buffet. Four tweed wingback chairs paraded by and through a doorway, to be arranged in front of the library's central glass display case of ancient maps. A production assistant handed Tash a lanyard, branding her as *Guest*.

"What is it called?" Olga smoothed her middle-parted, waist-length hair.

Tash stared back at Leo's wife. "The book? It's called *The Colony*. It's a feminist dystopian novel."

"I see." Olga's face showed no sign of recognition.

Leo smiled down at her beneficently. "We don't read like we used to." He smiled at Digby. "What with having so recently procreated."

In Tash's head, a celebrity sex designer rolled his eyes and groaned. Caleb had called this correctly—Tash had put a lot of pressure on this podcast appearance, forgetting how exhausting Leo's pomposity could be. It occurred to her she might want to save her strength for the actual interview.

She spotted the two other *Guest* lanyard-wearers. With a *Nice to have met you* wave in Olga and Digby's direction, Tash initiated a retreat. She'd confirmed Leo Rousseau could still trigger her sense of inadequacy with just a single sentence. How fantastic.

But as Tash reversed, Leo offered Olga further context: "Tash and I dated at the inception of the journal. I behaved badly." Leo delivered this as if a bit of theater. He turned to Tash. "You were right to move on."

Olga nodded. "It is terrible to be a young woman."

Leo nodded back at her, all dramatic solemnity, gazing to his loafers. "It is terrible to be a young man, too."

Olga rested her cheek against his chinos. She stroked a palm along his outer seam. Digby mewled, and Leo reached down to gravely pat his fluff.

And Tash could have left them to their moment, however ostentatious and false, but she recalled telling Caleb she'd come for a redemption—not to watch Leo let himself off the hook.

"You didn't 'behave badly,' Leo. You gave me chlamydia and slept with my thesis adviser." Every bit of blood in Tash's circulatory system rushed to her head. "I didn't 'move on'—I dropped out. You made things so bad for me, I had to leave the program."

Leo's expression stiffened with something distinctly base. "We both suffered. We were young."

But Tash refused it, a reckoning hammering behind her rib cage. "You were almost thirty. It didn't put a damper on your career at all." It was all she could do to keep her voice even; she reminded herself not to let him rob her of her grace. "You launched a journal with university money. You became celebrated in your field."

The conceptual artist Olga Horvat stood and interrupted, slotting herself between her husband and Tash. Like a bouncer, assessing Tash: "But you're a guest on his podcast. People must celebrate you, too."

"They don't." Leo flicked it witheringly, a cigarette butt of critique. "Not in any substantive arena." He bent haughtily, retrieving Digby from the floor.

Olga laced a Swedish-looking fabric sack between her shoulders. Leo completed the ritual, helping their child scale his mother's hip curve, lacing him into the backpack. Over his family's heads, Leo glared at Tash.

He glared as an assistant materialized with a brown corduroy blazer, slipping Leo into his costume, delivering a binder, ostensibly nudging interview information at its host.

Leo glared as he was hustled into his wingback armchair, to one side of the library's display case, and as Tash and the two other authors were arranged in their arc of equally tweed seating on the other side.

He glared at her through the sound check, four humans with microphone cages angled overhead like personal recording chandeliers.

Leo glared, and it began to fill Tash with foreboding. She should have waited to get combative. She considered leaving before the taping started, while there was still time. She searched the crowd, now fully assembled, anxious to locate Janelle.

When Tash finally caught her eye, Janelle waved her butterfly sleeves overhead. Tash smiled weakly, fighting the urge to hurl. The moment arrived, and Janelle hooted as the library doors sealed closed.

An audio engineer shushed the whole place, gesturing at Leo with green placards.

"Today, the journal finds itself taping live, in the state of Florida." Leo's podcast persona embarked. "The physical, and the metaphysical state of Florida: key lime pie and NASCAR; alligator wrestling and orange groves; theme parks, beaches, and the laxest gun laws in the nation. Florida is where right-wing backlash roams free and shouts loud. It was our country's last frontier, its inland swamps subdued long after the fabled cowboys and gold rushes of the American West."

The room had ceased to rustle.

"This state—this metaphysical state—figures in the work of three area artists joining our conversation today." Leo paused to swing his smile magnanimously from the rows and rows of listeners around to the authors. "Kris Lemur-Whitting, whose genderqueer memoir of a childhood spent in the Tate's Hell doomsday cult on the Florida Panhandle won the Seminole Prize."

No applause; the audience had already been instructed to refrain for the sake of the audio recording.

"Alette Decuir, whose Creole-inflected poetry of the water margins between Florida and the Caribbean islands received the prestigious Fontaine Award." Leo paused for a millisecond, flipping the page of his binder.

"And Natasha Grover." He turned the binder face down. "A Florida native whose small-press debut brought feminist dystopia to a mass-market audience."

Mass-market—Leo's favorite slur. Tash knew he meant it vindictively, a spiteful reference to her undiscriminating public. She'd encountered the insult often when they were a couple, especially when she proofread his harshest journal rants.

Tash began to sweat.

He opened the discussion with a question about "cultural memory"— inquiring about the way "the political and emotional terrain of Florida" appeared in each author's work. A left-to-right question-and-answer pattern ensued. Because Tash sat farthest away from him in the guest semicircle, she was the last to answer:

"I think for me, it's the natural cruelty of Florida." Her nerves constricted—a pit in her stomach and a tightness in her throat. She sensed Leo's animosity daring her to say the wrong thing. "There's a beautiful hostility to the Florida environment that seethes inside the land. Fruit that can maim you, for example—Florida grows the original poison apple."

The audience tittered. Tash forced a grin. Red ON AIR plaques fluttered their extraneous-noise scolding in the library footlights.

"It's called the manchineel." She tried to relax into her local knowledge. "It's a green beach apple on a gorgeous tree, and eating it will kill you. Touching even just the bark will make you blind."

As she spoke, Tash locked on the top of Janelle's head, aware meeting her eyes would be too much; her best friend's mahogany whorls, however, were an ideal focus.

Tash continued. "I think the 'emotional terrain' of Florida has to include the water, too. Our swamps, obviously—but also the way the ocean tempts us with its beauty and then threatens to drown us. It's flash floods and rain that rips your roof off. There's a deeply wronged feminine power in the Florida environment daring us to give it a reason to unleash its might. It scares me, honestly. But it's also awe-inspiring."

Janelle raised two thumbs-ups over her head again.

"That's on-brand." Leo said it flatly into his microphone.

It might have been another dig, but Tash didn't try to decode it; she'd managed one question deftly. She gave herself a trophy while Leo busied questions at the other guests.

To the doomsday-cult memoirist, he posed:

"Kris, as I mentioned, Florida was our country's last contiguous, physical frontier. Its wetlands proved nearly impossible to, quote-unquote, tame. Can you talk a bit about the generational, atmospheric traumas that resulted from this beating into a submission? In end-times religion, say, or apocalyptic communities."

To the water-margin poet:

"Alette, your latest collection draws on a little-known 'Saltwater Railroad,' which sailed escaped slaves from Florida to the majority-Black, British-controlled Bahamas, in the period before the American Civil War. Can you talk a bit about the folkloric echoes of that journey and how you weave their politics into your verse?"

Tash was sure Leo was running down the clock, sure he'd planned to ice her out of the remaining conversation—and perhaps that was okay. Perhaps a single high note was a good way to skirt his firing squad. But no. To Tash, Leo finally asked:

"Natasha." His voice booming into the microphone. "The idea of tokenism strikes me as something you might want to address."

Once again, Leo had set aside his binder. His eyes speared her; he was not reading from a prompt. The pit in Tash's stomach clenched. This was far worse than being ignored.

"Alette vocalized a suspicion that the bound and printed versions of her poems are often used to signal anti-racism—in essence, people buy her book to use it as a prop. The paper manifestation of her collection becomes alibi for an entrenched class."

Tash braced in her wingback. Her mind puzzled over what "token-ism" in her book's case might imply. She considered cultural appropri-ation, or a comment about her dropout credentials.

"In the same way, the commercial spread of your book invites readers into a kind of dangerous McFeminism, don't you think?" Leo's accent danced, clearly delighted with himself over the phrasing.

Tash had forgotten his tendency to "Mc" things—in two letters, he could turn her into dust. Still, she forced herself to deny it, whatever it was he was suggesting. Carefully: "No, actually. I don't."

"Really." Leo only cocked his head. "Well, I'd be happy to explain it to you." As he all but cracked his knuckles; as he all but bent his knees and took a practice swing.

He leaned into the microphone. "*The Colony* benefited from sensationalized press, yes?" He peered at Tash, dropping the formality he'd used with the other guests. "Pop-culture reportage characterized the work as radical because a maternal protagonist murders her child at the end."

He made no apologies for this spoiler.

"But your mother character is not really controversial. She's a copycat dark sibling to the conventional Earth Mother, whom we all regularly embrace. The plot of your novel never deviates from standard romantic tragedy—packaging the climactic non-scandal in a familiar chew-and-swallow pill." He shrugged arrogantly. "Hence the McFeminism. Hence the token." Conceit bloomed in his features. "Your book pretends an adjacence to radicalism, but it isn't radical at all. There's no originality in its writing."

Tash blinked, tasting the room's silence. The mic hovering by her forehead began emitting an electric buzz. She didn't dare glance at Janelle.

"And on the flip side of this tokenism, there lies commodity."

Leo was actually continuing to riff. It transported Tash back to his lectures, back to their bedroom—to the mistakes she'd made at twenty-four. To the mistake she'd made now, by thinking she could manage this podcast. By provoking him before it had even started.

"And then, of course, whatever shreds of integrity the work purported to have are lost when it's synthesized for the screen. Your book is being made for television—that postmodern cliché. A cultural product cosmetically enhanced." He gripped the mic rig. "A desacralized replica. An empty frame, which once flattered itself by boasting it was art."

Tash stunned, shaken by his tirade. She scanned the horizon beyond Leo's armchair, beyond the audience's vision, searching for someone from the podcast staff to dart him with a tranquilizer; someone who registered the deviation from his usual, collected tone. But all she found beside the dimly lit soundboard was Olga Horvat—standing laced to her child, staring triumphantly at Tash.

Meanwhile, the shards of Leo's takedown glittered everywhere they'd landed—in Tash's hair, down the front of her dress, strewn across her lap.

She picked up one of the fragments—"Desacralized replica," he'd said—turning its edges over with shaky fingers. When her eyes could focus, she saw the words for their distorted froth. She registered the evidence that Leo had not only read her book but all its reportage, too.

"Hold on." Tash banged her lips against the microphone's cold metal crosshatch, grasping to recover. "I'm hardly the first person to sell the film rights to a novel."

But Leo preempted her rally. "True. But you *might* be the first person to predicate a novel on radical feminist ideals, then sell it to an entertainment-conglomerate superstore." He paused, paws together, snidely savoring his kill. "Specifically, to its most mainstream, most sexist male director. A man best known for close-ups of girls in hot tubs and action pyrotechnics—"

His mic cut.

Only Tash and the two other guest authors heard Leo spit "Ram Braverman"—as, blessedly, someone on the podcast staff realized the onslaught had gone too far.

One after another, in a hesitant, confused game of visual telephone, the corded sideline techs lowered their red ON AIR plaques. Leo twisted gruffly in his wingback, failing to comprehend the sudden loss of his voice booming across the room. He banged frustratedly at his switched-off output.

A senior producer crept over, whispering in Leo's ear.

The skin once graced by luxuriant muttonchops mottled a deep red. Leo elbowed at his recording-rig halo. "Goddammit, Derek! Turn me back on!" He moved to get out of his chair.

Before he could leap all the way up, the producer threw his arm over Leo's shoulders, bustling him off toward the greenroom.

A tech scuttled in front of the glass display case. "We've got a glitch, folks!" Suggesting the podcast's recording equipment, and not its esteemed host, had just melted down. "Let's take five while the engineers reset."

Library ushers unsealed the corridor to the museum's main hall. The front row of audience began to stretch. Tash's view to Janelle was blocked off.

Tash sat, still in shock, reverb addling her inner ears.

She'd come hoping to distance herself from Braverman, hoping to position herself back on a high ground—but Leo had smacked her with the Hollywood association. He'd guessed where she'd be tender, and his allegations were correct. Radical ideals sold to a superstore—Tash had seen the result already, in Episode Nine's unresolved mess.

She turned to the soundboards, sickened and spinning, needing to disintegrate. She fixed on a large steel rectangle inset in the library's wallpapered damask—an emergency exit. The path toward it was littered with cabling obstacles, but otherwise abandoned.

Tash did not deliberate; Leo Rousseau could go McFuck himself.

She snatched up her handbag hastily, held her breath, and, with two hands, shoved through a heavy, levered warning on the steel door, triggering a skull-puncturing alarm.

The exit spit her to the bright scrub of the museum's exterior landscape, where her heels sank into industrial crabgrass, the emergency bleat still roaring.

Tash tripped. She yanked off her shoes. She fled from the lanyard-wearing faces watching her curiously from the exit. From the gorgeous library where Leo Rousseau had just labeled her a sellout and a fraud.

She trembled in the sun, fumbling for her phone, texting Janelle, finding the minivan; then hiding in its shade, awash in the overwhelming relief Caleb hadn't made it to the taping.

"Tell me that didn't just happen." Tash monotoned to Janelle when she finally arrived and unlocked the car. Tash closed her eyes against the hot plate of the passenger-side window, absorbing the scent of sun-seared dashboard.

"Which part?" Janelle maximized the air vents, turning down the kiddie tunes competing with the still-bellowing alarm. "My discovery that you used to have a taste for reverse-cancel-culture gasbags?" She wrenched over the console to buckle Tash in, like one of her kids. "I bet that guy made you call him Jacques Derrida while he jerked off to a desacralized replica of his ballsack." She put the car into reverse. "If I'm right, you're paying for drinks."

Tash would have loved to laugh. Instead, she looped on a mental replay of Leo's sneer. Janelle piloted the minivan until the museum sirens had faded; then she pulled into a strip mall, idling the car in front of a tanning salon.

She shifted in her seat, facing Tash head-on. "Hey. Listen. The only person who looked bad back there was that asshole of a host."

Tash shook her head in shame. "He called me a fraud." In case her best friend had missed it. "He called me a sellout. On tape. It'll end up on the fan forums. No one understands Braverman wasn't my choice—"

"Nope." Janelle put her hand up. "Enough about the online twatter—that stuff is out of your control. You are *not* a sellout."

"I am." Tash stated the logic flatly: "I'm helping the studio with scene direction that undermines my message. There are all kinds of changes—it's exactly what Leo was talking about."

"Fuck Leo!" Vehemently. "Honestly, who even is that guy? Tash, all you're doing is avoiding a breach of contract. That's kind of a fundamental thing."

That her readers would never know about.

Tash's humiliation mingled with an existential disappointment. "You know what my last press event was? Before this? That panel for Off-Center Arts. Do you remember? The entire place was women."

Janelle nodded. "I remember."

"Girls came up afterward and cried, right? It felt meaningful. That's what I wanted for today. I wanted to talk to Leo and feel proud about how far I've come—I wanted to be smarter than I was in grad school." Flaggingly. "But I just looked compromised."

Janelle reached awkwardly across the center console to grab both of Tash's shoulders. "Babe, your ex-boyfriend is a misogynistic hack. He took potshots at you because he felt threatened. You are not a sellout—you are a legend, and you wrote an important book."

"Based on your ideas." Tash's long-standing insecurity.

"Based on *our* ideas. Are you kidding?" Janelle poked her, hard. "You know where *my* ideas go? I take them to an occasional academic conference. They circulate at our crappy, sweet little school. Meanwhile, you put *our* ideas in a book that's reached more people than I could ever imagine. You think 'mass-market' is an insult—I know you—but I'm telling you, it's praise. That guy has three basement trolls for listeners, and you're about to have a TV show. You have eclipsed him, and he can't stand it. Creating art that people actually read and watch doesn't make you lowbrow, Tash. It makes you relevant."

No more pep talk—Janelle had reached her limit. She put the minivan in gear and turned her kids' music up again. "I'm going to let you feel bad for yourself for exactly three songs while I process my extreme feelings about the men you used to date. But then we're finished. We will expunge this from our memory because it isn't worth it. Onward."

Tash pulled the lever to lay her seat flat, wishing it could be that quick to forget.

Chapter Fourteen

The Sweetwater Film Festival's fete of Ram Braverman's *Big Gun* took place at an historic bougainvillea-covered Spanish-revival castillo in Coral Gables, within a mojito-muddling wrist-flick of the surging, star-swept Florida sea.

From the backseat of the car-and-driver gifted along with Astrid Dalton's VIP pass, Tash soaked in the winding drive lined by uplit frangipani. She hoped the venue's romance would soothe her podcast bruises. She hoped Caleb had convinced the studio to revise its notes on Episode Nine. She hoped he'd be waiting for her by the party's entrance; as he'd predicted, two days apart *had* been a long time.

And he appeared like a hipster Gatsby, in white-blazered shoulders and navy trousers, a pocket square in the same blue highlighting the glint in his tortoiseshell-framed eyes. Mid-century Cuban horns crooned as Caleb helped Tash from the car, taking a moment to appreciate her gauzy gown and stilettos. The sky smudged above them like fine cigar smoke. They passed under ornamental balconies that waited for the woo of sweet nothings from below.

Beyond a fountained inner courtyard, a celebrity step-and-repeat marked the grand entrance to a ballroom, flanked by billboard-size glassed posters from *Big Gun* and paparazzi-style camera crews soft-balling inane questions at the party's guest list.

Surprisingly, Caleb steered Tash in a different direction.

"Before we have to be professional." He led her to the twinkling shelter of a topiary-fenced side patio.

A jazz band played somewhere not far off, trombone and double bass, and Caleb stepped into the hidden plaza's painted-tile center, sweeping Tash into the high school samba he once mentioned. His palm went to her lower back. He tucked her hand against his heart.

They swayed as tres guitar strummed, and fluted terra-cotta water features burbled, and sculpted hedges threw shadows on their private candlelight.

"I hated the way I left your place the other night," Caleb whispered against the floating pluck of strings. "I wanted to remind you that you like me when we're not wrangling about your adaptation."

In her heels, Tash's temple touched his cheek. "You sure about that?"

"Yes." His smile grazed her skin. "And I like you, even when you're riled up."

Her unease began to settle. She pulled back slightly to examine him. "Why?"

He held her in place, shrugging white-blazered self-possession. "I don't know, I think it's kind of hot. You *bodily* inhabit your convictions." He raised rakish eyebrows. "It speaks to me."

Guitar chords thrummed between them. "Oh." Tash said it slyly, like discovering a scandal. "You like my female monster."

Caleb owned the charge. "Maybe. Since I know what's behind those fangs."

Tash hid his sweetness away, to savor later; other men had been scared off. She skirted her brimming feelings. "You like the baring." Another favorite from their Episode Five work: "The will-they-or-won't-they tension."

Caleb's laugh came on a whisper. "Tash. I'm pretty sure they will."

"No, I get it—a childhood in a burlesque bar. You imprinted on 'The Tease.'"

"Are you done yet?"

She smiled up at him. "That's the female lens, though. For real, what I was going for in the book—all the sexy stuff that isn't explicit. The lead-up." She brushed a lock of hair off his forehead. "I'm making fun of you, but you have good taste. 'Before' is the best part."

"I mildly disagree." He took a moment. "What about the 'after'?"

Tash thought, trying to lighten a heavy answer: "Historically? That part hasn't gone that great for me."

Caleb stopped swaying. "Come out to California." Direct, as ever. "Before your semester starts. I'll find you inauthentic chai, and we'll walk Iggy to the farmers' market from my boho-modern home in Silver Lake. We won't write a single line of blocking."

A picture formed, Tash's longing for it luminous and right-there.

"Would I get to meet your father? Maybe see that tool belt Ilsa went on about?" She said it only to prevent herself from grabbing her phone and booking a ticket immediately, from dragging him to a taxi and heading for the plane.

"Would you control yourself around him?" Caleb tugged her closer, an assurance they'd be late to any meet-the-parent lunch.

Fragility dazzled in Tash's rib cage. "I promise nothing."

He cut through her shield of banter. "Just say yes, Tash." Sincere and solid. "I have my own opinions about 'after.'"

His candor went to her head. It burst into her locked room of secret wishes, splinters flying everywhere. Other decisions rushed in to clamor—whether she would teach in the fall, whether she should try to write another novel, whether she could manage the unfinished business of *The Colony*.

The urge to silence all the questioning was overwhelming. "Okay. Yes."

The patio sighed around them, then, a moonlight shift of paradigm. Havana claves knocked a new rosewood rhythm. Tash rushed not a single note of song.

Eventually, they moved toward the ballroom, where a red-carpet bottleneck forced them to stop and admire the corridor of posters from *Big Gun*.

Caleb kept his face blithely neutral, eyes on the billboard-size cannons. "How long do we need to stay here to get credit? Twenty minutes?"

Tash steadied her gaze on the same still from Braverman's film warfare. "Seriously? You're the one who wanted to come."

Caleb inched them closer to the ballroom's grand doors. "True. But we've danced, and you said yes to California." He waited politely as an attendant checked their names off a list. "I've seen your dress. Mission accomplished. Let's go get naked and order pizza. You can tell me about yesterday on the way."

Tash bypassed that last bit—she refused to let the memory of Leo ruin her just-recovered high. Instead, she focused on *California* and *naked*. "Go work the room, then. You have fifteen minutes. Find me when you're ready."

Inside, Tash noted Caleb's cohort was far more polished than the ragtag Biscayne Coastal adjuncts she'd introduced him to at Manta Ray's. Baritone amor sounded from the bandstand instead of a jukebox; the high-ceilinged ballroom was heady with jacaranda instead of cheap tequila and keg sweat. Bronzed, glorious mile-tall waifs and Miami stallions rubbed elbows with Braverman aficionados.

Through a moving maze of passed hors d'oeuvres, Tash spotted the guest of honor—just as the guest of honor spotted Tash. From across the room, Ram raised a cordial pinky ring, acknowledging Tash's presence with a civil nod. She dipped her head in return, grateful not to have to fake enthusiasm for a more thorough greeting.

Grateful not to have his mirror held up directly to her face. In the month since the piano bar, she'd gone from guarding her characters militantly to letting them strip naked on the sand, from dodging production company emails to sleeping with their sex designer. From uptight to the dirty version—exactly as Braverman had asked.

It tied Tash in a knot: The work she'd done with Caleb felt elevated, and she knew they needed the studio to be pleased, but Braverman's approval also gave Tash pause and made her doubt her instincts.

A brunette at Ram's side took his arm for a question, her lowlighted curiosity having followed his gaze to Tash. After he answered, the woman began to glide in Tash's direction. She wore an expensively embellished cutaway shift dress and terrific peep-toe pumps. She held a double vodka rocks with a lime twist.

Tash knew this because the woman ordered another from a passing waiter, at the same time she stuck a toned arm out.

"I stopped adding tonic—carbonation is terrible for the gut. Regina Bond." She shook Tash's hand adroitly.

Tash smiled, noting neither the waiter nor this stranger had asked if Tash would also like a drink. "Tash Grover."

The brunette sipped her vodka. "I know." She tilted her head, waiting for Tash to catch on: "I head the Braverman streaming vertical. I'm loving your rewrites, by the way—you and Caleb have whipped up some great stuff."

Tash could not make heads or tails of this; she couldn't place her, and the woman's expression was a shiny, smiling rock. "Caleb is a pleasure to work with." He'd said the same thing about Tash in his comments to the Story Edit team.

Regina Bond stepped closer, her brow appearing to want to lift. "Are you kidding? Caleb Rafferty is a fucking dish. I'd gladly write a book for him to translate into movement." She leered, as if she and Tash were girlfriends giggling in the corner, as if she'd calculated that an author of feminist fiction might find delight in a reverse locker room.

But Tash had only awkwardly frozen, her feelings about Caleb not lecherous and much too delicate to share.

Regina carried on heedlessly, going for managerial next: "No, really. Ram and I are lucky to have Caleb on the project. He takes four wildly different opinions and gets us all to agree. He's a lion-tamer."

Tash smiled wanly, close-lipped. She wondered if this woman meant to imply that Tash was a tamed lion. She wondered if she was taunting her—or just making random, vodka-tinged small talk.

"These days, agreement is key on a project like *The Colony*. Our production has to be seamless—budget is everything right now. That's why what you two are doing is so important." Regina leaned in conspiratorially. "So, tell me. How's that new ending coming? Caleb's playing hard-to-get about it, but I'm dying to know."

New ending.

It took a moment for Regina's meaning to sink in; but when it did, Tash's suspicions clicked perfectly into place.

The studio had planned to change the ending all along; Ram had even said "save the baby" to Tash at their first meeting. But she'd allowed herself to get preoccupied with Caleb. And now her worst fears had become reality.

"Reggie! I thought you couldn't make it." One of Caleb's white-blazered shoulders sliced between their tête-à-tête.

Regina. *Reggie.*

Of course.

Executive producer *Reggie*. Story team *Reggie*. This bullish woman in thousand-dollar footwear was *Reggie*—Regina Bond.

Tash's dense preconceptions collapsed inward. Whenever Caleb had mentioned *Reggie*, Tash had imagined a dumpy dude. Not a woman with expertly engineered Hollywood Hills contours, who'd called Caleb a *fucking dish*.

Who greeted him dulcetly. "Would you believe my mom got stuck in Saint-Tropez? She called yesterday from someone's yacht, insisting I come here in her place." Reggie dismissed the thought with an entitled quirk of one embellished cap sleeve. "She and Ram were only married for a minute, and she only had a small role in *Big Gun*—but she's bizarrely sentimental about it."

Busy monologuing her dynastic family drama, Reggie might not have clocked Caleb's ashen expression—but Tash saw it plainly. He hadn't expected Reggie at this party. He had not intended for Tash and Reggie to ever meet. Because Reggie Bond had sights set on *The Colony*'s "new ending"—a detail Caleb knowingly kept from Tash.

Reggie Bond was also Braverman's stepdaughter. Reggie led Braverman's Executive Production team. The only decision-maker to outrank Reggie was Ram himself—who just then arrived stoutly beside them in his tuxedo.

Tash's tailspin gained speed.

"I sense young people discussing me." Ram had a young, blond person on his arm.

Regina raised her double vodka in a glib greeting. "I was just telling Caleb and Natasha that I'm your Ghost of Starlets Past."

Ram obliged the reminiscence with a theatrical nod of his silver head. "Regina's mom was terrific in *Big Gun*. We fell in love on that set." He patted the hand of his companion absently. "You know, back then, I thought *Big Gun* was the most exciting thing I'd ever do. Then I discovered peyote."

Regina pointed at him. "And I discovered your stash."

They both laughed, as if the one-two had been practiced, as if Doolittle had written them a partner stand-up routine to use at formal events.

"Now here we are, decades later, and the stepkid who used to sneak around my pool house runs our fastest-growing division." Ram spoke in rehearsed tones, delivering a cocktail keynote, the sentences tired from making the rounds. He angled his lowball glass at Regina. "She tells me blockbusters are dead and the market only wants streaming content."

Regina's élan picked it up unabashedly. "Streaming content with universal themes that drive consumption, and a finale that draws us crazy buzz. Like the one I'm waiting to hear about." She pushed her impatience at Tash again, and then at Caleb, a chummy smile on her face.

Caleb's own expression approximated winsome, even though his color was still gray. "Reggie, come on. You know we're off the clock."

Tash's filmy dress suddenly felt like a cinched-tight corset, making it difficult to breathe. She surveyed Caleb's facade, watching him balance on the knifepoint of this melee. Then she turned to Regina, putting on false innocence, deciding to plunge to the bottom of everyone's maneuvering. "And what finale could draw you crazier buzz than throwing a baby off a cliff, anyway?"

Reggie pursed consummately lined lips. "Well—as Caleb has heard me say too many times—human sacrifice doesn't play well to women between the ages of twenty-six and fifty-nine. Which is the demographic your show needs to satisfy so we can sell the next two seasons. Creatives don't like to hear this, I know, but actual humans don't decide what gets renewed—the numbers do." She shrugged. "We have to please the data."

Tash had gone cold. "If you wanted to please the data, perhaps you should have bought a different book."

Reggie countered affably, reaching a hand to Tash's arm. "Oh, no! Alternate worlds are entertainment gold! They're our bread and butter. Sci-fi series have some of the longest runs, especially when they tap into retellings. That's why I had to have *The Colony* in the first place—you gave us a Garden of Eden, a Red Sea . . . It's the type of broad, biblical underpinnings the data eats up!" Reggie crossed her fingers. "Honestly. We could be sitting on a smash."

Her profound misinterpretation rendered Tash absolutely speechless.

Reggie continued to pick up steam. "Now just imagine if someone saved the baby—then we'd have a Moses!" The loaded glance she darted to Caleb suggested she'd floated this before. "Trifecta, right? And a *literal* cliff-hanger."

Tash's eyes began to water. Her body was lead weight in a gown.

This woman had disemboweled her book's meaning and replaced its insides with algorithmic stuffing wrongly mapped to theologic themes.

The volume of Tash's voice rose argumentatively. "You can't change the most important part of your source material, though. Not when the ending is integral to the plot."

Regina looked at Tash with pity. "Oh, hon. That hasn't been true since they changed the ending to *Forrest Gump*."

The blonde on Braverman's arm perked. "*Forrest Gump* was a book?"

The ice cubes in Regina's vodka rattled, pointing the verdict at Tash. "Exactly."

Through the narrowing tunnel of her vision, Tash recognized Reggie's ilk—she was that special strain of woman who had the means and education and the network, but made the wrong choices, for the wrong reasons. In another life, Regina could have championed *The Colony* and been a friend. But in this life, Regina sold herself to the data.

And for sure, the data was compiled by a guy.

Tash persisted in quarreling. "Okay, but—"

"Wasn't *Big Gun* based on a book, too?" Caleb's palm landed in the middle of Tash's back, the same place he'd held her when they slow-danced. Only now it had a different purpose, guiding her slightly away from Reggie, signaling for Tash to *Shut. Up.*

"Actually, it's based on a Japanese cartoon. The term we use is 'manga.'" Unselfconsciously, Ram began to extemporize.

Tash disassociated from the conversation.

She knew—for certain now—that Braverman Productions would change the underpinnings of her story. Their take on *The Colony* would celebrate male energy that Tash had set out to exorcize. The same male energy Tash meant to purge with the novel's writing.

She came back to her body only when an industry crony dragged Braverman and his budding blonde away, and when Regina Bond had coasted off, perhaps to butcher a new crop of literary content.

Leaving Tash and Caleb alone together, once again.

The romantic guise dropped. Tash stood, disillusioned—in a cacophony of caricatured Cuban music, in a sea of tasteless canapés, with the very real knowledge Caleb had just been busted. He'd tried to keep Braverman's plans under wraps. He'd silenced Tash in front of Ram and Reggie.

Tash's brain rebooted.

She found herself outside, where the red-carpet corridor remained floodlit and jammed. Paparazzi blocked her path to the valet, so Tash stumbled deeper into the fortress. She sensed Caleb following her, past wood-and-iron doors, against a stream of bow-tied waiters, through an industrial kitchen, around trays of lipstick-smudged glasses and ruined florist Styrofoam half domes.

Out to the waterside service entrance, to a driveway clogged with party-rental trucks.

"Tash, wait!" Caleb had trailed her across the street, down a grass slope bordering a bay with bobbing, tied-up dinghies.

She felt the night look on and laugh at them in mean déjà vu, ridiculing all the other times Tash had bolted and all the other times Caleb had chased her.

"Tash!"

She used to be angry; once upon a time, Caleb had urged her to dig beneath that fury, to tell him about her fears. Like an idiot, she'd laid them out for him on a platter. And apparently, he'd taken his pick of which to exploit.

Tash spun to face him now—too shredded to breathe fire, wishing for that old rage.

"You knew they planned to change the ending this whole time! You haven't been managing the studio, you've been managing *me!*" The enormity of what she'd yielded to him sent Tash reeling. "You got me to give Braverman everything he wanted!"

Wet grass clung to the ankles of Caleb's navy trousers, his white blazer flapping open in the wind. "No! That isn't—"

"Don't try to convince me it's okay!" Tash shook her head fiercely, not falling victim, guarding against more of his spells. "That's what you did with Episode Nine, and what you'll do to Ten, too—anything to make sure Braverman gets their finale. I should have just signed the decline and spared you the extra effort." She broke on the accusation: "But then you wouldn't have been able to fuck me to fuck me over, right? You must be so pleased with yourself."

Caleb took a step forward, his face in shadow in the unlit bay— and despite the catering clang and the noise of seagulls, despite the impromptu pursuit, he still wielded reason like a weapon. "Tash." Imploringly. "What you heard inside was office politics. That was Reggie flexing focus group numbers—which is her job, and *literally* her religion. You don't have to deal with Braverman, I do. I know Reggie has ideas about the finale. We can find a balance."

Tash ruptured further. "I thought Reggie was a guy!"

"So?" A truck rumbled past them, up the slope, spewing sports radio. Caleb waited for it to dissipate. "Who cares? She doesn't write the scenes—we do. Nothing is in ink until you and I decide it."

Tash's anguish gathered his words up and packed them bitterly into a grenade. "You mean until you manipulate me into yet another thing I don't want to do."

He stopped short then—his supplication turning into stone. "I have never manipulated you, Tash. Not once."

"Please!" She snapped at his sanctimony. "You got me to compromise on every line we wrote!"

Caleb's tone stayed infuriatingly even. "No, I guided you through script polishes. I kept lawyers from snatching *The Colony* out of your hands. I helped you find a way to maintain the story's integrity."

"You cut me out!" She jabbed indignantly toward the castillo. "You cut me off! Just like you did back there!"

"Tash." His hands went frustratedly into his hair. "You were about to blow your chances with Reggie—the same way you blew up your line to Ram. I covered for you then, and I covered for you just now. You should be thanking me."

"For what?" She was yelling, and she didn't really care. "Letting Reggie measure my book for Bible data? Letting Ram make this series into a tit parade? What do you want credit for, Caleb? Corrupting my book or demeaning my characters?"

He marched closer. "Hey. *The Colony* is not a political movement. *You* demean it when you call our work a 'tit parade.' The scenes we wrote are smart and careful, Tash. The fact they're sexy makes them skilled. Most people can't strike that balance. What we did was special." He retreated momentarily, just to challenge her again. "And what would even be so bad about more seasons? Don't you want to explore more of what you built? What if the property had real legs?"

She was disgusted with his word choice. "Don't call it a 'property'! It makes you sound like one of them."

Caleb finally lost his cool. "I *am* one of them!" He shouted it skyward. "You know that!"

The waiters dumping trays of half-eaten foie gras tartlets in the service alley paused their scraping. The bayfront water ceased to lap. All nearby creatures stunned at Caleb's outburst.

Tash realized she'd never really seen him angry; she took a disturbed satisfaction in finding the end of his rope.

Then she picked up the calm demeanor he'd discarded.

"I know that now." She remembered his claim to be the opposite, during that first, piano-bar parking lot brawl: "one of the good ones," Caleb had said. It turned out to be untrue. "But guess what, Caleb? The property isn't yours to give away."

A chapter closed. Tash was done trusting. She was done behaving.

She scrambled up the wet lawn and pushed past him.

Caleb wheeled around to follow. "Can you just listen? Tash! It doesn't have to be so black and white! I'm not giving anything away! There are lots of ways to solve for Ten's finale!"

Back on the service drive, she hitched her dress in two fists to mask their shaking. "I don't want to solve anything with you. I'm not your problem anymore. Don't come near me, and don't come near my book, Caleb. I'll finish what I owe Braverman without you."

She stumbled by a set of dumpsters, turning back to make sure she got the last, acidic word. "Actually, maybe I *should* be thanking you. You said to start with the emotion beneath the action, right? And I'm feeling perfectly violated. So thanks for that inspiration—I'm sure the writing will be great."

Chapter Fifteen

Tash survived the next days in a state between a smoke and a solid; she'd left her head on the bayfront grass outside that ballroom, and her heart slow-dancing on that hidden patio.

She'd left her collaborator shouting pleas at the taillights of her taxi.

She'd left herself with a ticking deadline she'd have to face alone.

The remainder of her had enough self-awareness to realize a single, stray thought of Caleb would destroy her ability to function—and Tash needed to function.

Specifically, Episode Nine needed her to function.

So she dragged herself to her desk and dove deep into *The Colony*'s script at the only marker she could manage—the Mother Beast's gorgeous, savage, retaliatory rising from the sea.

Tash zoomed in on Noab at the edge of the water, bloodied and forsaken and fathomlessly wronged. She poured a ballroom's worth of shattered trust into the Mother Beast's score-evening arrival—from her first sniff of blood in the water to her vicious ripple of gills. Tash let the island's demonic sea huntress be chillingly repulsive in her hunger for meat, figuring Braverman's one redeeming quality would be his special knack for cinematic destruction.

Tash piled on the helpful, descriptive minutia. None of which was necessary. The studio already had these broad strokes in their existing script.

The scene alterations Tash actually owed came earlier: what would turn out to be the farewell sex; then Hewett's deceit. Still, she passed whole mornings imagining Braverman's head atop a ragged pirate tunic and Reggie's lowlights on a scurvied form before Tash killed them off. Doolittle died, too—but with less fanfare because Tash had never met him in person. She could only picture a blinking cursor for his face.

This activity provided such immersive gratification that Tash got completely lost in it and distractedly, unconsciously, picked up the ancient landline in Rohan's apartment when it rang.

"Just checking to see if you're alive." Janelle's background clang indicated another summer playground. "You haven't called in days."

Afternoon light swamped the wall of windows. Tash wished it to dim. "I messaged you, though. I'm in a hole until this deadline."

A hollow, more like—which she would not discuss. She'd texted Janelle only to say that work required all of her attention; then Tash turned her phone off and buried it at the bottom of her bag. She'd shut the bag in a drawer, locking her pain in a limbo.

She'd unpack it once she settled her obligation to the studio—once she hit submit.

"But I haven't even heard about the party!" The rusty chain of a swing set creaked alongside Janelle's complaint. "I've been waiting for feedback on my dress selection."

Therapeutically, Tash glanced to the phantasmal homicide gracing her screen. "I have to send everything to Braverman on Friday. Can I come over then?"

"You better." A child squealed somewhere near Janelle's phone. "Also, invite Caleb."

Tash returned directly to her fictional carnage to keep him from her mind.

She took a breather only when the day stopped shining in the garden apartment and she could slink upstairs to her duplex in the dark. She wasted almost a week like this, pushing herself toward sleep on the unsolicited tweaks she'd made to the episode's closing moments: Tash had expunged all of Hewett's dialogue, rendering him voiceless; she'd made him set off straight for the horizon, sending Noab no last looks. Tash spared Noab the anguish of having to hear his voice, or allowing him to see how much he'd maimed her.

She let Noab mourn in private, her eyes leaking her secrets, as the man she'd foolishly dropped her defenses for sailed swiftly away.

Ultimately, Tash had to force herself to inch backward through Episode Nine.

Her cutoff date for Braverman loomed, and the responsible cells in her brain commanded her to put the Mother Beast's payback aside and deal with the treachery that caused it: the plot points between Noab waking warm in Hewett's arms one morning and shivering, abandoned by night.

Just a span of hours for Hewett to betray her; just a span of days for Tash to choreograph Noab's suffering. Problematically, Tash and Caleb had discussed the scene only long enough to fight about the reason for Noab's capture: for the slave trade, as Braverman wanted, or for Hewett's men, the way Tash wrote it in the book. She didn't have Story Edit's actual comments, and they suddenly seemed very necessary for Tash to successfully finesse the blocking.

And so, for lack of any other feasible alternative, at her most rock-bottom, she smothered her pride and emailed the only approachable story team contact in her possession, other than Caleb, forty hours before the deadline: Brian Doolittle, he of *Nice job getting the author to loosen up*. The same guy who'd messaged constantly, on Ram's behalf, in the month before Caleb arrived, and whose missives Tash had roundly ignored. Brian Doolittle would definitely not be inclined to help her; she knew the email was a long shot, and also pathetic.

Hey Brian! With an increasing panic about the time crunch, Tash attempted blasé. No big deal, just coolly begging him for the Episode

Nine notes, without offering a case for why she might need them. She prayed he could be discreet because Tash did not seek to open a channel to Braverman, and she wasn't interested in hearing anything more from Regina Bond.

Then she refreshed her inbox a thousand times.

After a thousand more, she had a different idea.

She reattached Rohan's landline to the wall socket and dialed the front desk of La Playa. This was official business—she called the hotel instead of Caleb's phone. Also, she wasn't sure he'd answer if he saw her name pop up on his screen.

She waited on hold. She cold-sweat convinced herself she'd be able to calmly ask him for the notes. She convinced herself she'd be able to hear his voice without shattering completely.

But her hand-wringing came to nothing—because Mr. Rafferty had checked out.

Tash slid to the floor.

Of course he'd checked out. Of course he'd gone back to California with the work they'd crafted together and the studio's congratulatory backslap for a job mostly well done. He'd packed up the freckles on the ridge of his shoulder and his bullshit about his dog. He'd packed up the gaggle of older women who adored him, and he'd gone home.

He wasn't coming near her—exactly as Tash had asked.

She wept on the sisal carpet in her brother's too-bright apartment, next to the sofa Caleb had sat on when he didn't know she lived upstairs. She howled into the jute cushions of an armchair, and at the corners of the tiny kitchen where she'd made them tea. She cried for all her hopeful soft parts, and for the hard shell he'd coaxed her to peel away, and for a dream she'd exposed to the elements, only to have it pummeled.

She cried because she was not strong, and because she'd forgotten her compass, or she'd misplaced it by choice. She'd dropped it into Caleb's pocket. And now she was adrift and alone.

Chapter Sixteen

Unsurprisingly, Brian Doolittle never replied to Tash's email. She understood she deserved it—after all, she'd initiated the bridge-burning from their first exchange. She accepted the karmic snub on the morning before her deadline.

Outside, on her balcony, the tree canopy dripped traces of a storm Tash hadn't heard. She dialed her brother. She'd unearthed and recharged her phone on the off chance Doolittle might call. When she'd turned it on, she discovered Caleb had not attempted to make contact; Tash churned with this knowledge, sad and angry and hurt and relieved. Crushed and used up and furious all over again, resolving once more to see her project through without him.

"Hey!" Rohan loud-whispered, Wesley still asleep. "I'm leaving for a shift. How nice to hear from the sibling who's been 'too tied up with work' to call."

"Rohan. I fucked up." Tash announced it hoarsely, lifting her face to the sky's disappointment, a trickle of whatever tears she had left dampening her cheeks. "I have a submission deadline in twelve hours. I don't know what to write, and I don't have the right resources. When I get this wrong, the studio will have another reason to do whatever they want with the script."

The sound of a drawer banging came across the line. "Shit! Hold on." A door shut solidly. After a minute, Rohan's normal volume returned. He put Tash on his car's speaker. "Start from the beginning. What happened to our handsome writing guy? Can't he help you?"

Tash had bandaged up that wound and had begged herself to keep it covered, just for the meantime. "He's not here. He turned out to kind of be a mole."

"There's *espionage?*" Rohan boomed like a diva. "What the fuck, Trash?"

On another day, it might have made her smile. "The bigger issue right now is that I owe the studio another scene—and I've been staring at a blank page."

"Which scene?" Rohan knew the book almost as well as Janelle.

"The assault, near the end. The studio wants to make it less upsetting." Tash had written everything else she thought Braverman might ask for, including Noab and Hewett's bittersweet goodbye sex—which actually had been easy, after her call to La Playa.

"And . . . ?" Rohan sounded confused.

"And I don't want to change it! It's supposed to be a symbol of what women endure every day. I've been trying to come up with something horrible enough to be worthy of the story that the studio will still accept—but I don't have their notes, so I don't really know what I'm doing." Tash began to cry again. "I'm going to disappoint so many people, and it's my own fault."

"Hold on. Just breathe." Rohan made his voice soothing. "Listen—if anyone can manage 'horrible' and 'upsetting', it's definitely you. You are the queen. You wrote a whole book about baby-killing just to get out of marrying that flaccid pediatrician."

Tash actually did smile then. "Zach broke up with me. And you know I wrote most of it before I met him."

Rohan's bias insisted. "That's what I'm saying—reverse psychology! You've always been very sneaky. And very, very talented. Just finish this. Then get out here and visit me."

In the end, Rohan's *sneaky* gave Tash the idea.

She decided on a hybrid solution. She let Hewett's crew ambush Noab but not physically harm her—they tricked her into a cage. Then Tash took her own words and stuffed them in the crew's mouth—making them describe their plans for Noab, the trauma all dialogue, maybe even a reverse riff on burlesque, the language unambiguous and awful, the fear it inspired ever visceral. The crew advertised the fact Hewett had done this many times before, regularly pleasuring himself with women he double-crossed.

Then Tash let Noab cleverly provoke them, earning a smack to her jaw with the butt of a gun. She wrote the slow spread of Noab's smile as she spit her blood into the water, summoning her fellow female monster. She wrote Noab's conviction that the Mother Beast would take her side and protect her—because they were Sisters.

And because the animal would sense she'd been depleted, now only a spent vessel, with nothing inside left to consume.

Tash half expected her laptop to explode once she'd uploaded the file. Or melt, or whimper, or ding with an immediate response. Instead, her computer just lazed there mutely.

She'd hit the finish line, and now she could fall apart. She parked her car alongside Janelle's manicured hedges, glancing down to assure herself she'd dressed. She made it to the front door without alarming the neighbors. She remembered it had to be naptime for at least one of the girls and let herself in without ringing the bell.

She found Janelle in the kitchen wiping counter crumbs and eating discarded grilled-cheese crusts, Denise by the Danish high chair in a pencil skirt. Tash trudged in and laid her head down on one of the brightly colored plastic place mats on their dining table. She dropped her haphazardly packed overnight bag with a quiet thud.

Without introduction, she launched into everything that had

happened, from the beginning of the *Big Gun* soiree—the fleeting fantasy of Caleb's California invitation; Tash's private moments with Regina Bond, who was also Reggie and who worshipped data. Tash recounted Caleb's lion-taming, and his double-dealing, and the way he'd used their relationship to nudge her toward Braverman's point of view. She told them he'd known about the studio's intentions all along and lied to her about them, while having the balls to sweet-talk at her with words like "trust."

When Tash finished, Denise uncrossed her arms, bending stylishly in three-inch heels to retrieve an errant raisin from the floor. Janelle avoided eye contact. The silence in the kitchen felt entirely too loud.

Tash had expected some supportive wrath. "Hello?"

Denise glanced to Janelle. "I don't know, Tash. As someone who negotiates fairly complicated shit for a living, I think you might be blowing this out of proportion. Just because Caleb heard other opinions and tried to find solutions doesn't mean he was manipulating you. It might mean he was trying to find a common ground."

Tash stared in ratty disbelief. "Denise! He was having full-on discussions about critical plot changes behind my back. He never told me any of it."

"But didn't you ask him to be the buffer? Maybe not telling you was a fair part of that game." Denise joined Tash at the table. "Who knows what goes on in those meetings. In my job, when I want a certain outcome, sometimes I ask every stakeholder for their two cents. I let them all yap into a pot, and then I throw in *my* solution—which inevitably rises to the top. And then a man tries to take credit for it."

Janelle chuckled, leaning back against the sink.

Denise said the next part carefully: "And while you do have a million amazing qualities, you also have a tendency to shoot first and ask questions later. Which, one could argue, is part of what got you in this bind. Maybe Caleb was scared of how you'd react to what goes on behind the scenes. Negotiations can be mental warfare."

Yet Tash couldn't forget the panic on Caleb's face when he saw her and Regina together. She rejected the suggestion she'd misconstrued it. "But it was calculated. Braverman had an agenda from the start. Caleb's first priority was always Astrid, and then the studio. Not me."

"Are you sure?" Janelle seemed unconvinced.

"Yes!" Tash flailed, growing more annoyed, grasping at more straws, her friends' doubt making everything much worse. "He even asked 'What would be so bad' about more seasons."

"But that's a great question!" Janelle exasperatedly shot back. "I mean, as long as you could keep the crux of the story. Now that we're on this road, we see that more seasons could equal more exposure for the book's ideas. And I thought Caleb really proved himself—I loved everything I read. There's no room for Braverman to twist the sequences you two showed me into something sleazy."

Tash dismissed this. "Episodes One and Five were less important. He was just working me to get what the studio wants for Nine and Ten."

"What, like a long con?" Denise made her skepticism obvious. "Doesn't that sound far-fetched?"

Tash glared at them on two sides of the kitchen. "What is going on here? The con was not that long! Caleb didn't even have to try that hard. I made it easy!"

Janelle moved to the table, reaching to squeeze Tash's hand. "Natasha, I love you. But you have *never* made anything easy."

Denise smothered a chuckle. "So what did he say after you ran out of the party, when it was just the two of you alone?"

Tash dredged up that last fight. "I don't know. I left."

"You left?" Janelle exclaimed. "Without letting him explain?"

Tash could not have predicted this. She'd envisioned a wallow and tequila, some man-bashing and hugs. "Explain what? The other ways he could get me to sell out?"

Denise intervened, putting an arm up, in real-talk lawyer mode. "*Compromising* is not *selling out*, Tash. You agreed to compromise when you signed a contract for the film rights to your novel. It's that simple. You gave someone else creative license, and this is how it goes. You need to stop being so precious."

"But it *is* precious!"

"It's precious to *you*," Denise corrected her, sighing, glancing at her wife. "Look." She turned to face Tash fully. "Janelle is too nice to say this—but you cling to exaggerated principles because you like to be mad. Rage is your go-to, and you're letting your feelings about Men stop you from dealing fairly with one particular man—who legitimately sounds like he was trying."

Tash swiveled to stare at her best friend. "Is that what you think?"

Hesitantly, Janelle fluffed her dark curls. She dithered, cocking one ear to the baby monitor and listening importantly to the end-of-naptime babble. "Well . . ." When no other plausible physical gestures remained. "I might have phrased it differently. Also, I would have poured us drinks before I brought it up."

This time, Denise laughed openly.

Janelle squeezed Tash's hand. "But yes. Caleb probably kept things from you because he was afraid of this, exactly." She indicated Tash's general state of decay. "He doesn't seem like a hustler. Manipulating you would be so much extra work. Just think about it—introducing you to his extended family? Breaking his code of professional ethics? I think he did that because he *likes* you. And your book. And me." Janelle preened. "Probably, mostly me."

Tash dropped her face back to the place mat, stinging everywhere that she'd been poked. She thought about Caleb trying to reason with her on the grass outside that party. She wondered if all her takeaways had really been mistakes.

Eventually, Denise spoke. "Are you mad I said you like to be angry?"

Tash cracked an eyelid. "Is this a trick question? Do you want to see if I prove your point?"

"It's Janelle's point, actually. She's the one who worries about your rage." Denise pushed back from the table and clapped efficiently. "I'm glad I could be useful, though. I have to get back to the office. I have a closing dinner tonight, so don't wait up." She blew them air-kisses as she hefted Tash's overnight bag. "I'll put this in the guest room."

Denise made her exit. The baby monitor broadcasted naptime-waking gab. Tash kept her forehead to the table and cast her eyes uncomfortably at her best friend.

Who tossed her shoulders back unapologetically. "Of course I worry about you! You let past relationships color your judgment, and you're wrong about Caleb." She glanced at the wall clock. "I need to get Zinnie and Twila. Then I'll put on the sprinklers. The girls can run around outside while I help you sort your life."

Before she walked out of the kitchen, Janelle engulfed Tash's slumped-over form. "I love you. It's going to be okay."

Tash trudged to the guest room and found her overnight bag at the foot of the bed. She dug out a random shirt. She washed her face and brushed her teeth again, feeling the need for a clean slate. Feeling the need for clarity. Probably feeling the need for decent sleep.

But mostly feeling for the truth in Denise and Janelle's lecture. Tash *had* been angry as a habit, for a long time; maybe it had become her default. Maybe it had warped her view of Caleb.

Her phone dinged on the nightstand. At this point, the world could wait. Still, Tash's finger hovered, her gaze snagging on the email icon.

Brian Doolittle

That asshole—he knew responding now was too late.

Tash opened the email. Brian had replied without text in the body, blankly attaching the Episode Nine pink draft—which, Tash remembered, meant three rounds of revisions and comments had rolled in since the original. She also remembered an emailed script like this was static—it only showed a snapshot of the margin conversation, without any click-through.

Just a day ago, Tash would have been ecstatic to have even that scrap; now, however, it had no utility.

She scrolled down anyway.

Just to see if she could tell how far from Story Edit's direction her blocking and dialogue had veered.

Tash thumbed until she got to Noab's ambush, finding a high-lighted comment from @ReginaBond:

> Sorry, boys, but depicting rape is off the table. The latest rider to Astrid's contract prohibits "portrayal of sex acts by force." I also reviewed *Transtempora* sequences and agree with @CalebRaffery—the sensitivity around assault scenes make it expensive and a possible bad fit for our bracket.

Tash read this twice more, going weak-kneed. There were no dates on the comments, but Tash gleaned that Astrid had amended her contract, barring her from participating in scenes depicting sexual violence. Tash also gathered Caleb had referenced his work on *Transtempora* as an example of what *The Colony* should avoid. She scrolled up and down again, scanning for other @s with Caleb's name.

A few lines down, from @RamBraverman:

> For the @CalebRafferty slavery/bondage idea: top notes of chained-up Princess Leia? The look is iconic. @BrianDoolittle please have Costume mock this up.

Tash connected dots.

The shift to bondage was Caleb's idea. Because Story Edit had wanted to push Noab's assault onto the screen. Caleb knew it would destroy Tash, so he steered the Braverman team toward a lesser evil by invoking his own work on *Transtempora*. He probably asked Astrid to add that contract rider, too.

He hadn't been manipulating Tash for the studio—he'd been manipulating the studio for Tash.

Sounds of discordant crashing ripped Tash from her daze. High-pitched wails tore through the baby monitor in the kitchen. Janelle shouted from upstairs.

Tash found her on the landing, holding a shrieking Zinnia, a bloody towel pressed to the four-year-old's head.

Janelle had paled. "I think she hit it on the corner of the dresser. She was trying to climb into Twila's crib."

Tash toughened for Janelle's sake and peeked under the towel, taking in the inch-long gash. "She's going to be fine. But this probably needs stitches."

Janelle couldn't look. Her lips were white. She hated blood, and Zinnie's was soaking through. Two year-old Twila bawled from her bedroom, standing on her mattress.

Tash went to the crib, lifting Twila by the armpits and swinging her onto a hip. "Janelle, where are your car keys?"

Tash grabbed Janelle's purse. Pulled an ice pack from the freezer. Located the diaper bag. Picked up a spare towel.

Then she did not breathe again until they were seated in the ER's pediatric triage.

She'd white-knuckled the drive there, thanking the stoplight gods for streaks of green. Beside her, in a row of waiting room molded-plastic chairs, goosebumping in the industrial air-conditioned chill, Janelle cradled the back of Zinnie's head with shaking fingers. Blood crusted in the collar of Zinnie's pajamas, and on the top of Janelle's sundress, and on Tash's sleeve.

"I bet she has her ringer off for that closing dinner," Tash assured Janelle when they still could not reach Denise; Tash had gone into an emergency-command mode, taking charge as her best friend completely freaked. Tash held a tearful Twila in one arm and had the other around Janelle's shoulders. "They're going to call Zinnie's name soon."

After forty minutes, a friendly nurse curtained them off in an antiseptic nook. She checked Zinnia's pupils and her pulse, then peeled away the ruined towel. Janelle hovered over the exam bed nervously, continuing not to directly look. With Twila koala-bear attached to her torso, Tash ferried juice boxes from a nearby vending machine.

"Hm. That's quite deep." The nurse clicked off her penlight, glancing at her watch. "Luckily, Pediatric Plastics is right here in the building." She ducked to wink at Zinnia. "I'll page one of my favorites. Someone real nice. Don't worry, sugar, we'll make sure this hardly leaves a mark."

Once they'd been left to wait again, Janelle stared flatly at Tash across the mint-green space. "Well, at least we know it won't be Zachary. He can't be anybody's favorite."

Tash hitched Twila closer, glad Janelle could joke in her current state. Tash had previously been ignoring the fact they'd come to the hospital where Zach worked, not wishing to calculate the odds of seeing him. "You never know. He could be that nurse's favorite."

"No way." Janelle dismissed it, stroking hysteric-sweaty bangs off Zinnie's face gently. "Her clogs showed power. That lady has standards."

But Tash braced herself. She'd driven to the hospital at warp speed and on autopilot. She could have done it in her sleep because she knew the roads from memory.

She heard the slide of steel curtain rings.

And watched as Dr. Zachary Vandenberg took in her presence, Zinnia's chart held in his hand, his auburn side part combed exactly as it was the day he'd dumped Tash outside a public radio sound booth, engagement ring returned irately to his pocket.

His scrubs spanned a tennis player's lithe build in manly forest-green camouflage, which, Tash would guess, would reveal to be made up of something like silhouettes of smiling puppies upon closer inspection.

"Tash." His stammering gaze darted to Twila, thumb-sucking, tucked beneath Tash's chin. His eyes moved to Janelle and Zinnia.

"Don't worry. Both of the kids are mine." Janelle said it to him dryly, her historical dislike reappearing. But then she backtracked, perhaps remembering the reason he'd just arrived. She craned to give Zinnie a pretend, scolding scowl: "This one did some naptime acrobatics and managed to hit her head."

Zach's expression unwound only slightly. "Congratulations. On growing your family, I mean. Please tell Denise I said so, too." He looked down at Zinnie's chart.

Tash's instincts longed to suggest more stickers from the nurses' station, or any other excuse to leave the room. But she'd fled too many scenes lately. The strategy had stopped working.

Or had never worked in the first place.

And Tash was an adult—she could adequately manage an interaction with her ex-fiancé.

Zach's doctor persona took charge. "Let's see, Miss Zinnia." He rolled a stool to the exam table, charmingly shutting out the other adults. "I'm Dr. Zach. Our names start with the coolest letter in the alphabet, don't you think? Can you help me find a zebra on here, so he can join our club?" He offered her a cardstock cartoon-animal eye chart. "Can you read this to me?"

He tugged an oversized, floor lamp magnifying glass over to the table, but before he looked at her head, Zach let Zinnia stick her bare feet under the plate-size lens. He met Zinnie's eye with faux gravitas. "As a medical professional, I think you need to cut your toenails, sister."

Zinnie giggled.

"For real." Zach played at sniffing her feet. "If these didn't smell like tiny human, I would think they're pterodactyl." When Twila laughed, too, Zach included her in the game. "Hey, I'm serious! I had twin pterodactyls in here yesterday, right where you're sitting! They tripped on a trampoline."

The girls cracked up. Even Janelle seemed to relax. Tash stayed put, begrudgingly admiring his pediatric competence.

He easily persuaded Zinnie to lie face down, her head in a massage-style doughnut pillow at one end of the bed. He propped a tablet screen beneath her and pressed play on an animated movie so Zinnie could watch it on the floor, and then waved Janelle over, finger to lips, miming stitches with his other hand. He showed her the three large needles he'd need to numb the site.

He did not know Janelle well enough to realize her fear of needles far surpassed her fear of blood. She began to buckle just as Tash popped forward to catch her with the arm not holding Twila. Twila locked her knees even tighter around Tash's stomach and began to wail.

"You know what, Miss Zinnia? I have a great idea." Zach folded a blue hospital blanket into a pillow and placed it on the floor beside the screen. "Your mom's going to lie here so you two can have a staring contest through that funny face hole. Your Aunt Tash is going to sit next to me. And your sister is going to be in charge of everyone."

Zach produced a kid-size stethoscope and entrusted it to Twila, who stayed clamped to Tash but shushed immediately when Zach explained the importance of her duties. "You put the chest drum right here, and then you listen." He fit the earpieces, showing Twila austere patience as he spoke. "Once you're done with your heartbeat, start looking for one inside Aunt Tash." Under his breath: "It might take you a while."

The glimmer of humor on his face stopped Tash from prickling at the insult. Also, she'd very recently decided to reevaluate her temper. This seemed like it could be good practice.

Zach rolled another stool over, flanking his instruments. He motioned for Tash, with Twila, to sit down. He raised the volume on the floor screen, backdropping the exam room with cackling kangaroos. He filled the three syringes with anesthetic.

"Okay. Zinnia, if you feel any pinches, you just squeeze Aunt Tash's hand. But I think after this first pinch, you should be fine."

Tash realized Twila could see the needles. "Is it okay for her to watch this?"

Zach bent, checking in with Twila, who'd moved the cold metal stethoscope into Tash's shirt. "Little kids actually love watching stitches. It's just like arts and crafts. Right?"

Twila nodded shyly. Zach brought a light closer to where he'd draped a sterile window around Zinnie's gash. Zinnie's small fingers squeezed Tash only once, with the first injection; then she was lost to her cartoons, while her mother lay woozily on the cold hospital floor beside the tablet.

Zach flicked his gaze to Tash. "So? How are you?"

She absorbed the absurdity of the situation. Her head ached with left-over adrenaline. Zachary Scott Vandenberg, whom she'd once planned a life with, currently wanted to chat—after he'd just made a cute quip about Tash being heartless. And although some new self-knowledge might have made her willing to revisit her role in their very acrimonious breakup, Tash wasn't sure she owed Zach any of her updates.

"I heard they're making your book into a TV show," he prompted. "That's awesome. Sounds like things really worked out."

"She has a boyfriend." Janelle reported this overstatement recumbently, with closed eyes. "But don't let that affect my child. Stay focused. Please."

Zach's brows rose, but only slightly, his scissors and suture forceps smooth. "A boyfriend, huh? Like, a real guy? Or a book boyfriend? Is that what we used to call them?" He glanced at Tash almost nostalgically, as if reliving a fond memory, as if her characters hadn't been the very wedge that drove them apart. "I'm happy for you. But if it's a real person, someone should tell him it gets hard playing second fiddle. You're pretty loyal to your fiction, if I remember right."

Tash nearly responded by telling Zach it wasn't hard for Caleb.

And that Zach should watch out—a framework that included "second fiddle" gave his insecurities away.

But instead, she sparked with revelation, recalling a conversation she'd once had with Caleb about anger and fear: Zach had probably been *scared* back then. He probably worried for his place in an imaginary ranking system of his own creation. He probably feared Tash wouldn't choose him, and he'd expressed that fear as anger.

Suddenly, Tash felt generous. She'd played an equal part in their bad dynamic. They hadn't known how to excavate their anger, and it burned their house down from the inside.

Bizarrely, she flushed with relief. She felt like crying, or laughing out loud, despite the exam room and the needles and Janelle on the floor. She wanted to tell Caleb about this full-circle, evolved moment.

And even if Zach made a flawed yardstick, Tash still couldn't help but compare: this man stitching, who'd shunned her for something she'd written, and the man she'd just been writing with, who didn't feel threatened by her work.

Who'd only ever been supportive.

The blocking of Tash's next steps became instantly crystal clear. She needed to pen an end and a beginning. She needed to write a way out of the mess she'd created.

She needed to do it skillfully, with great care—because it occurred to her that Caleb's loyalty might have been to Tash's fiction, too.

Chapter Seventeen

Two weeks later, as Tash and Rohan laced up their sneakers, he claimed to not have done any cardio since the last time they ran the oceanside pavement path from Santa Monica Pier to Venice Beach.

"Unless you count that vibrating-plate class Wesley drags me to on Sunday mornings." Despite the coastal highway fumes and scent of dried kelp, Rohan had been managing a steady stream of chatter. "And the rowing fundraiser I did with the transplant team."

Tash played at pushing her younger brother off the early-morning concrete lane. "What, and the marathon training you squeeze in before work?"

Rohan dodged her, running ahead, spinning to jog backward so he could jeer. "Trash—don't insult me." He winked beneath his Lakers cap, smug as ever. "I only train that hard if it's an Ironman."

Tash scoffed at him mid-stride, then darted around, trying to sprint past him—but Rohan's legs had practically surpassed the length of her entire body by the time he was sixteen. He kept pace easily, barely out of breath. Tash would definitely not beat him.

Trying to trip him, however—or trying to peg him with the trail mix his boyfriend had thoughtfully packed alongside her water bottle— provided an excellent distraction from the day's upcoming event: New light winked on the Pacific, and the wind tried to shake off its dawn cold, and the next Story Edit meeting would commence in six hours.

"How are you feeling?" Rohan could be silly, but he also was stead-fast. He trotted beside her with an excellent antenna for her stress.

In fact, he's assumed responsibility for her downtime since she'd arrived. Yesterday, Rohan whisked her out of his perfectly restored West Hollywood bungalow to search an Indian grocery store for ingredients for their dadi's famous curry. Afterward, they swung by a new La Brea goat-yoga studio. Then, in the tiny guesthouse that had once been the bungalow's garage, they continued their process of combing through Tash's box of letters from their mother. Rohan's delight in Mary Gro-ver's blue-ink fossils was instructive—he allowed their childhood de-tails to amuse him instead of getting annoyed. In the evening, Rohan and Wesley had read Tash's final pages for Story Edit.

Both of them had cried.

"Trash! I asked you how you're feeling!"

Tash startled from her split-second reverie. "Rohan! I'm trying to keep my shit together!"

"Yikes." He slowed their tempo. "Toning down the yelling might be a place to start."

In truth, Tash's hopes for her Hollywood pilgrimage blanched at the prospect of going up against Reggie and Ram. "I can't tell if my grand plan is dumb or brilliant." She dreaded the idea of dealing with Brian Doolittle in person. "I might not even make it past the parking lot. Braverman security might try to drag me out."

"I'd pay to see that."

"Thanks," Tash deadpanned. She slackened their jog to a walk.

Rohan slung a sweaty limb around her neck, tucking Tash into his disgusting armpit as only a giant little brother could. "We both know you've got this! You wrote everything they asked, and more. You're brave and creative. And like we said last night—existentially, the outcome of this meeting doesn't matter. What's important is that you state your case."

Such high-mindedness had felt genuine at a drink-in-hand cruising altitude of thirty thousand feet, and it had continued to feel genuine on Wesley and Rohan's designer sofa. But in the harsh light of the day-of, Tash knew the outcome of the Story Edit meeting absolutely mattered. Risking her pride was one thing; it was another thing entirely to risk *The Colony*'s legacy.

Tash yanked her sunglasses from where they'd been squished by Rohan's embrace. "I think I'm scared this is my raw chicken."

"What?" Rohan craned to see her face.

"From Mom's letter—the raw chicken. The chicken-plucking." Tash waited for him to catch on. "It's a metaphor. For thankless female sacrifice."

Rohan stopped short, still holding her in his loving headlock. "No. Raw chicken is a great way to get salmonella. That's all."

Tash huffed. "You think that because you're a man."

"I think that because I work with immunocompromised renal patients, and salmonella can be fatal." Rohan released her momentarily, only to gather her cheeks in both his hands. "But, hey. I'd pluck raw chickens for Wesley. Maybe one day I'll pluck raw chickens for our kids. Mom and Dad's chicken-plucking dynamic doesn't have to be your model for relationships—that's why you're going through those letters, right? To free yourself from the vestiges of being judged, and to rewrite your relationship with Mom? To find peace with making vastly different decisions from her, while still appreciating her presence in your life?"

Tash sputtered between his palms as Rohan congratulated himself on such profound insight.

"If you need chicken-plucking to be a metaphor, let it be a metaphor for love. Loving someone doesn't have to make you weak, Trash.

Just choose the right person." Rohan gestured at blowing both their minds. "And the right chickens to pluck."

Tash laughed then.

She wondered if it could be that simple.

Actually, she'd come to California in the hope it was that simple—she reminded herself of this all afternoon, right up to the moment Rohan wished her luck and shoved her out his front door, into the sleek temperature-control of Astrid Dalton's SUV.

Tash hadn't seen her since their disastrous parting from *Vaudeville Striptease* at Miami Arts. When Tash arrived in Los Angeles, she'd questioned whether Astrid would even take her call. But then they'd spoken on the phone, and the star of *The Colony*'s adaptation had been thoroughly cordial.

"Caleb doesn't know you're here? Really?" Idling her car at Rohan's curb, Astrid moved a huge purse from her passenger seat onto the floorboard.

"Not yet." Tash sincerely wished this not to backfire; the drive to Culver City would take less than thirty minutes, and Caleb would find out then.

Astrid pulled her SUV into traffic. Tash adjusted her seat belt over a one-shoulder printed-silk top and across the waist of cigarette pants curated especially by Janelle. Tash had woken to three missed calls from her best friend, but between the run with Rohan and trying not to vomit, she hadn't had a chance to try her back.

Right now, Tash's immediate Sisterhood consisted solely of Astrid. "Thanks again for doing this with me." She'd be grateful for safe passage onto the Braverman Productions lot.

Astrid pushed white sunglasses up into her topknot. "Don't thank me yet. All I heard is that the meeting's in an EP conference room. I don't know which one." She stopped at a red light, glancing over to Tash wryly. "But I *do* know I need to apologize. I embarrassed myself in Florida. It's hard to have a crush on someone who used to change your diaper—they tend not to love you back. At least, not the way you're hoping. I don't recommend it."

Tash found herself in the odd position of having to reassure another woman of Caleb's affections. "Caleb cares about you a lot."

"Like a baby sister. I know. I'll get over it eventually." Traffic began to move again. "I also need to say that Noab is the role of a lifetime. There aren't a lot of parts like her, and I appreciate the opportunity."

Tash returned the olive branch. "The series is lucky to have you." She decided to take Astrid at face value, even if she was only flexing her acting skills.

"Let's see if that's true—first I have to get you into this meeting." Astrid changed lanes, stepping on the gas.

Tash had only ever visited a film production office once. The first showrunner to buy the screen rights to *The Colony* worked from an abandoned flagpole warehouse in Philadelphia's colonial neighborhood—all red brick and soaring, single-pane windows, open to the scent of river sludge and expired kegs and generational revolt. If that team's headquarters signaled indie protest, then Braverman's gave off aging action star—its labyrinthine workplace a jumble of worn artillery-vest pockets and gruff corporate lobby.

Astrid swept right through it, charming the standing-desked receptionist. She retrieved a visitor badge for Tash with minimal cajoling, rendering concerns about Tash's admittance moot. Then Astrid marched them toward a creaky elevator, chose a button, and led Tash into an empty conference room.

"Shit." Astrid began to fluster. "I knew this would happen."

They tried a different, creakier elevator, and then a different flight of stairs.

Astrid cringed apologetically, speed-walking them through a ragtag cafeteria. "Maybe it's in Ram's suite."

Tash gritted her teeth. The sky-high heels on her strappy sandals were not built for stairwell trekking. Also, her aesthetic sensibilities had been shocked at what she'd discovered beyond the lobby—she'd imagined Braverman Productions as overtly gloss, all packaging, like Ram; not as a maze of water-stained drop ceilings and beige Formica and dusty cubicles and sagging ficus plants.

After a much-longer-than-intended tour of the office, Astrid finally led Tash to Reggie's conference suite—twenty-seven minutes late for the meeting and definitely frazzled.

"Good luck." Astrid thumbs-upped toward the doorway, retreating without a drawn-out farewell. There was no time to grapple with conciliatory send-offs, which maybe was for the best.

Through a glass wall, Tash spied an oval table surrounded by eleven white men hunched over their screens, nodding to where Ram held court from an ergonomic office-chair throne. He appeared deep in conversation with a squawking, triangular speaker in the center of a long table. Beside him, her cardigan clasped with a diamond broach, sat Reggie—executive producer consigliere.

And on a bench windowsill, with his back against the sprawl of low-rise industry horizon, Caleb Rafferty sat with his ankle on his knee.

He looked a little washed-out—his hair drooped and his eyes had dimmed; his tattoo had faded, elegant black to depressed gray. He wore dark jeans. Even his sneakers seemed somber—glum with a heartbreak-purple sole.

Tash knew she wholly projected these symptoms of their mournful time apart. In real life, Caleb's mouth moved merrily, now appearing to address the room. Reggie glanced up from where her thumbs flew furiously over her phone to listen to him, then to toss him an inside grin.

I'd gladly write a book for him to translate into movement—Tash remembered Reggie's words.

Except Tash had exactly done that. She'd very literally, actually written a book. Maybe not for Caleb, and maybe they'd translated only parts of it together. But now she had more words she wanted him to read.

An unadulterated thirst for it propelled her through the door.

Perhaps too quickly—Tash stumbled over a panel leaning against the threshold, papered with blown-up character hair-and-makeup test Polaroids. The commanding entrance she'd envisioned for herself gave way to plain gawping: In the largest photo, Astrid's coif gathered in gold-ringed, postmodern Noab cornrows, her cheekbones fierce, her lips reflecting a black shine. Her eyes were shadowed into catlike angles that gloated magnificently, her entire expression a majestic dare.

It left Tash breathless, lost to the depth and pride of Noab and Astrid intermingled.

While the members of the Story Edit team openly stared at her bumbling arrival; and Caleb jumped up, keeping Tash on her feet.

The speakerphone call must have ended.

Reggie smiled at her, thumbs paused. She greeted Tash in the otherwise deafening silence. "Tash! What a cool surprise."

"What the fuck?" The muttering had come from Ram.

Two seats over from him, a saggy twerp copied Ram and performatively scowled. "This is a closed meeting. People can't just barge in."

Tash took a wild guess the twerp was Brian Doolittle.

"It's okay." Reggie waved a stylish hand. "Gentlemen, this is Natasha Grover, author of our source material." Taking a moment to gesture around the oval: "Natasha, these are not gentlemen."

Even as she said it, it was clear Reggie was one of the boys; their leader, even, the bro in charge after Ram. She dangled a heeled mule off one toe as her chair swirled. "Please, join us."

No one interpreted this welcome to mean they should offer Tash a seat. Which she pretended wasn't awkward. She pretended she preferred it that way, on display in the middle of a meeting, while puzzled gazes rolled off the sex designer dreamboat standing guard at her side.

Tash curved her mouth upward. She aimed a falsely chipper tone at Reggie and Ram. It went sideways to Caleb also, as explanation: "I wanted to be here for the Episode Ten review. To pitch some ideas for the finale."

Probably-Doolittle snarked. "You're not on the agenda."

Reggie twisted to consult a meeting schedule tacked to a rolling whiteboard. "Tash is the reason we're here, though. We can make time."

"But Caleb gave his notes already." This dude did not stop.

"One idea leads to another." This came from Caleb—apparently still on her side.

At least creatively.

"That's how the best work happens." Caleb missed no beats, easing Tash's envelope of printouts from her shaky hands and passing the contents to an assistant for distribution around the table. He kept a set of the stapled sheets for himself, immediately paging through.

"I wrote the last scene as narrative." Tash began to overexplain to the room. "That's the way we built Episodes One and Five—which everyone liked—so I continued in that vein."

The many other fervent declarations she'd rehearsed swarmed at the starting line in her brain, but they were only for Caleb, and they'd have to wait now—Doolittle's hostility threatened Tash with imminent derailment, and Ram had frowned at her on sight.

Reggie was not an ally, either.

In fact, at the conference table dais, Reggie pushed Tash's hardcopy paragraphs away. "Why don't you just walk us through it? We'll take advantage, since you're here."

Tash exhaled. Before flying to LA, she'd examined her idea endlessly with Janelle. Tash wished she'd also been able to bounce the scene off Caleb instead of barging in to Story Edit blind—but then again, she'd committed to concluding the story by herself. And for herself.

To pluck the chickens for herself.

Later, Tash could tell Rohan and laugh.

Now, she mentally teleported to the place she felt the most in control: to a coconut-oil-scented classroom, with Ram and Reggie as burnout surfers, and board racks crowding the faculty parking, and an aloe plant on her desk.

"Fraternal twins." Tash anchored, as if beginning just another "Heroes and Villains" lecture. "Reggie mentioned how well audiences respond to 'broad biblical underpinnings.' If Noab gives birth to a boy *and* a girl, we can use the tragedy of the son and the cliff-hanger of the daughter. We get a finale that's doubly dramatic—"

"But you're still killing a baby," Ram interrupted, a pair of rimless reading glasses on his nose. He examined the printout in irritation. "This is going backward. I thought we moved on from human sacrifice."

Tash did not know what he meant, exactly, but she'd come prepared with argument. "It isn't 'human sacrifice'—it's a parable of siblings. It's a 'slaying of the firstborn.' Fraternal twins gives us a modern interpretation of Cain and Abel, which reframes the finale into wide, cross-cultural legend." Tash aimed for Reggie's viewership jargon, hoping it could sway Reggie to her side.

Ram glanced to Reggie skeptically. Doolittle observed this and mimicked the same qualm. Reggie tapped one French-manicured finger pensively on the table.

"I'm not sold." The diamond pin holding Reggie's cardigan in place sparkled beneath fluorescent lights. "I liked my Moses idea better."

Doolittle leaped onto the bandwagon. "Me, too."

Ram's dictatorial mouth opened, seemingly about to concur.

Tash raised her voice over the next objection. "The baby girl is resurrection. She's redemption. She's hope and beauty rising from Noab's pain. It's your strongest storyline, because the action stays with your lead, who we've just followed for an entire season. She's made terrible mistakes and suffered. But audiences love a comeback. Let her give them a show."

She hoped Caleb caught her reference.

Then Tash homed in on Ram. "Let the finale's momentum stay with Noab, who embodies sex in every sense—lust, seduction, fertility. She's so close to a cliffside climax. Now isn't the time to cut away." Tash pushed her next words at Reggie. "In terms of retellings, what's better than a story of redemption? It's relatable to every demographic. It's algorithm gold."

What these algorithms might be, Tash could not quite say. She knew literary tropes and she knew archetype. She knew Reggie liked the lingo, which right now Tash tried desperately to speak.

Reggie prevented Tash from spouting more by leaning forward, pegging Tash with a request: "Repeat what you said about resurrection."

Tash retraced her riffs, sensing a foothold. Sensing Reggie's curiosity. Sensing she'd hit upon a nerve.

She knew the data celebrated allegory. She remembered what Caleb once said about lush imagery. "The girl-child is narrative rebirth. She's spring, and dawn, and resurrection." Tash summoned her verbal pyrotechnics. "She's the virgin breaths after a sexual release."

Reggie stopped her. "Right there—I like that part."

Doolittle spoiled the moment. "Still, you'd be killing a kid."

"We'd be killing the boy and keeping the girl, though. Something for everyone." Reggie rotated to confer with Ram. "It gives us good material for world-building."

Which Ram seemed to consider. He pulled off his reading glasses, ignoring Tash, looking to Caleb for a guarantee. "Virgin breaths? You can write that?"

Caleb's solid form flanked Tash. "Absolutely."

Ram metabolized the plot change, commandeering the new direction in a span of seconds, suddenly behaving as if it was his idea. "We can tell press I liked the story so much, I expanded on it. I'm a champion of women's television."

Tash moved not a muscle in reaction—not even to roll her eyes.

Ram ended the meeting. Reggie glided from her chair. Doolittle shut his computer.

He addressed Caleb. "Please make sure Episode Ten is polished before it goes in." Pointedly, definitely at Tash: "Because Nine was a disaster."

But she would not be lured into altercation.

She let Story Edit disband around her, leaving behind a faint tang of lab-administered testosterone. She hung back by her leading lady's victorious test photograph. She noted an intimacy coordinator's lingering retreat to the window.

She held her breath, refusing to jinx this outcome.

She searched for the emotion beneath the action, outlining her next move.

Chapter Eighteen

Once Ram and Reggie made their exit, the conference suite drained quickly.

No one stayed behind to question why Tash loitered, or why Caleb returned her gaze so intensely from his spot on the sill.

When the hallway outside had cleared, too, Tash finished pretending to fiddle with her one-shoulder top's silk knot. All that remained were the character photos and the Culver City skyline and the exhilaration of having vanquished her own python. And the tender loose threads of unfinished business.

Caleb broke the ice.

Ten feet away from her, he perched on the window's bench seat, arms folded across his white button-down, his posture a defensive hedge. "'A cliffside climax'?"

Unsure if it was praise or ridicule, Tash shrugged self-consciously. "Someone once told me each department has its own language. And I had to really use it if I wanted these guys to listen."

His mouth stayed neutral. "You did a good job." His gaze stayed politely aloof. "How do you feel about the changes? Fraternal twins is a big shift from the book."

"I feel great about it." Tash felt the wave of apology and resolution that had carried her from one coast to another. "Once I got past being precious about the plot, fraternal twins seemed like a smart way for the property to go."

Behind his glasses, Caleb's eyes flickered. He nodded slowly, perhaps picking up on her clue. "You gave the baby girl some interesting symbolism."

"I did." Tash inched forward in heels she could not wait to unstrap. "She's supposed to signify second chances." When Caleb just blinked at her, she took a more overt angle. "I know about the rider to Astrid's contract. She told me it was your idea."

Her tactic had the wrong effect. "You spoke to Astrid?" His bearing tightened.

"She got me in here. I wasn't sure I'd make it past reception."

"Well, the rider was a last resort." He'd stiffened into a stoic barricade. "Story Edit seemed hell-bent on shooting something graphic, and I knew that was the last thing you would want. I'm sorry if you're angry. I had to find a middle ground—"

"Caleb. I'm not angry." Tash cut him off, her cataclysmic track record seeing it would need to make amends. Of course he assumed she was angry—he expected it, just like Denise and Janelle.

She dared another step toward his stronghold. "I'm grateful. I saw the pink draft of the script. I understand that we were cornered. I understand you did it to help me. Again." She remembered Doolittle's parting quip. "Although it sounds like I butchered Nine's execution. Writing it without you kind of sucked."

Limb by muscled limb, Caleb became familiar to her again. He leaned back against the plate-glass window. "Did you know I pitched half of your finale idea before you walked in?"

Tash shook her head, not following.

"The baby as a girl. I thought of it last night. I wasn't sure it was okay, so I left Janelle an extremely long-winded message." He shrugged humbly. "But it didn't matter because I couldn't convince the team. So this save is all you."

The three missed calls from Janelle suddenly made sense. "Janelle's probably laughing—I got the twins idea with her, too. I made her go over it with me a thousand times." Tash would owe her best friend an update.

First, she owed Caleb something else.

She reached for the monologue she'd practiced. "I know I ruined things. We were supposed to have a safe space, and I filled it with my hang-ups. I jumped to conclusions, and I got mad, and I ran away instead of letting you explain. These are habits I'm trying to break." She gave him a self-aware smile of entreaty. "At least with you. I mean, if you're into comebacks. Which, I hear, are trending pretty hard."

His expression thawed. "What, like, tales of redemption?"

She nodded.

Caleb uncrossed his legs, purple soles planted on beige carpet. "Then I'll respond by saying I could have done a better job of laying out the Braverman dynamics. I shouldn't have kept you in the dark. I did it because you'd had such a bad experience with them already, and the inside of story negotiations can be such shit." He blazed with sincerity. "I should have been more open. I wanted to spare you the aggravation."

"I get that now." Tash found herself in the shelter of his knees.

He pulled her toward him gently. "Although. You handled things perfectly today. You pitched like a natural."

Tash balked. "I am never coming to one of these meetings again."

"You might have to." Caleb pointed to the conference oval. "You probably just got yourself a second season."

Tash trapped his shoulders against the window, silencing his wit. "The thing is, I'm difficult to manage. I need special collaboration. The only person I can really work with is very in demand."

"I might know someone. I'll introduce you."

Tash climbed into his lap.

She kissed him in reacquaintance, the choreography all hot celebration.

His smile for her was private. "How long can you stay?"

Tash shrugged, high on his scent, already. "Until my brother and his boyfriend kick me out of their guesthouse?"

Caleb must have done the math. He withdrew for a moment. "Don't you have to get back to your classes?"

She took in his mussed hair, his dilated pupils, the scruff on his jaw. "I'm on leave for a semester. To work on something new."

He absorbed this. He stood then, grinning, fixing her legs around his waist. He walked them toward the exit. "So there's enough time to help me write the virgin breaths after a sexual release? Because you just promised a bunch of people that dialogue and blocking."

Tash laughed. "*You* promised."

"Same thing."

She pretended to mull it over. "What you're saying is—you need specific words and movement."

He pinned her against the conference room wall unabashedly, right in front of *The Colony*'s blown-up Polaroids. "Yes, but it has to be excellent. Hope and beauty. Cross-cultural legend. Spring, and dawn, and lust."

Down the corridor, the elevator dinged open for them; beyond it, the California sun.

Tash smiled, certain what Caleb asked for wouldn't be a problem. "Sure. I think I can help you flesh that out."

Epilogue

Tash had once dreamed of Gayle and Oprah hosting an all-girlfriends watch party for *The Colony*'s premiere.

She'd imagined celebrating her book's Hollywood debut with all its fanfare. She'd pictured Rohan and Wesley as her dates. She'd envisioned Janelle decked out in gloriously consequential clothing. She'd visualized herself swanning through cocktails and applause.

She'd never once considered swapping that pageantry for sunrise over a secret beach.

Or limestone crueler than her Biscayne Coastal lagoon instead of the red carpet, or a riptide so dangerous she could only view it from a tamarind-treed hill, or pelicans instead of paparazzi, or the scent of hibiscus and ginger massage oil still fragrant on her skin.

Gayle and Oprah would have been amazing; but Tash had chosen a different premiere-night fantasy.

She wrapped one of the villa's blankets around her naked shoulders, matching her breathing to the tranquil wind.

"There you are." Rumpled and shirtless in the half-light, Caleb walked barefoot across the lookout garden's grass. He'd left the villa's French doors open. He slotted behind Tash in the hammock without upsetting its swing.

He retucked their blanket. Tash snuggled in, his broad chest warm at her back. They watched the day break over the ocean, Bali's sky cracking a volcanic scarlet-gold.

"Jet lag?" Caleb rested his chin on top of the wildness of Tash's hair.

She nodded. "I didn't want to wake you."

His arms cinched tighter. "The LA premiere is today."

Tash craned around until her smile found his incredible blue-eyed gaze, still a little bleary above a pillow imprint slashed across his cheek. "Do you wish we hadn't missed it?"

"Oh, absolutely." Caleb deadpanned, voice husky over the distant marine crush. "One hundred percent. I'm hating every moment of this Season Two fine-tuning." His hands dragged lazily over the blanket; beneath it, his legs harnessed her hips. "This project continues to be awful."

The project had landed Braverman Productions an early renewal deal with the streaming platform, and knee-deep in two more seasons of groundbreaking feminist TV. Caleb and Stacy had been renewed, too, for the whole run. Advance press hailed Astrid's performance, and her media blitz included several podcasts in addition to the usual round of late shows.

Tash did not know if Leo Rousseau's podcast had made Astrid's cut; once Braverman's lawyers blocked Tash's episode from airing, she'd stopped paying attention.

"I'm so sorry you have to stay here for some of the filming, then." Tash's contract for *The Colony*'s extension granted her a similar script oversight to Season One. The cast and crew were due in Bali soon, but she and Caleb had flown out early—to refine certain story elements that could only be finalized on-location.

Even if, so far, the only setting they'd diligently researched was their villa's four-poster bed.

"Me, too." His kiss was not at all apologetic. "Which backdrop should we knock off today?" Caleb's official duties included tour guide. He'd visited during the first season's taping, after Stacy contrived a consultation, insisting Bali was too spectacular to miss. "The forest around the mountain temple, or the forest around the waterfall?"

Tash had stayed behind for that first trip. She'd returned to Florida to give herself a concentrated focus on a next book. She and Caleb tried long-distance for a few interminable months, before Janelle helped Tash pack up the duplex and put her on a plane to California.

"Which forest goes with which episode again?" Tash laughed; they'd begun the same conversation yesterday. But the travel to Bali had been exhausting, and they'd both recently been working so hard, and the villa had a pool and butler service. They'd abandoned their responsibilities, and not left the resort's grounds.

"I don't remember." Caleb scrunched sideways in the hammock, sliding down until they angled face-to-face. He'd left his glasses inside, and his eyes glimmered. "Let me think through the scenes."

He affected scruffy contemplation. "Okay. One forest is where a cynical detective with a penchant for mathematics goes undercover at a burlesque club, only to fall for a con man who frequents it, becoming his latest mark."

He'd mashed the plot of Tash's new novel draft into *The Colony*'s landscape.

Tash raised her eyebrows. "Sounds like a must-see."

"A must-read," Caleb corrected. "It's a love story—even if the author tells you the genre's called Florida Noir." He continued to sweetly trample several rhetorical devices. "The other forest is where a beautiful literature-professor-slash-novelist gives up her rental in Venice to move in with her boyfriend and his handsome dog in Silver Lake." Twinkling. "Also a love story."

Tash grinned. They'd begun part of this conversation yesterday, too. She wove their bodies closer together. "Wow. These forest sagas are so compelling."

"I know." Caleb lowered his voice to a persuasive murmur. "But the second forest has space for Janelle to visit. And your brother loves the kitchen in the second forest."

"My brother loves every kitchen, as long as it has food."

Caleb pressed on. "The second forest could also make room for a writing desk, if you wanted." He kissed her again, smiling the possibilities. "Or you could keep Venice as your office."

Truthfully, the prospects thrilled Tash too much to play coy. "Let's do that one."

Caleb pulled his brawn back. "Really?"

"Yes. Just please stop disrespecting the wordplay. I'll come to all your forests." And his canyons and his cliffs, and probably even his secret groves and warrior islands. "But it's still early. Let's go back to bed."

Acknowledgments

In romance terms, this book has been my Slow Burn—and as I stroll hand-in-hand into the sunset with it, I'm grateful for every brush with love I've had along the way.

Thank you to Aurora Fernandez, my First, for plucking up a blind query and deciding to champion a romance about female rage. Thank you for the early structural feedback that made the story stronger. Thank you for being a sounding board and an advisor. I am so lucky to have jumped off this cliff with you!

Thank you to David Howe, my One Who Got Away, for bringing this book to HarperCollins. I still think about our instant chemistry and What Could Have Been! I love our loose thread out there in the world.

Thank you to Caroline Weishuhn, my Blind Date—who knew a set up could ever be this good? Thank you for embracing this story and for loving us so well. Thank you for the thoughtful, sharp editing that burnished and clarified my manuscript. You make me believe in Meant to Be.

Thank you to Kathryn Dodson, my Long-Distance—I very literally could not have written this book without you. Thank you for every comment, every bit of thinking-along, every wise word, every piece of feedback, and every drop of your endless patience. You are the Best Thing That Ever Happened, a gift of kismet, and a cherished guiding light.

Thank you to Edward Gunawan, my Platonic, for the infinite drafts you read of a different manuscript, which taught me many lessons. Thank you for your aspirational creativity. I treasure our kinship and our connection, no matter how far away.

Thank you to Robbie Taylor Hunt, my Star-Crossed, for your behind-the-scenes Intimacy Director expertise. Your articulate generosity with me and with this manuscript was beyond a Hollywood fairy tale.

Thank you to the Cuddle Puddle of brilliant professionals that escorted this book into the world. At Trident Media Group, thank you to Alice Berndt, Julia Maziarz, and Olivia Vella. At HarperCollins, thank you to Doug Jones, Amy Baker, Dori Carlson, Michael Fierro, Megan Looney, Heather Drucker, Rachel Molland, Suzette Lam, Mary Beth Constant, and Joanne O'Neill. At Verve Books, thank you to Jenna Gordon, Lisa Gooding, Ellie Lavender, and Demi Echezona.

Thank you to the three women this book could not live without, my Love Triangle:

To Nirali Shah—you said Guest Star, but I say North Star. Your sensibility gave me a goal, and your keen eye and smart critique were invaluable to this story. You remain ever pinned to my vision board.

To Lisa Goeller for being my earliest reader—of the treatment for this book but also of the many narratives that got me here. You are both the bar and the person I want to sit next to at the bar. Yours is the mind I wrote to please and the voice inside my head and the fellowship in my heart.

To Neha Patel for walking beside me through every moment of crafting this book and for inspiring the soul agreements in its pages. You are the sun beneath which my entire family warms itself. You are my compass and chosen companion. No one knows how I got behind your velvet rope, but good luck kicking me out.

Thank you to the two women who tend the charmed garden from which MmmHo sprung, my True Loves, Lindsay Ernst and Ada Loi. You are the gorgeous monster in the sea; and you are the glowing flame beneath the tea. Thank you for an ever-evolving Sisterhood and our steady, sacred clasp of hands.

Thank you to Shaun Bernier, my Office Romance, for your unflagging camaraderie on this path we trek together. Thank you for being an endless font of resources and for talking over every detail. Thank you for standing next to me while we ate the same lunch for months and months and months.

Thank you to Marilyn Laves, Lee Stern, and Michele Witlieb—my Childhood, High School, and College Sweethearts—for being my life-long bedrock. Decades later and look at us! Still keeping it fresh.

Thank you to Amelia Sewell, my May-December, for valued feedback on a previous project and for our globetrotting, passionate affair. A ten-year age gap! And yet the love is real.

Thank you to the men I steal bits and pieces of to write my heart-throbs: Myles Goeller, Darren Massara, and Ferish Patel. Other people probably think you're just Arm Candy, but to me you are genuine Brotherly Love.

Thank you to my many other Friends with Benefits:

To Ajna Pisani for your ongoing invitation, which reunited me with joy.

To Molly and Linda Bondellio for the seat in your circle, which returned me to myself.

To Nia Hughes for your kindness in connecting me to Robbie Taylor Hunt.

To Tracey Morton for our immediate harmony, which bloomed during this process.

To Emma Nanami Strenner for our safe-space dialogue.

To Andrea Cavallaro for your incredible open-heartedness, and for letting me grasp onto our Babysitter Romance, and for flying in to celebrate that Adult Romance! May we always raise our glass.

To Debbie Laves for your future vision, for knowing this would happen, and for proclaiming it with such certainty.

To Brigitte Kahn for sweeping me up into your love of the arts in those early days in New York City; and for continuing that cocktail conversation with me over our many years.

Thank you to the teachers who shaped my young adult romance with literature and words. At Marjory Stoneman Douglas High School, thank you to George Mitchell for imparting a deep, lasting affinity for archetype and female legend and cultural mythology. At the University of Pennsylvania, thank you to Rita Barnard for blowing my mind in a freshman English seminar, and thank you to Peshe Kuriloff for opening my eyes to craft.

Thank you to the studios and instructors with whom I've practiced the Self-Love of yoga. Thank you to sweat and flexibility and balance and ujjayi breath. Thank you to a special back balcony on Robertson Quay where much of this book was written.

Thank you to the matriarchy for the hearth fires that came before me—to the historical romance I grew up watching in the Gabel blood-line and to the Turner female-warrior roots.

Thank you to my children, my Great Loves—who lose me to this love and welcome me back again.

Thank you to the Love That Makes My World Go Round:

To my husband, the Guardian;

To my brother, the Caretaker;

To my father, the Appreciator;

And to my mother, the rare-magic medley of all three.

About the Author

Turner Gable Kahn grew up in the extra-hold-hairspray ribbon of sunshine between the Everglades and the Atlantic's best beach. Her higher education took place along the banks of the Schuylkill and then the Hudson. She commuted endlessly across the East River in the blood, sweat, and tears of a design career before leaving her heart on Victoria Harbor's dance floors and the South China Sea's cliff hikes. She now writes in the bright heat near the Singapore Strait during the school year; in the summer, she greets the sunset with her family on a back deck overlooking the Puget Sound.